# no place like you

## Emma Douglas

St. Martin's Paperbacks

NO PLACE LIKE YOU

Copyright © 2017 by Emma Douglas

All rights reserved.

For information address St. Martin's Press, 175 Fifth Avenue, New York, NY 10010.

ISBN: 978-1-250-11102-9

Our books may be purchased in bulk for promotional, educational, or business use. Please contact your local bookseller or the Macmillan Corporate and Premium Sales Department at 1-800-221-7945, ext. 5442, or by e-mail at MacmillanSpecialMarkets@macmillan.com.

Printed in the United States of America

St. Martin's Paperbacks edition / December 2017

St. Martin's Paperbacks are published by St. Martin's Press, 175 Fifth Avenue, New York, NY 10010.

10  9  8  7  6  5  4  3  2  1

*For my Dad.*
*And for everyone who's chasing their dream.*

# acknowledgments

Books don't grow on their own. Thank you as always to Eileen Rothschild and everyone at St. Martin's Press who help me bring them into the world. Thank you also to Miriam Kriss, my fab agent. For my family and friends, writerly and non-writerly, who put up with writer weirdness and keep me going through these interesting times.

To team torti who provide vital feline services. And lastly, to all the wonderful readers out there who love books like I do and give all the characters we writers have to tell stores about a place on their bookshelves and in their hearts, you rock.

*Once upon our time*
*You remembered me*
*Yet somehow I forgot you, baby*
*But now you're all I see*

From "Me after You," Track 3,
*Lost in the Undertow*, Blacklight 1995

# chapter one

"Now there's a sight for sore eyes," Billy Lawler said, sounding, for once, completely sincere.

Zach Harper glanced back at him. Billy stood at the wheel of the yacht they were sailing back to Lansing Island, gray hair spiking from the salt spray. He wore an old CloudFest T-shirt and a manic grin.

Billy adjusted course and pointed past Zach. "Home sweet home."

Zach rolled his eyes and turned back to study the view that lay ahead of the boat. Cloud Bay. A small town on a small island. But it nestled around a very pretty harbor and yes, with the boats that were bobbing around in the sunshine, backed by the town and the hills beyond, it looked like it had been staged for the perfect tourist snap. Cozy. Welcoming. Pity that the reception waiting for him once he set foot back on Lansing might not be quite so friendly.

"Home sweet freakin' home," Eli Lawler, seated beside him on the bench below the wheel, muttered.

Zach nodded in agreement. "How long since you've been back?"

Eli pushed his sunglasses up his nose. "Couple of years, maybe? I think we had Thanksgiving at Danny's. When was that?"

"Dude, that was nearly six years ago."

"Nah." Eli frowned and shifted his right foot—currently encased in some sort of complicated-looking medical boot—a little. "Can't be."

"Not a date I'm likely to forget," Zach said.

Eli cursed. "Sorry. I forgot."

That had been the first Thanksgiving after Zach's dad, Grey Harper—rock god, legend, less-than-perfect father—had died. Danny Ryan, who'd been the guitarist in Blacklight, the band Grey and Billy and Shane King and he had formed over thirty years ago, had insisted on holding Thanksgiving at his place on the island.

He'd probably been thinking that it would be easier on the three Harpers—Zach and his half sisters Faith and Mina—to spend the holiday somewhere less familiar than their own house. But the truth was that Danny's house was just as haunted with memories of Grey as their own had been. Danny had done his best and all the other Blacklight families had showed up but it had been a subdued holiday. After that, Faith's mom, Lou had insisted that the four of them get off the island for Christmas. They'd gone to Tuscany, somewhere they'd never gone with Grey. It had been a little easier that way, but still not great.

Grey Harper, hard as he had been to live with at times, left a big hole behind him. He'd also cast a long shadow, musically. One that Zach had been trying to fight his way out from under for nearly ten years now.

Leaving Lansing Island behind had been a first step. He'd spent less and less time here as the years passed.

But now he was back. About to confront some of the things he'd left behind.

Which included Faith and Mina.

"You think they'll be rolling out the red carpet for you?" Eli asked, staring at the rapidly approaching island.

"Mina might. Think Faith is more likely to set the dogs on me." Not that he knew whether or not Faith had dogs right now. Grey had collected stray animals, but surely they'd all passed away by now. Mina would have told him if Faith had bought a dog. Of course, Stewie, Mina's big yellow lab could probably do some damage if he decided he didn't like someone. Not that Stewie ever did. Zach folded his arms, trying to ignore the growing desire to ask Billy to turn the yacht around and take him back to the mainland. Not an option. So he was just going to have to man up and face his sisters.

"You still haven't patched things up with her?" Eli said. "You didn't tell me that."

"You've been a little busy recovering from nearly killing yourself coming off that damn bike of yours," Zach pointed out. "Didn't seem like the time to share."

"I don't know," Eli said easily. "Watching you fuck things up is always kind of entertaining."

"Right back at ya," Zach said.

The boat hit a wake trail left by a smaller craft and bounced. Eli winced and sucked in a breath, lifting his injured foot off the deck.

"How are you holding up?" Zach asked.

"Kind of wishing we'd opted for that chopper," Eli said.

Billy hadn't wanted to take the ferry—the island's sole form of connection with the California coast—claiming he didn't want to deal with fans. He and Eli had been heading for the island when Zach had announced he was heading home to Lansing. Billy had talked Eli into spending a couple of months on the island to complete his rehab. They'd of ered Zach a ride.

Eli had vetoed the helicopter idea.

Zach wasn't sure if it was because of his injuries or because his best friend had never really liked helicopters since the first time Grey had taken them on a sightseeing flight over Hawaii and the pilot had decided to play a little game of "impress the rock star client" with some acrobatic moves. Grey had loved it. Zach had thought it was pretty cool too. Eli, on the other hand, had lost his lunch all over the chopper's cabin.

"Won't be long now," Zach said. "We can always get a cab from town up to the house." Billy's master plan was to moor at the harbor, stock up on groceries at Cloud Bay, and then sail the rest of the way around the island to where the Blacklight guys had all bought land and built houses after the album they'd recorded on the island had turned into their first multi-platinum all those years ago. Why, when Cloud Bay's stores were perfectly happy to deliver—after all, the island wasn't that big—Zach wasn't sure. Maybe Billy just wanted to show off his new boat.

"I might take you up on that," Eli said as the yacht bounced again. He braced himself with his right hand; the left was bandaged halfway up his arm. It was supposed to be in a sling but Eli kept slipping it free, claiming his shoulder ached.

The boat jolted a third time. This time, water sprayed over the side of the yacht, half-drenching them both.

"Dad, I'd prefer to arrive un-drowned," Eli called up to Billy.

"You're not going to melt, princess," Billy yelled back.

Zach grinned. It was mid-May and the California weather was warm enough that getting wet didn't bother him much. And he was starting to realize just how much he'd missed Eli's company. Zach had spent a big chunk of the last three years touring with his band, Fringe Dweller. The relentless schedule didn't leave a lot of time for friends and family. Or hadn't until two weeks ago when their lead singer, Ryder Lange, had suddenly announced he was taking a year off to "find himself"—whatever the fuck *that* meant. In Ryder's case, it wasn't code for going to rehab, as it often was for other musicians. But Zach hadn't been able to get the reason out of him and neither had anyone else in the band. They'd played the last two shows on the tour they'd been finishing in a stew of seething resentment and then they'd gone their separate ways.

Fucking Ryder. Always a drama queen. Zach had joined Fringe Dweller as a fill-in guitarist. He'd stuck. But Ryder and he had never truly become friends. Probably because Ryder belonged to the "I'm the lead singer and I run the band" school of musicians. They worked well together and stayed out of each other's way the rest of the time. But pulling this crap was just not cool. Not when it looked like they were finally building to something bigger.

Not cool at all.

And now, thanks to Ryder, he was back on Lansing. Home sweet freakin' home indeed.

Holy crap, Zach Harper. Leah Santelli stared out the window of The Last Crumb, where she was waiting in line for a sugar fix and her second coffee of the morning.

Then she stepped a little closer to the glass so she could watch as the man who wasn't supposed to be anywhere near Lansing kept walking down Main Street toward the bakery.

Double holy crap.

It was definitely Zach. It wasn't as though you could mistake the guy. At least, she couldn't. She doubted any other woman with working eyeballs could either.

Zach Harper.

One long tall streak of trouble. Too talented and too hot for his own good. His hair was longer, falling around his face, and he wore sunglasses, hiding the amazing gray-green eyes he shared with his sisters, courtesy of their father Grey, but there was no mistaking that loose-hipped stride. Or those shoulders. Or the three guitars tattooed on his right forearm.

*"Born to prowl."* She'd heard one of her mom's friends call Zach that once at a party. And maybe she'd been mostly basing that off her assessment of Grey, who was born to do many things, prowling definitely among them, and had perfected his rock-god persona many years earlier—but she had been right. Like father, like son, maybe.

Zach kind of glided across the earth, moving like a cat who knew he was king of the jungle, and not much caring about those left stumbling around in his wake when he left.

Once upon a time, Leah had been one of those left behind.

But not any more.

She rubbed the spot on her finger where the missing weight of her recently discarded wedding ring still bugged her. She'd moved on from Zach Harper. Turned out she hadn't exactly chosen the perfect man to do it with but that wasn't anybody's fault. Her marriage to Joey Nelson had kind of faded away, ending not with screaming fights and tears but with Joey announcing that he wasn't happy, that he'd met someone else, and with Leah realizing that she felt more relieved than any other emotion when he did so.

So they'd divorced. And she'd finally pitched her wedding ring and her engagement ring into the sea one night six months ago after she and Faith had been drinking champagne and she'd been cursing men—even the friendliest of divorces came with some pain after all. She hadn't thought she'd miss them.

But she did.

Every now and then she'd look down at that finger and wonder how she'd screwed things up. Twenty-eight years old and one marriage down. Not exactly her life plan.

Zach and Eli—God, Eli as well—were almost at the bakery now. Eli had his left arm in a sling and was limping in a walking boot, looking too thin. Right. He'd crashed his motorcycle. Faith had told her he'd banged himself up pretty good. But he was laughing at something Zach said, and Zach was grinning—dammit, that smile should be outlawed. And dammit, she was staring and they'd be able to see her any second. She ducked back out of sight, heart pounding.

Dealing with Zach took some prep time. She hadn't seen Faith's brother very often since Grey Harper had died. Zach hadn't been back to Lansing much over the last six or so years. But the few times he had come home, she'd learned that she needed to steel her defenses when it came to him.

Because he was still funny and charming and well, to be honest, smoking hot, but none of those things had been appropriate to think about when she'd been married to Joey. And now she wasn't married to Joey and they still weren't appropriate to think about. Because Zach Harper was born to prowl and born to leave and she wasn't going to let him wreck her a second time.

What she was going to do was call his sister and find out what the heck he was doing here and why the hell Faith hadn't told her he was coming.

But not here in the middle of Stella's bakery with six other people ready to listen in on the conversation.

She'd grown up in Cloud Bay and yet there were still times when small-town life annoyed the crap out of her. Mostly when it involved everyone knowing your business.

Not that Zach was her business. But he was Faith's.

By the time she was back in her car, loaded up with doughnuts and muffins for today's studio session, she was still trying to process Zach being back. Gobbling down one of Stella's best apple cider doughnuts—okay, two—in record time didn't help. So she licked sugar off her fingers, wiped her hands on her jeans, and dialed Faith on speaker as she backed out of the parking space.

"Hey, Leah." Faith's voice was a little tinny through the car's speakers. She sounded distracted.

"Hey," Leah said. "Um, is there something you forgot to tell me?"

"Not that I can think of," Faith said, voice sharpening. "Why? What's wrong? Did someone show up at the studio you weren't expecting?"

"No. Everything's fine at the *studio*." Leah ran the recording studio that Harper Inc. operated on the island. Did a lot of the sound engineering too. Even a little producing when she got the chance. She had the place running like clockwork. Well, as clockwork as a business that regularly had to deal with rock stars and other musicians—who, in Leah's experience, could have a flexible relationship with the concept of "on time"— could get.

"Good." Faith said. "I can't think of anything else. Wanna give me a hint?"

Did she really not know Zach was back?

"Well, I'm not sure if this counts as a hint, but I just saw Zach and Eli walking down Main Street."

"What?" Faith's shriek made the car speakers squeal. Okay. So that was probably a "no" to her knowing about Zach's return. "So you didn't know he was back?"

"No." Faith sounded pissed. "Are you sure?"

"As I haven't recently hit my head on anything, yes, I'm sure that I recognize your brother and his partner in crime."

There was silence on the other end of the line.

"It might be good," Leah offered. "Maybe he's realized he's been a jerk and has come home to apologize." She tried to sound convincing, but it was a struggle. She'd always thought there was a good guy underneath the swagger and the burning desire to prove himself, but over the last few years Zach had put himself and his career ahead of his sisters too many times. Totally didn't matter how hot the guy was, a pretty face and abs of steel didn't make up for being a dick.

When it came to Faith versus Zach, she was firmly Team Faith.

"Always the optimist," Faith said. "If Zach's back, then I'm guessing he wants something."

"Fringe Dweller just finished their tour, didn't they? Maybe he needs a vacation."

"I don't think Lansing is high on Zach's list of prime vacation spots."

Leah sighed. Nope. Zach had been keen to leave Lansing in his rearview mirror since he'd been about thirteen. She hadn't really believed he'd do it when she'd been young and stupid. Or rather, she'd known he'd go, but she'd always thought he'd come back regularly like Grey had. But now she knew better. "Okay, you're right. But I thought you should know. Just in case he turns up on your doorstep or something."

"Thank you," Faith sounded sincere. "It's nice to get a heads-up."

Because her idiot brother hadn't given her one.

"Call me if you need anything," Leah said. "I'll be at the studio in about thirty minutes. Are you coming down today?"

"Yes, I want to hear Nessa again." Faith said, sounding more cheerful. "I'll try to get away from the office for an hour or so this afternoon."

"See you then. I'd offer to save you a doughnut but with the ravening hordes at the studio, I'm not sure I can promise anything."

"Damn. Though Lou brought pie over last night when she came for dinner. Which means I had pie for breakfast."

"Healthy." Leah laughed.

"Just making sure I get my share. Caleb loves Lou's pies so much he'll eat the whole thing before I get home otherwise. And anyway, you're the one eating doughnuts at eight a.m."

"Who says I was eating any?" Leah said, checking her mouth for sugar in the rearview mirror.

"I know you too well, Santelli. See you this afternoon."

# chapter two

Zach wasn't surprised to find Faith and Mina sitting on the front step of the guesthouse he usually stayed in when he was home.

The main house on the Harper estate felt like Faith's now. Had kind of been that way since Grey had died and Mina had gotten married. He assumed it would only feel more so now that Faith's fiancé, Caleb, lived there too. He knew his old room upstairs in the big house was still waiting for him if he wanted it, though he'd hauled all his stuff out of it several years ago. But the guesthouses were more private. More space. If he was going to do what he had come here to do, he'd need more space. So here he was.

And here were his sisters waiting for him. Identical pairs of gray-green eyes watching him with carefully neutral expressions. His sisters didn't much resemble each other. All three had different mothers, though Faith with her long brown-blond hair and tanned skin looked

more like him than tall, dark-haired, pale, and slender
Mina.

But the eyes—their father's eyes—marked them as
siblings.

Would Grey be disappointed to see the three of them
now, silent as a group of cats sizing each other up?

Probably not. He would have told them all to pull their
heads out of their asses, have a drink, and make up.

He could try suggesting that tactic, but Zach doubted
it would work for him.

For one thing, Mina didn't drink.

So here they were, the three of them. Face to face
for the first time in a . . . well, longer than he was
proud of.

He'd known they'd be here.

Once he'd walked down Main Street in Cloud Bay
there had been zero chance of his sisters not hearing that
he was home before he made it to the house. He was
guessing it had taken no longer than ten minutes for one
or both of them to get a call from some well-meaning
resident to let them know that the black sheep of the
family was headed for the old homestead so to speak. He
was probably lucky that Faith's mom—his stepmom—
Lou hadn't joined in the less-than-welcoming com-
mittee.

"Okay, who ratted me out?" he said, dropping his
duffel bag at Faith's feet. He smiled, hoping to lighten
the situation.

His sisters exchanged a glance that basically said that
wasn't going to happen.

"Too many people to mention," Mina said, tone cool.

"And really, the bigger question is why anyone had

to tell us at all?" Faith added. "Did California lose all means of communication or something?"

Faith was more pissed than Mina. That had been true for nearly a year. Mina was usually the peacemaker. But from the frown she was directing at him, she was clearly on Faith's side.

"I've been on tour," Zach said.

"Tour ended two weeks ago, didn't it?" Faith asked.

He should have known that she paid attention to those things. "Yes. But you know what it's like when you're done. There's still shit to do. And sleep to catch up on." Also there was figuring out what the hell it meant if your lead singer suddenly wanted a year off. "I'm sorry I didn't tell you. But I'm here now. So are you going to let me inside?"

"Be my guest," Faith said. But neither of them moved.

"What?" he asked. "Is there a secret password I need to know?"

"Why are you here, Zach?" Mina asked. "Is everything okay?"

Definitely less pissed than Faith.

"That depends on your definition of okay," he quipped.

Faith paled. "You're not sick?" She reached for Mina's hand, knuckles white as she squeezed it.

Crap. He hadn't thought that they might leap to that conclusion. After all, the thing that had sent Grey running home for good in the end had been cancer.

"No." He held up his hands, palms out. "I promise you, I'm fine." He looked down at his sisters' linked hands. "Breathe, Faith."

She blew out a breath, looking slightly embarrassed.

Then tossed her hair back over her shoulder as she let go of Mina's hand. "Good. So then, what?"

He'd been hoping to put this conversation off for a few days. He needed to sleep some more, shake the exhaustion that had been riding him since even before Ryder had dropped his bombshell, and then get his plans clear in his head before he brought them to his sisters. But apparently there was no grace period for the not-so-prodigal son.

"Can we talk inside?" he said. "It's hot out here and my guitars will cook." He pointed back at the pickup he'd borrowed from Billy to cart his gear over.

"You brought guitars?" Faith's brows rose.

"A few," he said.

"Does that mean you're staying awhile?" Mina asked. Her expression was still neutral, but was that maybe a hint of hopeful in her voice?

"Did you two join the Spanish Inquisition while I was away?" Zach asked. He took a step back, angling himself toward the pickup. "Look, we can talk inside, but I'd like to bring my bags in first, if that's okay?"

"Fine." Faith climbed to her feet. "We'll meet you inside."

The implication being that big brothers who'd pissed off their sisters got to carry their own damn luggage.

Well, maybe he'd earned that much. He watched his sisters disappear into the guesthouse, united in their disapproval, and then turned to deal with his stuff.

Ten minutes later he had a pile of gear in the entry hall and no more excuses to avoid explaining why he was home. He could hear Faith and Mina out back in the kitchen, laughing about something. He headed in that direction.

One of them had opened the place up. The house was cool, ceiling fans circling lazily in each room, catching the air coming through the windows. It was warm outside but not hot enough to need air-conditioning, and the sea breeze brought the smell of salt and the flowers in the garden. A familiar smell that settled over him, making all the tense muscles down his spine relax fractionally. What he really wanted was to swim. Dive into the ocean and let it wash his problems away for a few minutes. The water would still be on the cool side, but that was oddly appealing.

But first, his sisters.

The laughter died when he walked through the door to the kitchen. Mina and Faith sat at the small dining table near the windows that looked out over the patio to the ocean beyond. They'd made coffee, they both had mugs in front of them. And, hallelujah, there was a third mug on the table. So either they weren't completely annoyed at him, or maybe they'd put arsenic in his cup. Either way, he needed caffeine, so he'd take the risk. He'd caught a red-eye to get into L.A. to meet up with Eli and Billy the day before, and they'd been up early today to get to Billy's boat.

He was running on fumes. The smart thing to do would be to sleep of course, rather than pour more coffee down his throat, but if his sisters were determined to talk, then coffee it was going to be.

He sat, reached for the mug, drank about one third of it in several rapid gulps.

"Billy been keeping you up late?" Faith asked. "Or was it Eli?"

"How is Eli?" Mina asked, her tone a shade warmer than Faith's.

"Recovering," Zach said. "His ankle is still healing but he's getting around. He's got a decent amount of physical therapy in his future but for now he mostly just needs to rest up. I think that's why Billy dragged him out here."

"Dragged? That's an interesting description of coming home," Faith said.

He put his coffee down. "Eli has a life outside Lansing. Some people do, you know. I'm sure he would rather be back in L.A., doing his job."

Faith didn't bat an eye at his sarcastic tone. "Which brings us back around to the subject of why you aren't off somewhere exotic doing your job, brother mine? Care to share?"

He thought he saw Mina wince slightly as the air between him and Faith turned a little electric. They'd always been the passionate two, arguing about music and life. They'd always been able to hug it out and forget at the end of the fight too. Until last year. Zach had pulled out of appearing at CloudFest at the last minute and Faith had not taken it well. In fact, she'd pretty much ripped him a new one. Perhaps deservedly. After all, he'd kind of done to her what Ryder had just done to Zach and the rest of the band. Left her high and dry.

Fuck. He rubbed a hand over eyes that increasingly felt like sandpaper. "Look, Faith, I know I'm not your favorite person right now but how about I just tell you why I'm here and we can fight about whatever you want after I've had a chance to get some sleep?"

Faith's lips pressed together, but then she nodded.

Mina finally smiled when she saw Faith relax back into the chair.

"Okay, that's a temporary truce," Mina said. "So, spill."

He took another swig of coffee. Mostly to make sure the string of curses that floated through his head whenever he thought of Ryder weren't the words that came out of his mouth when he started to talk.

"Ryder wants to take a year off. Fringe Dweller is on hiatus for that time. So Jay thought it would be a good time for me to record a solo album."

Faith's brows shot up. Mina's mouth had made a perfect O.

"You want to record *here*?" Faith asked.

He understood her surprise. He'd always been determined not to ride on Grey's name, and Grey and Blacklight were indelibly linked with Cloud Bay and Lansing.

"Jay thinks it's a hook. Give us some leverage with a label to get a decent deal if we can appeal to some of Blacklight's audience."

"You want a label deal?" Faith asked, still looking startled.

"If it's a good one. Still hard to beat the marketing power of a label even if I don't need their money to record." Zach said. "Jay says they'll fall over themselves at the whole 'second-generation Harper going back to his roots' thing."

Faith pursed her lips. "I'd have to agree with that."

Her expression had changed from annoyed to interested. Ah, he'd engaged her business brain. A good tactic to remember.

"So, I thought I could record a short set—five or six songs maybe—and debut them at Cloud Fest. Take the

Blacklight slot." He paused. "I assume none of the others have asked for it?"

The band members had started CloudFest together all those years ago. These days, even though Harper Inc. ran the festival, there was a standing agreement that any of them could take a slot at the festival if they wanted. None of them had, and instead Faith had been keeping up Grey's tradition of sneaking a big name onto the CloudFest schedule without announcing them to fill the space in the schedule. The fans loved the surprise—and the online speculation about who might be appearing each year made for excellent free promo for the festival.

"What makes you think I haven't filled the slot already?" Faith asked.

Which didn't exactly answer his question, but if she was talking of filling the slot, then he had to assume Danny, Billy, or Shane hadn't asked for it.

"Tradition," he said. "You usually schedule it late."

"I respect tradition," Faith said. "But with tradition comes a little thing called loyalty. We gave you the secret slot last year, Zach, and you left us—left *me*—in the lurch at the last minute. It was only because Danny stepped up that the whole thing wasn't a total disaster. Why should I trust you this year?"

Because this year he needed it? That was a hell of a thing to think. And he wasn't going to say it out loud to his sisters, even if it was true. It made him sound like a total self-centered prick. Maybe he *was* a total self-centered prick. "Last year was different," he said. "And this year, obviously, Fringe Dweller isn't going to be picking up any last-minute gigs at Madison Square Garden."

Faith shook her head. "It's still a couple of months away. What if Ryder changes his mind? You going to abandon this little side project of yours and go running back?"

Maybe he deserved that. He took a deep breath. He was here to make peace, not get into yet another argument with Faith. "Firstly, it's not a little side project. I've been writing songs for this for a while now. Secondly, no. If Ryder changes his mind, then he'll have to wait until I finish. He can't have it both ways."

"I see," Faith said. "So, who's your producer? And who are you using for your band?"

Yep, definitely in business mode now.

"I have some feelers out for producers," he said. *Feelers*. That sounded casual. Hopefully Faith wouldn't ask who. He was trying not to think about it. He was going after his two dream producers. There was a good chance they'd turn him down. He hadn't decided what he'd do if that happened. "Eli has heard a couple of the songs and is going to work on two of them with me. And I'll figure out the band. It's a low-key sound so I can start with getting my guitar parts and vocals down."

He waited to see if Faith was going to offer any suggestions on the band front. Not because he needed her to but because, if she offered, it was probably a sign that she was thawing a little. But she just sipped her coffee instead. "If you want studio time, then you need to talk to Leah. I'm not going over her head to give it to you."

Maybe "no" on the thawing then. "I'm going to use Dad's studio to start, but sure, I'll ask Leah, get a feel for timeframes."

Grey's private studio was small, sized for four or five people max to work in. It had a single practice room and a small recording booth that you could just squeeze a drum kit, a drummer, and three other people into. The size didn't matter. The place had great acoustics, decent equipment. Not quite as new as the set up at the Harper Inc. studio, but it would do.

Blacklight had recorded their first album in an old house overlooking the cliffs up this end of the island, but by the time *Cloudlines* had catapulted them to fame, the house had burned down. The four of them had all bought land on this part of the island and Grey had built the studio on the spot the old house had stood long before he'd decided to expand and build a proper recording facility so that other bands could record on the island too.

As a kid, Grey's studio had been sacred ground to Zach. Grey hadn't liked to be disturbed in there, and Zach would sit outside, hoping that the windows would be open so he could listen to his dad and the guys messing with songs, knowing he wanted to do that too one day. Once he'd learned to play, Grey had let him in to jam a few times. Those moments were some of his best memories from his childhood. He and Grey speaking the same language, sharing a fierce love for the magic that could be made with guitars and voices. He and Faith hadn't rehearsed their stuff there; they'd stuck to the rehearsal rooms at the Harper studios instead. Unless Faith ever set foot in Grey's studio, it was unlikely that anyone had been in there, other than maybe to clean, since Grey's death.

Maybe he could be a fresh start for it. And vice versa.

"Unless either of you have a problem with that?" he added.

"Of course not,' Mina said quickly. "Dad would want

you to use it." She shot a "don't argue" look at Faith. And, Faith, to his surprise, didn't. Mina had always been the quiet one, deferring to Faith most of the time. She didn't often call the shots. Maybe he'd missed more than family time in the last few years.

"Good," he said, smiling at Mina. "Thanks. So, does that end the inquisition for now?"

Faith blew out a breath, but then nodded. "For now." She rose. "We should let you unpack." She hesitated. "Do you want to come up to the house for dinner tonight? Lou is coming over."

That was an olive branch. A teeny one, given the tacked-on comment about Lou that he was pretty sure was to make sure he knew Faith wasn't making any special effort for him—but he'd be dumb to turn it down. "Sure," he said easily. "Sounds great." He'd only met Faith's fiancé twice in person—once at Mina's art show in L.A. and once when Lou had asked him to lunch in New York and had turned up with Faith and Caleb in tow, presumably in an attempt to start the reconciliation ball rolling. It hadn't worked. But maybe if he could bond with Caleb that would also improve Faith's current opinion of him. Though it might also be nice to have a buffer between him and Faith. Or several buffers. He turned to Mina.

"Mina, can you come? Bring Will. It would be good to see him again." Mina's new guy, Will Fraser, ran a bar and whiskey distillery on the island. Zach didn't know him that well either, but he'd drunk at Salt Devil a few times in its early years when he'd still been coming home a few times a year. He'd liked Will then and he liked him more now that he'd seen how happy Mina was with him. Will had shadowed her around that same gallery opening, giving Mina space to shine but always there when she looked around for him.

Mina shook her head. "I can come for a while but I have the graveyard shift at search and rescue tonight. And Will is working at the bar. Maybe we can figure something out later this week? But you can come see me at the cottage, I'm there painting most afternoons. I'll tell Stewie not to bite you."

"The way to a Lab's heart is through his stomach," Zach retorted. "One cookie and that dog is mine." If only sisters were as easy to win over. Though Mina was smiling properly now.

Faith linked her arm through her sister's. "Come on, Mina. Let's give the prodigal son some space."

He followed them out to the front door. Mina kissed his cheek and hugged him tight as she said goodbye. At first he thought Faith wasn't going to do the same but then she stood up on her toes and kissed him quick.

"Welcome home, you big dumbass," she said quickly then ran down the stairs before he could respond.

"So, spill," Leah demanded as she passed Faith a cup of coffee the next morning. She'd come armed for their weekly review of the studio's schedule with salted caramel lattes and a box of pastries. All the better to weasel information about why Zach was home out of her best friend. Maybe that made her sneaky, but forewarned was forearmed and all that. If Zach was only here for a few days then she could just keep her head down and stay out of his way and there'd be no way of getting herself into trouble with nostalgic longing for the man.

If he was going to be here for longer however, that required a different plan. She opened the bakery box and pushed it across Faith's desk. "Fresh from The Last Crumb this morning."

Faith tried to look stern but failed miserably. "Don't tell Caleb. He thinks I have a doughnut habit."

"He'd be right," Leah said. "But where he's wrong is in thinking that there's anything wrong with said habit. You run and do all that healthy stuff. The odd doughnut isn't going to kill you."

"I agree," Faith said as she took one and bit into it. Her eyes closed in pleasure. "Plus, God, Stella is the best at doughnuts. If there was a doughnut Olympics, she'd win gold."

"Totally." Leah lifted the lid on her go cup, blowing on the coffee. Working in the studio for so many years had accustomed her to leaving her coffee abandoned way too long before she got around to drinking it. Call it supreme laziness in not wanting to get up and re-nuke it to heat it but she preferred it lukewarm these days. A fact that horrified her parents to the very core of their Italian American hearts but what they couldn't see couldn't hurt them.

She waited for Faith to finish chewing. "So, Zach?" she prompted as Faith wiped her mouth with a napkin and eyed the remaining contents of the box.

"You're harshing my doughnut high," Faith protested. "It's too early to talk about my idiot brother."

"There are always more doughnuts." Leah pointed out. "And you're going to have to tell me sooner or later. So get it over and done with and we can put him back on the 'do not discuss list.' What's convinced the great Zach Harper to grace us with his presence?"

"Cone of silence?" Faith said.

Leah nodded. "In the vault." She drew her hand over her lips in a zipping motion.

"Ryder's having some sort of crisis. He's decided to take a year off."

"Shit," Leah said. "That's . . . not great for the rest of the guys. They must be *pissed*. They've been going from strength to strength. Bad enough to miss the summer touring season let alone a whole year. They'll lose all their momentum."

"Yep," Faith agreed. "It's kind of a dick move if you look at it from their perspective."

"So Zach's back to what—lick his wounds and make plans?"

Faith's long blonde-brown hair bounced as she shook her head. "No, he wants to record some songs here. He's thinking of making a solo album. Says he's been writing."

Leah almost spat out her mouthful of latte. Wow. So that was "no" to Zach only being on Lansing for a few days. Damn. She hadn't expected that. And she was definitely going to need a Plan B for dealing with the oldest Harper.

Then the more sensible part of her brain caught up with what Faith had said. Zach wanted to record. Here on the island. Most likely in her studio. That was potentially complicated, but also potentially a fantastic opportunity.

"Who's producing for him?" she asked, hoping she sounded casual.

Zach Harper making his first solo album in the same place where the album that had made his dad so famous had been recorded. That would sell a squazillion easy, as long as the music was good. And she knew Zach's

music was good. Ryder was the main songwriter for
Fringe Dweller, but she'd heard enough of Zach's music
over the years to know the man had plenty of talent. The
fact that he and Faith hadn't taken off immediately
had been more a product of youth and being slightly
out of pace with where the market was at the time
rather than their music being bad. If she could produce
his album—or even some of the songs—then that would
be the break she'd be looking for to take the next step in
her career.

"He said he had feelers out. And that Eli was going
to work with him on a few songs."

Crap. She'd forgotten about Eli. He was also a sound
engineer, one who was making a growing name for himself as a producer. Doing exactly what *she* wanted to
do, in fact. And he was Zach's best friend.

So that was a wrinkle in trying to get a toe in the door
with Zach on his album.

She loved her job, but the itch to produce had been
growing over the last few years. It had been a bone of
contention between Joey and her. He didn't like the idea
of her doing something that would likely take her off-
island for long chunks of time. She'd managed to do a
little here and there but so far hadn't found an act to take
a chance on her who could give her the boost she needed.
Faith had asked her to work with Nessa recording a few
songs, but Zach was a whole different ballgame.

She chewed her lip.

"What?" Faith asked.

"Just . . . thinking," she said. "About when we might
have a studio for him," she added, not ready to share her
budding plan with Faith just yet.

"He's going to use Grey's studio to rehearse, maybe

record some demos," Faith said. "So it's not an immediate issue."

"Still, it might take some juggling. We're booked pretty solid up until CloudFest." She had another thought. "I take it he wants a CloudFest slot too?"

Faith nodded. "Yep. Haven't promised him anything yet though. I don't need a repeat of last year."

"Sensible," Leah agreed. She took a brownie from the box. Bit into soft squidgy chocolate deliciousness. Faith was sensible not to trust Zach right away, but she had a feeling Zach would get his way if he played his cards right. The guy was way too charming for his own good. Even Faith, pissed as she was, wasn't going to be able to resist him forever if he set out to prove he was reforming his ways.

Zach Harper on a mission to win someone over was a force of nature.

Which just meant that, now that she knew why he was here and what that might mean for her, she was going to have to give him absolutely no reason to want to charm her. Her hormones, if they decided to get stupid over him all over again, were just going to have to suck it up.

# chapter three

It took a night of tossing and turning, and a day of being unable to shake the idea, for Leah to work up the determination to go find Zach and sound him out about producing. She couldn't wait too long. If he got some big name to agree to take him on then that would be that, even if he brought them to work here on Lansing.

Worse, a big-name producer might even want to bring their own sound engineer, and she'd be locked out of any involvement at all.

She'd spent the day obsessively making a list of the arguments in her favor, drinking too much coffee, and fighting the urge to bite her nails to the quick. Nessa Lewis, Faith's first foundation-grant recipient, had been in the studio but she and her band were rehearsing, not recording, and the other group wrapping up a recording stint had declared a day off while they worked out an issue with their last song. Which left Leah with just enough extra time on her hands to drive herself crazy.

When she'd found herself scrubbing the toilets in the

studio, she'd known she was only going to drive herself crazy if she put off asking Zach for even another day. She'd chased Nessa and her bandmates out right at five o'clock.

So now, here she was, walking down from the studio to the guesthouse, taking the long way through the gardens around Faith's house in the hope that maybe she wouldn't be spotted.

The days were growing longer, the heat of the day starting to linger into late afternoon. It was still technically spring, but the approaching summer was starting to make itself felt. She took a breath of warm air, let it soothe some of her nerves. Lansing's climate was hardly freezing through the winter, but Leah was a summer girl. She liked the beach and wearing silly flirty sundresses and flip-flops and drinking cool beers on warm nights. Liked the heat of the sun on her skin.

Maybe it was the Italian side of her. Born for the Mediterranean climate or something.

She'd been to Italy twice and had loved it both times, but it wasn't home. No, she wanted sea air and surf with her sunshine, not the weight of history and culture, as fascinating as that was.

The breeze flowing through the garden was full of salt and the tang of the ocean, ruffling through her hair. She'd tied it back in a ponytail after a day of running her fingers through it as she tried to figure out how to talk to Zach had turned her curls into a tangled mess. Wild-eyed Medusa wasn't the look she was going for, so the ponytail seemed safer. Along with her favorite long red cardigan over the black T-shirt and skinny jeans that formed the basis of her studio uniform most days in the colder months.

The edge of the garden came faster than she would have liked, and her stupid heartbeat picked up a little when she spotted the guesthouse.

They had history, she and Zach and that guesthouse.

She'd been inside it since, of course. The guesthouses were most often used by Grey's rock-star friends or clients of the studio who were famous enough to require the security the Harper estate offered while they worked.

That had happened more often when Grey had been alive. These days, any of the big names that came to the studio were just as likely to use one of the Blacklight guys' houses. Danny and Billy and Shane were infrequent residents of Lansing now, all busy with the projects they'd taken up after Grey's death.

It had been hard on all of them, losing Grey. Leah had watched Faith and Mina battle the grief close up. She'd shared it with them—having grown up with Grey, pretty much the most fascinating of her uncles even if he was an uncle in name not blood. She'd envied the guys, Zach included, who'd all been able to leave the place that held the hardest of the memories behind them, who hadn't had to face them every day.

It was harder to forget when you couldn't leave.

And now, staring at the guesthouse and wondering why her feet had suddenly frozen and left her rooted in place, she knew there were other memories that she thought she'd dealt with a long time ago, just waiting to pounce on her once she stepped through the white door.

So. Keep her head. Keep her cool. Keep her mind firmly in the moment.

She was here for business.

Nothing more.

Zach could be a client. He might even be a friend

again if he could prove that he hadn't turned into just another self-obsessed rock star chasing the dream. He hadn't done much in the last year or so to make her think he hadn't. Not with the way he'd neglected his family, let alone the stunt he'd pulled with CloudFest.

So a friendly acquaintance perhaps. She wanted to hold out a small shred of hope that somewhere in there was the Zach she'd known. But part of her thought there wasn't. Not the laughing older boy who'd been part of the landscape of her life for eighteen years. Definitely not the man who'd been the first to break her heart.

That Zach Harper belonged in her memories. Locked away in the deep recesses of her brain where she rarely dared to think about him.

He had no place in real life. Real life, where he'd be leaving and she'd be staying right here on Lansing.

She straightened her shoulders, forced herself to move. Strode across to the guesthouse door. Only to realize that the place was deathly quiet. Zach rarely existed in silence. There was always music playing in any space he was in. It was like oxygen to him. Even when he was out in public, he hummed under his breath or tapped his fingers in endless rhythms when he wasn't thinking about what he was doing.

Faith did the humming thing too, but not to the same extent.

Wired for sound, the two of them. And Zach had been able to indulge his passion. Hadn't had to learn to put it aside like Faith had. So he never really tried to hide the fact that part of his brain was almost always listening to some melody only he could hear.

She pressed the doorbell, wondering if maybe he might be asleep. The sound of the chime came through the door but there were no answering footsteps or movement in response. She waited, but that didn't change. There was only silence beyond the door that stayed stubbornly closed.

Dammit. Where was the man?

It had taken her this long to get up the nerve to face him, she didn't want to have to do it all over again tomorrow.

"Where would I be if I was Zach Harper?" she muttered to herself. Grey's old truck—presumably borrowed from Faith—was parked in one of the covered spots off to the side of the guesthouse, so somewhere on the estate seemed like a safe enough bet. Unless he was with Eli. But counting that out for now, then the most likely places were the beach or . . . Grey's studio, she realized.

Zach was a night owl. It was close to six now, which for him was more like lunchtime.

If he was settling into the studio, he'd just be getting started.

She should have thought of that earlier. Another quick detour, retracing her path through the garden a little faster, and she was past the main house safely again and heading down the opposite side of the garden, following the narrow cliff path that led down to the small studio building and then onward to the property line where the Harper estate ended and Shane's land began.

A line of salt-and-wind-battered bushes formed a wall between the path and the house, so she was hopefully still incognito and safe from Faith's eagle eye. In fact, at this time of day Faith was probably still working in the Harper Inc. offices. With less than three months now until CloudFest, Faith was starting to hit the pointy end of the mountain of organization that lay behind pulling off a massive music festival.

It meant long hours and working nights while she was trying to deal with musicians and management located all over the world.

And this year she was throwing a wedding into the mix. She and Caleb had set the date for the start of September.

Personally, Leah thought that was insane. Faith usually took a few weeks off to recover after CloudFest, and this year she'd have to roll straight into final countdown for her wedding.

But maybe Faith was thinking longer term. She and Caleb could take a vacation each year that culminated in their anniversary with no need for any kind of excuse. There was some method to the madness when you thought about it that way.

Leah reached the end of the path, rounding the last slight bend, which brought Grey's studio into sight. Now she could hear music, the sound of a guitar. Definitely Zach, she thought, listening to the melody. She didn't recognize the song but she knew the style of the musician. He must have the windows open, airing the place out. The studio was well soundproofed, so she wouldn't hear him otherwise.

It was tempting to stay right where she was and just listen to him play. He might be a dick, but he was a great guitarist. And the music he coaxed from six simple strings always had the power to steal her breath and her common sense. It would be all too easy to stand here and let herself be a lost-in-a-crush teenager again.

But that wasn't going to get the job done. She wanted to work with him, not jump him.

So when the music stopped abruptly, she walked over and knocked on the door.

It swung open faster than she had expected and there he was. Zach Harper. Large as life.

Larger, maybe.

"Leah," he said, sounding surprised. Then he smiled, and her pulse sped up all over again as the force of that grin hit her like the kick of a bass drum to the back of her head.

Larger than life and still freaking hot.

Dammit.

"How the hell are you, Santelli?" Zach said, stepping back to let her in.

She skirted around him. There would be no contact.

"What, no kiss hello?" Zach said, closing the door behind her. Leah kept walking. No contact and definitely no thinking about kissing. Of any kind.

"Let me guess. Faith is mad at me, so you're mad at me? The old best friend solidarity thing?"

"Faith is mad at you," Leah agreed. She stopped and turned to face him. Took a breath while she figured out what exactly she was going to say. That was a mistake. The studio smelled like Zach.

How was that even possible? The man had only been in residence a little over a day. The studio had been, as far as she knew, closed up for years. Maybe Faith had it cleaned now and then—it didn't looked covered in dust. It shouldn't have smelled like much at all. But it did. Another breath. Yep, there it was. A scent so familiar she would have known who it was with her eyes closed. Spice. Salt. Zach.

It made her want to close her eyes and breathe deeper. *So not going to happen.* Business. It was all about business. She straightened her shoulders. "I, on the other hand, am willing to maintain a neutral stance."

"Neutral, huh? Sounds interesting."

He was still smiling. Zach Harper's smile had always made it difficult to concentrate.

She turned back to face the studio. She hadn't been in here in forever. There was a tiny recording booth and board in the next room, but this main room was rehearsal space. A guitar case lay open by a stool and a mic stand. The guitar itself was resting carefully on a stand.

"Is that your dad's old Martin Shade-Top?" she asked. "Nice." She wandered over to look at the guitar, but didn't touch it. She'd seen Grey play this guitar a hundred times. Rarely on stage, but it was one he reached for when he was jamming with friends or working out an idea in the studio or just roaming the house trying to work up a song.

She hadn't realized Zach had kept it.

"Yes," Zach said. "I brought a few of his with me. Thought I could warm up the place with some sounds it remembered. Kind of reintroduce myself."

She understood. A studio was more than a room. Every space had its own personality, the little quirks and foibles that gave it a unique sound. Musicians were superstitious about such things. There was a reason Grey had rebuilt a studio in this spot after all. She knew every inch of the studios at Harper Inc., knew how to coax them into behaving and giving her back some glorious music.

She'd never recorded here though. Maybe her dad had, but she couldn't remember him mentioning it. This had been Grey's space. Blacklight space. Sacred Harper ground. So how did Zach feel standing here?

"Sounds like a good idea to me," she said. "Get a feel for it again."

She circled the guitar, which brought her back face to face with the man. Who looked almost . . . relieved? Why? Because she'd told him that what he was doing made sense. Wait, was Zach nervous about recording an album?

He stood there, barefooted, wearing worn jeans that hung loose around his hips and a plain white T-shirt. Textbook. He looked good but up close, tired too. There were some shadows under those Harper eyes—more gray today—that didn't usually mar his face. Well, he'd been touring, and that was exhausting even if he hadn't been screwed over by his bandmate at the end of it.

"So," she said. "Faith said you're planning on being here for a while."

His face tightened. "She told you, right? About Ryder?" His shoulders tightened. She tried not to look at them. He wasn't taller than when he left—and definitely not since the last time she'd actually seen him—but he was broader now. Stronger.

All traces of the lanky teenager of her memories gone. Leaving only a man.

A distractingly good-looking man.

*Don't think about that.*

"She may have mentioned something." She held up a hand as his brows drew together. "The news is going to be out soon enough, Zach. You can't keep something like that secret for long. Frankly, I'm surprised you've managed it for this long. It's what . . . two weeks since your tour ended? Long enough for your management to be spinning bullshit about you all being out of town on vacation or something, but if you guys had anything lined up over the summer, they're going to have to start canceling soon. Then it will be all over the place. Have you got your stories straight?"

He grimaced. "I'm still not sure what the damn story is. Fucking Ryder." He shoved his hands into the pockets of his jeans. Which only drew her attention to the tanned muscle of his arms and wrists.

Dammit. Guitarists had good arms. His were no exception. In fact, they were a pretty damn good example of that particular piece of male anatomy. Maybe even a perfect one. The guitar tatts on his right forearm only highlighted the delicious lines of muscle. And the edges of a tattoo she hadn't seen before poked beneath the edge of the left arm of his T-shirt, making her fingers itch to push the soft white cotton up and see what he'd marked his skin with. And then she could—no.

*Mind on the job.*

Shoving thoughts of other things musicians were good at out of her mind, she made what she hoped was a sympathetic face. It wasn't that she was pleased that Zach's band was imploding around his ears, but the part of her that was Faith's best friend had to admit to a tiny bit of satisfaction that karma was coming around. Zach had bailed on Faith when they'd tried to get a career off the ground. They'd been struggling and then their dad had gotten sick. They'd taken a break to figure out their next steps, and Zach had been offered a temporary gig filling in for Fringe Dweller's guitarist. Temporary had turned to permanent, leaving Faith stranded, dealing with the brunt of Grey's illness, and stepping up to gradually take over running the business side of the Harper Inc. empire as he faded. Not to mention looking after Mina, who'd still been a teenager when Grey had first been diagnosed with liver cancer. And who'd then decided to marry her high school sweetheart at eighteen. Only to lose him in a car accident three years later.

Through all of it, Faith had stood, stayed. Been here. Zach, on the other hand, had run. That was his choice. And hey, maybe in his shoes she might have done the same. But maybe now he was going to have to make some different ones.

"Did Ryder say anything about what brought this on?" she asked.

"He's not using. If that's what you're asking. Not as far as I know," Zach said. "None of us are into that shit." He hitched a shoulder, mouth grim as he stared down at the guitar. Which had been owned by a man who hadn't exactly had "Just say no" as his life's motto. Not until it was too late.

Then he looked back up. "So no, Ry hasn't really offered an explanation. There was a girl about a year ago that he was mooning over and she split, but if that's what brought this on, then it's one hell of a delayed reaction."

His voice had turned frustrated. And she was here to ask him to take a big chance on her. So perhaps steering the conversation back into safer waters might be a smart idea. "Well, I think you're doing a smart thing. Coming back here, I mean. Get some songs together. See what happens."

"Faith told you that part too, huh?" He looked amused.

"Dude, of course she told me. She can't vent about you to Mina, she's trying to be fair."

"I don't see why she needs to vent about me wanting to record here."

"Did I say 'vent'? Maybe that's too strong a word.

Bounce stuff off of, maybe. Mina's not the best outlet for that when it comes to you. For one thing, Mina doesn't give a crap about the music industry. I do."

"Yeah, the studio seems to be doing great," he said.

She tried not to beam with pleasure. "Didn't think you paid much attention to the figures." She'd been working her butt off the last four years, hustling to keep the studio going as her dad had stepped back to retire. Sal Santelli's legendary skills at the board had been a big draw for artists interested in recording on Lansing. She'd been determined to show the world that nothing would change when he left. She thought she'd managed it in the end, but it had been a long hard slog to convince people that she could do the job just as well as Sal.

"I'm not stupid, Leah," he said. "I might not have the hard-on for the detail that Faith does, but I read the reports."

O-kay. She didn't want to think about Zach and hard-ons. In any context. "Oh. Good," she managed as she struggled to wipe the sudden memory of Zach naked that flashed before her eyes. "That's good." Gah. Now she sounded like a moron. To cover herself, she walked over to the French doors that overlooked the cliffs. Maybe if she opened them, the sea air would clear her head. Clear that damn scent of him out of her lungs. But then she remembered the pile of papers by the guitar. Sending a bunch of his stuff blowing around the room wasn't going to impress him.

She turned back. "So, you're here. And you're going to write. Then record some new material?"

He nodded. "Yes."

There was no good way to ask. Better just to get it over with. "Who are you working with?"

"As a band?"

"No." She shook her head, feeling kind of sick and hoping it didn't show. "Who's producing?"

He spread his hands. "That's not set in stone yet. I have a few people in mind. Why? Did you want the job?" He grinned at her, clearly finding the idea amusing.

She stuck out her chin. "Why is that funny?"

Those salt-water eyes widened. "Are you serious?"

"Why shouldn't I be? I'm a sound engineer. A very very good one. You know who trained me. You know my experience. And I'm producing now too. And no one knows our studios better than I do." She bit her lip, not wanting to say more. Like "No one knows you like I do." Once upon a time that might have been true. She'd grown up with Zach, used to know the ins and outs of his life like she knew her own, but that wasn't true any more. The man was a stranger. But maybe the guy she'd known before was still buried in there somewhere.

Zach's arms folded. "Leah, I—"

"Do you want me to send you a resume?" she said. "I can. I'm good, Zach. We'd be good together, I know it." Damn. That last part came out wrong. Because his expression turned wary.

"I'm not even ready to record," he said.

"But you're looking for a producer. You need that sorted out. So, I'm here. I'm available. I'm good. And I'm asking."

He shook his head. "Like I said, I have feelers out. I'm not making any decisions yet."

"Does that mean you'll consider me when you do?"

No answer. And his face changed to the patented

Harper politely-neutral-and-giving-nothing-away expression that all three siblings had learned from their dad.

Which meant that the answer was really "no."

"You want to tell me why not?"

He didn't move. "I just don't think it's a good idea."

"Why not? Because I don't have enough experience? You need something new. Something different if you're looking to make a splash."

"It's not that."

"Then what?" Realization dawned. "Oh God, please don't say it's because we slept together once upon a time?"

"Leah—"

She held up a hand. "No. Because that's crazy. It was one night. It was a long time ago, and I don't know about you, Zach, but I haven't spent the last ten years pining over it. I moved on. Hopefully you have too. So that has nothing to do with this conversation."

"I'm sorry, but no," Zach said.

She stared at him. He looked determined. Stubborn. Just like his sister. Which meant that "no" really meant "no." At least, for now. And that if she didn't want to end up doing something entirely unprofessional, like punching him for being so goddamn shortsighted, she'd better leave.

"You're making a mistake," she told him and headed for the door.

# chapter four

Zach stared at the screen door, still vibrating after Leah had slammed it.

Leah Santelli asking to work with him.

He hadn't expected that.

Hadn't expected her, which was dumb because she worked on the Harper estate, and where Faith was, Leah and Ivy Morito—the other member of the trio of trouble as he and Eli had called them back in the day—were rarely far behind. Presumably they weren't still quite as in each other's pockets as they had been as teenagers, but it was still a small island.

Leah Santelli.

Dammit.

He should have handled that better.

But when it came to Leah, he'd always had a way of sticking his foot in his mouth.

And she'd blindsided him with that producing question. Of all the things that might have brought Leah back to his doorstep, he hadn't imagined that particular scenario.

Still, he'd delivered his "no" in a manner that had distinctly lacked chill.

And now she was pissed.

Big green eyes ready to spark, hands on hips. Leah wasn't tall—maybe five foot five if she was lucky—but what she lacked in size she made up for in attitude. Or temper, perhaps.

He should have thought before he'd answered, let her down more gently. Because now Leah was mad at him, and that was going to make Faith mad at him all over again.

Well done. Back home for just a couple of days, and he was already screwing up.

He seemed to have developed a talent for that over the last few years.

Or he'd inherited it from Grey and it was just now making itself known.

Leah Santelli.

Some might say she was one of his first big screw-ups. He never should have slept with her all those years ago. Not when he was leaving and he knew she had a crush on him. But she'd been gorgeous—not quite as gorgeous as she was now—and she'd asked. And he'd been young and stupid. Now, apparently, he was older and still stupid.

He thought again of those big eyes flashing at him and the curving fullness of her mouth when she'd said hello. She'd been beautiful at eighteen but so very young. Though pretty damn persuasive. He'd seen her in the intervening years, of course. Not much in the last few years. She'd always been perfectly polite and friendly to him. Of course, this was the first time he'd seen her since she'd gotten her divorce. Maybe that was the difference.

Current-day Leah wasn't just gorgeous, she was fierce. She knew what she wanted. She had gone after it. No beating around the bush. No game-playing or flattering or sucking-up, the way most people in the music industry seemed to go about trying to get something from him. Leah had just laid out her offer. Just like she had at eighteen. It was undeniably hot—which was all kinds of wrong because she'd been pitching him professionally, not personally. And now she was pissed off at him. Had she marched straight over to Faith's place to tell her about him being a dick? He winced. He hoped not. Because that was likely to bring Faith marching right back here to read him the riot act.

He didn't think he wanted to be yelled at twice in one night. So maybe it was time to beat a strategic retreat. The watch on his wrist told him it was closing in on dinnertime anyway. And he hadn't yet made the effort to stock his fridge. He reached for his phone. Eli. Eli wouldn't mind if Zach invited himself for dinner.

"Bring forth the beef," Billy bellowed from out on the deck.

Eli shook his head in mock-exasperation. "Give the dude a grill and he thinks he's suddenly a five-star chef." He picked up the platter of steaks that lay on the counter in Billy's kitchen. "Hope you like yours well done. Dad's grill skills seem to lack a certain finesse."

"That's because Shane always used to work the grill at Blacklight parties," Zach said. "And if Billy is anything like Grey, then he doesn't do much grilling on his own."

"No," Eli agreed. "Plenty of ordering of takeout though. Good at finding the best barbecue in any given town, but I'm not sure I've ever eaten a meal that Dad cooked from scratch."

"How long is Nina going to leave him unsupervised?" Zach asked. He'd come to Eli's seeking dinner and a place where Faith couldn't find him if she tried to yell at him about Leah. It was, as usual, a little chaotic. The place looked like five people were living there with shit strewn all over the place. And Eli seemed to be cooking for five, judging by the amount of food and the size of the steaks.

Eli shrugged. "Mom will be out every other weekend, I guess. She's got a couple of big cases running at the moment, she's probably glad not to have him underfoot."

Billy's wife, Nina, had decided in her mid-forties that she was tired of just following her husband around the world and raising kids, and had gone back to college, followed by law school. These days she was a very successful lawyer. Zach had never been sure how their marriage survived being split into two very different worlds and very different schedules, but they made it work. Billy said he kept asking Nina when she was going to retire. Her answer was that she'd started late so she still had years to make up for.

"At least he's only attempting the steaks," Zach pointed out. He looked at the rows of bowls holding potato salad, green salad, pasta salad, and something made from one of those hippie grains he could never remember the name of lined up on trays ready to be taken out to the deck. He was pretty sure they'd all come from one of the delis in town. Fine by him. As a tourist town, Cloud Bay did food well. When he'd been a kid it had been more basic, burgers and pizza and Chinese and one nice French restaurant. But every time he came home there seemed to be a new café or restaurant. And the food was getting trendy. "And we're not going to starve if he burns them. Hell, we can go to a bar and get a burger if we need to."

Eli nodded, though the movement was half-hearted to Zach's eye. "Maybe." He rolled a shoulder, and a muscle tightened in his jaw.

Zach frowned. Was Eli in pain?

He was supposed to be recuperating. Zach took that to mean resting. But if Eli and Billy had been sailing half the day then that hadn't happened.

"How's the arm?" he asked and picked up the tray with all the salads before Eli could attempt to carry that and the steaks.

"Fine. Thanks, Mom," Eli said sarcastically as Billy yelled "Beeeeeffffffffff!" from beyond the door.

"A guy is allowed to ask how his best friend is feeling when said best friend is a klutz who manages to smash himself up a little too often."

"Three times isn't often. Besides, the first time wasn't my fault."

True. That had been Billy. Who made a bet with the boys that they couldn't climb the massive oak tree that dominated half the lawn to the side of the house. The same tree that Zach could see in the distance now.

It hadn't grown any smaller and it had already been a monster when they'd tried to climb it. Apparently Billy's skills hadn't stretched much to judging the climbability of trees. Or knowing that ten-year-olds couldn't defy gravity. That had been the first time Zach had seen Eli snap a bone. Not his favorite memory. Not the scream as Eli had slipped off the branch they'd been balanced on, or the sickening thump as he'd hit the ground, or the sickly white of his face when Zach had finally gotten down to him. Or the quiet fury on Nina's face as she'd come running out onto the lawn to see what had happened as Billy had carried Eli back toward the house.

"The second time wasn't either," Eli mused. "Someone skied into me, not the other way around."

He'd fractured a cheekbone and a few ribs and sprained an ankle in that collision if Zach remembered correctly. That had been the year they'd both turned twenty. Eli had spent Zach's birthday in bandages.

"Maybe not, but you'd think a guy with your history might not think a motorbike is a good idea."

"You owned a bike long before I did."

"Stopped riding it too," Zach said. "Once I realized how easy it would be to kill myself on it." He slid the door to the patio open and waved for Eli to go in front of him. "But you don't seem to have learned that lesson yet. So I get to keep asking you dumb questions."

"What dumb questions?" Billy asked, blue eyes lighting as he saw the steaks in Eli's hand.

"Zach was asking if he could have his steak rare," Eli said, grinning at his dad. "I've been telling him that your prowess with this contraption means that it's pot luck around here."

"Oh ye of little faith," Billy said. He slapped the steaks on to the grills with a grin that matched his son's. "I am the grill-meister."

"Okay, but if you're the grill-meister then you're also an alien who replaced my dad last night. Because last night, the steaks my real dad cooked were mostly charcoal."

"No one ever said I was a slow learner," Billy said. "I've got this now." He waved an arm at the table. "You boys sit and watch and learn. Zach, you want a beer?"

Zach shook his head. "Thanks, I'm good."

Billy frowned. "You saying that because you don't want one or because you're trying to spare my feelings?"

"I'm good," Zach repeated. Eli was still taking painkillers. Billy was a recovering alcoholic. Zach didn't need a beer. He didn't drink much these days anyway. Didn't like the way it messed with his playing if he got loaded. Damned if he knew how all those legendary musicians with equally legendary drug and alcohol problems managed to perform every night. Grey had pulled it off, but he wasn't here to ask any more. And he definitely wasn't going to ask Billy.

Besides, Zach had tied one on the night the tour had wrapped up, drowning his sorrows in very good tequila with Ian and Austin, the three of them venting their mutual frustration with Ryder. That hangover had taken nearly three days to get over. He was getting too old for that shit. And it was way too soon for him after that to have any interest in repeating the experience. He'd stick to soda. He wanted to start work in the morning. Hole up in the studio and start digging into some of the ideas that had been running around in his head the last few months.

The studio.

That reminded him of Leah. Of their exchange. Of the flash of hurt in her eyes when he'd said "no" to her proposal. Of how much he'd been enjoying looking at her before they got to that part.

"Something on your mind?" Eli asked as Zach followed him back into the house to finish bringing out the rest of the food. They made two trips, then Eli went back in a third time and came out bearing two bottles of some hipster-looking soda. He held out to Zach

Zach took the drink and glanced sideways at Billy. He loved the man as an uncle but he wasn't going to talk about Leah in front of him. "Nah, I'm good."

Eli looked doubtful, but then he gave a small nod and changed the subject to gossip about a band one of their friends was currently touring with as a substitute bassist.

By the time he'd eaten Billy's not-too-terrible steak, Zach was feeling a little mellower. Apparently more so than Eli, who, when Billy wandered back into the house to watch TV, grabbed a beer from the small fridge built into the stand that held the grill. "You sure you don't want one of these?"

Zach shook his head. "I'm good." He tipped his head at the drink. "Are you meant to mix booze with your painkillers?"

Eli rolled his eyes. "I'm off the strong stuff now, Mom. I can have one beer."

"It's *your* liver," Zach said.

Eli shrugged and opened the bottle. "So, you want to tell me what's actually bugging you?"

"Who says—"

Eli lobbed the bottle cap across the table, and it landed right where Zach's fingers were drumming against the tabletop. His next reflexive finger tap sent it bouncing back toward Eli.

"That," Eli said. "You only turn into a wannabe drummer when you're stressed."

Damn best friends. They knew all your tells.

"I'm supposed to be relaxing. So you have to tell me before you give me a relapse trying to figure it out," Eli said, leaning back in his chair and propping his bad foot up on another. He looked pretty relaxed to Zach.

"You're not that sick."

"Maybe. Maybe not. Are you really willing to risk it?" Eli smirked at him.

"Anyone ever tell you you're a drama queen?"

"Not often."

"Only because you look comparatively sane next to Billy."

"Hell, everyone looks comparatively sane next to Billy. Except maybe Danny." Eli lifted his beer in a toast. "To mad musicians." He took a long swallow. "But anyway, back to you." He gave Zach a smug "betcha thought I'd fallen for your change of subject" smile.

Zach contemplated trying to continue avoiding the subject. Eli could be as single-minded as Faith when he wanted something. It would be less hassle in the long run to just give in. "Leah came to see me earlier."

Eli's smile turned from smug to genuinely pleased. "Leah? How was she? I haven't seen her in . . . well, far too long." He paused for a moment, expression contemplative. "Wait, she got divorced, didn't she? Is she single?"

Zach felt himself bristle. Tried to ease it down. "Strangely enough, the subject of her sex life didn't come up."

"Damn." Eli sipped his beer again. "She was always gorgeous. Too bad she was kind of in love with you."

Zach flinched, then tried to hide it and almost knocked over his soda. Eli had thought Leah was in love with him? That was crazy. And why hadn't he ever mentioned it to him before? "Bullshit. Leah has better taste than that." He'd never told Eli about what had happened on Leah's eighteenth birthday. So he didn't need Eli poking around the subject.

"Maybe," Eli said. "So, is she still gorgeous?"

"Wherever your train of thought is going, I suggest you change tracks," Zach said, the words far closer to a growl than he intended.

Eli's brows lifted. "Why? You want to visit that station yourself?" He smirked at Zach, saluting him with the beer.

"No!" Zach straightened. "That station deserves better than either of us. And, in case it has escaped your noticed, that station is a Cloud Bay station. Not going anywhere. So she doesn't need to be derailed by either of us."

Eli held up his hands in surrender. "Okay. Kidding. Mostly." He frowned at Zach. "Either of us? Does that mean the thought has crossed your mind?"

"No," Zach said firmly. "Nor is it going to."

"Okay, then I guess you should tell me the rest of the story. Like why your encounter with the fair Leah has left you so cranky."

Zach blew out a breath. "Faith told her I was planning to record."

"Of course she did," Eli said. "That was always gonna happen."

"So Leah asked me if she could produce for me. And I turned her down." He shifted in his seat, hiding a wince as he remembered the hurt on her face again.

"Huh. Didn't see that one coming. Which was dumb. Totally should have seen that one coming. Do you mind if I ask why you turned her down?"

"Firstly because *you're* supposed to be producing for me."

"Not all the songs," Eli said. "Billy is going out on tour in a few weeks. You won't be done by then."

"You're going with him?"

"Yeah, he asked." Eli shrugged. "If I don't go with him, he'll just be bugging me every day checking up on me."

"Is your ankle up to touring?"

"Well, I don't have to work sound if I don't want to. And there are plenty of people around to carry my luggage and that kind of shit. Besides, it's not like Billy travels by bus these days."

No, the days of any member of Blacklight needing to tour by bus to save money were long gone. It was more like private jets all the way.

"So I can take it easy," Eli continued. "Lounge by the pool of whatever hotel we happen to be staying at. Check out the shows. Sleep a lot."

"Wait, does that mean you'll miss CloudFest?"

Eli shook his head. "Nope. Billy made sure Erroneous structured the tour around it. He feels bad for missing last year . . . says he wants to try to get Faith to sing again."

Erroneous was the band Billy had joined after Grey had died and Blacklight disbanded. They played a brand of rock a lot heavier than Blacklight had, bordering on metal. He doubted Faith would want to sing any of their songs. "Yeah, good luck with that."

"That's what I told him. Apparently Ben had all sorts

of enquiries for her after she sang with Danny at Cloud-Fest last year. She turned 'em all down flat."

He hadn't known that part. Ben Flaherty had been Blacklight's manager. Still was, in as much as he helped Faith out dealing with the money side of managing their catalog. And people had been asking Ben about Faith? Fuck. Faith was a natural musician. Like him. Hell, she was a way better singer than him any day of the week. And the reason she'd never really done anything with her music, was him. He scowled.

"Thinking about Leah again?" Eli asked with another grin.

"Fuck off," Zach said, trying to keep his tone light.

"Not until you tell me why you said no."

"This is too important," he said. "She's a rookie."

"A rookie who was trained by her dad—and Sal's one of the best sound guys out there—and has grown up living and breathing music production at the studio. Plus she's produced bits and pieces here and there. I've heard some of it. She's got a good ear. And good instincts."

Zach shook his head. "I'm sure she has. But I need more than good. I need superstar. This album has to fly. It's the first impression I get to make with my own stuff. And who knows if Fringe Dweller will resurrect itself. I don't want to find myself back on the hunt for a replacement gig."

"I think you're a bit beyond that now. Plus, you're forgetting the part where you actually don't have to work."

"Tell me again about that part, Eli. Then tell me how you spend your days swanning around the world sipping cocktails like a trust fund baby. Oh right, you can't. Because you're either working for Billy or hustling your

own stuff practically twenty-four seven." The last part
came out crankier sounding than he'd intended.

Eli's hands lifted again. "Dude. Chill. If you don't
want to work with Leah, then you don't want to work
with Leah. I think it's a mistake, but it's your career."
He eyed Zach cautiously. "Though if that's the case, I
think you need to think a little harder about why the fact
you said 'no' to her has you so churned up."

Oh, no. He definitely wasn't going to think too hard
about that. Not beyond the part where it was going to
piss Faith off when she found out about it. "She's Faith's
best friend. Faith doesn't need another reason to hate me
right now."

"Well, that particular hole you dug for yourself, man.
You're going to have to figure out how to dig yourself
right back out on your own."

"Faith likes you, you could put in a good word for me."

"Hmmm. Go poke the bear on your behalf? Especially when the bear now has a huge blond fiancé in
tow? Somehow that just doesn't sound like a fun time
to me." Eli grinned, waved his bandaged wrist. "I don't
need to add to my collection of these, thanks very much."

Zach couldn't blame him for that attitude. "It was
worth a shot."

"I'm sure Billy has a shovel somewhere."

"A shovel?"

"To help with the digging yourself out part," Eli said
and then laughed as Zach pitched the bottle cap back at
his head.

# chapter five

"That's some voice."

Leah jumped, her hand knocking one of the knobs on the mixer out of place. *Zach*. That was all she needed.

She was already running on a night of broken sleep, having been too angry when she'd arrived home to do much more than toss and turn. Facing Zach again so soon was the last thing she needed. So what the hell was he doing here?

It wasn't as though they had anything to talk about.

She reached to turn off the recording—Nessa having broken off mid note to wave her guitarist, Clay, over—and the sound from the booth, moved the knob back to position for the next take, and swiveled around in her chair to face him.

"Yes. She can blow the roof off." She narrowed her eyes. Why was he waltzing into her studio after telling her she wasn't good enough for him last night?

Her glare was wasted. Zach was staring through the glass at Nessa, who was talking with Clay, curls bouncing as she gestured enthusiastically and talked a mile a minute. He looked . . . impressed. He also looked good.

Dammit.

She was mad at him. She shouldn't care what he looked like. She should be immune to his stupid charms. But he was kind of hard to ignore. His jeans were battered and torn—and not the kind that came that way from the store—and he wore a T-shirt that had seen better days and his hair was all over the place and he still looked like he should be on a billboard or a magazine cover.

She, on the other hand, looked like normal everyday Leah. Jeans. Converse. T-shirt that was hopefully unstained with coffee. She glanced down at her chest. Yep. Stain free. And at least she hadn't worn yoga pants to work today.

"Who is she?" Zach asked, tipping his chin toward the booth.

"That's Nessa Lewis."

He looked blank. "Should I know her?"

Leah stared up at him. "Are you kidding me?"

"What?"

"She's the first singer Faith's been working with for her new foundation."

Zach hitched a shoulder. She took that as musician code for "Nah, I got nothing."

Okay, so maybe Faith was right and Zach was just another self-absorbed wannabe rock star these days. Maybe she'd dodged a bullet last night. "Wow. I knew she was pissed with you but you two really haven't been talking, have you? Or have you just not been paying attention?" The last part came out sharper than she'd intended. She took a breath, rubbing at the bare place on her finger where her wedding and engagement rings used to be. She couldn't afford to get into an argument with Zach with a roomful of musicians standing just a few feet away, separated only by glass. She doubled-checked that the intercom was off.

"I know she started another foundation. And that she's running a development program for female musicians. I just didn't remember the chick's name."

*"Chick?"* Ugh. "Double wow." She didn't know exactly what to say. Everything lingering on the tip of her tongue was bound to start the fight she really didn't want to have. Too much chance of saying things she couldn't risk saying to him if they had a real argument.

"Are you mad that I didn't know her name or that I turned you down last night?"

"Triple wow." She gritted her teeth, then forced herself to relax. "And you know, right now, Zach, three wows and you're out. I'm kind of busy here."

"I wanted to talk to you."

"Well, I don't particularly want to talk to you right now. So, please go." She made a shooing motion toward the door to emphasize the words.

Zach stayed right where he was. "Why not?"

"Leaving aside last night? There's the fact that Faith's my best friend. You haven't exactly been setting yourself up to win any brother-of-the-year awards over the last few years. You hurt her. So you figure it out." She rubbed her thumb over the base of her ring finger again.

"No rings, huh?" Zach said. "I heard you got divorced."

"You remembered *that* but you didn't know the name of Faith's protégé?" She wondered who he did keep in touch with on the island. Lou—Faith's mom and his step-mom—she supposed. Mina, knowing Mina. Some of the other kids he'd gone to school with, maybe? All of whom were well aware that Zach and Faith weren't talking. So maybe it made sense that they'd stick to island news and not get in the middle of anything by talking about Faith to him. Though that also meant he hadn't asked about Faith either.

"I've been busy," Zach said. "Touring a lot."

"Like father, like son."

Zach frowned, gaze sharpening. "What's that supposed to mean?"

"You know exactly what it means." She swiveled back to the mixer, trying to keep her temper in check. She had a job to do and it didn't involve Zach Harper. Far better to focus on the musicians who were thrilled to be working with her. Inside the booth, Nessa and the guys were milling around in a way that suggested they were ready to go again. She hit the intercom. "Another take?" Nessa looked around, then nodded. She and the band began to move back to their places as Leah switched the intercom off again.

"Can that wait a minute? I really need to talk to you," Zach said.

She turned her head to look at him over her shoulder. "I'm working. These guys are working. You, on the other hand, are not. You already made it clear you don't want to work with me. So you can wait until I'm done. Preferably somewhere else." She turned back to watch the band settling into their places. She ran an eye over the mixer. Everything looked good.

"You know, technically, I own part of this place," Zach said. "That makes me your boss."

"Faith's my boss," Leah replied. "If you have a complaint about my attitude, you can talk to her. Tell her I have a complaint about yours while you're at it."

"C'mon, Leah, I was joking."

"Well, maybe I just don't find you very funny," she said, giving Nessa a thumbs-up through the window. She hit record as the singer stepped up to her mic. "And maybe you should go wait out in the foyer. This is a private session, after all. Nessa's new at this and she doesn't need any distractions."

"Am I a distraction?" Zach asked.

He was smiling, she could tell from his voice. Trying to charm her. Well, she wasn't in the mood to be charmed. She wasn't going to so much as look around.

"Not to me," she said as she turned her attention to the music.

Zach strode out of the recording booth, annoyed. Though mostly with himself. He'd convinced himself that Leah would be okay after she'd had nearly twenty-four hours to cool down. He'd been wrong.

At this point, a smart man would probably retreat and try to redo the whole conversation tomorrow.

The main problem with that theory was that he didn't think that Leah would be any happier with him tomorrow. And that apparently he wasn't so smart.

He rolled his shoulders. Maybe it wasn't so bad. He didn't need the big studio yet. He had Grey's. He just needed to work his way into his songs down there. Get used to the idea that he was finally going to do this.

He was halfway down the hall that led to the front of the building when the door at its far end swung open and Faith walked through, balancing a bakery box on one hand. She stopped when she saw him, looking startled.

"Zach," she said warily.

"Faith," he said back, mimicking her tone. He wasn't really in the mood for another argument.

"What are you doing here?" she said. Absently she set the box down on the long counter that ran along half the hallway. The rest of the surface was covered with empty coffee mugs, neatly piled stacks of mics and cables, abandoned magazines, and all the other crap musicians left behind during the day. Faith didn't seem to notice any of that. She just opened the box and withdrew a doughnut, biting into it. The smell that wafted over to him was amazing.

"Can I have one of those?" he asked.

She shrugged, still chewing, but pushed the box so it angled a little more toward him. Not exactly enthusiastic agreement, but he'd take it. He grabbed one of the doughnuts and took a bite.

As doughnuts went, it was pretty damn good. "Where are they from?" he said. "I don't remember anywhere making stuff like this."

"Stella Campbell took over the bakery on Main Street two years ago. She's a genius," Faith said.

"Don't let Lou hear you say that," Zach said.

"Well, if Lou ever decides to open a bakery, then I'm all hers," Faith said. "But I don't think that's going to happen, and she insists on being a teacher instead of baking for me all day, so Stella is the next best thing."

"I'll say," Zach said. He finished off the doughnut in two bites. "She could make a fortune if she moved to L.A. Or maybe San Francisco," he amended. Los Angeles was full of health nuts these days. Ryder even drank kale smoothies. Maybe that was what had sent the guy off the deep end. He reached for another of the pastries. Faith smacked his hand away. "These are for Nessa and her band. And Leah."

Well, that explained what Faith was doing here. Checking in on her pet project.

"She has a great voice," he said, nodding his head back toward the door that led through to the rehearsal rooms and the booths. "Nessa, I mean."

"I'm aware," Faith said, lifting her chin. "Kind of why I chose her."

"You have good taste. And it's a good idea," he said. "Your foundation. It's tough out there."

"Something else I'm aware of, Zach," she said, and he winced.

Of course she knew. After all, he and Faith tried to make a go of it back in the day, touring as a duo. It hadn't gone so well. And he'd jumped ship. Now didn't seem like the time to talk about that though. "I was just leaving," he said. "You should go on in."

Faith didn't budge. "You didn't answer my question."

"About?"

"What you're doing here?"

"In the studio that I'm part owner of?"

"Yes."

He shoved his hands into his back pockets. "Came to talk to Leah about booking some studio time but she was busy with Nessa. So I'll come back some other time."

Faith frowned. "What did you do?"

"Excuse me?"

"The only reason for Leah to send you packing is if you did something to piss her off. So what did you do?"

"Who said she sent me packing?"

"Well, you had annoyed-Zach face when I walked in. And you're too nosy not to hang around a studio session and watch what's happening for at least an hour if no one chases you out."

"Maybe I've been here an hour."

"I talked to Leah about fifteen minutes ago when I was driving back from town. She failed to mention you were here, so I don't think so." Faith put her hands on her hips. She wore jeans and a T-shirt that were almost the mirror of his own outfit, if the mirror was a very girly one.

Faith and he were too alike in many ways. Maybe that was why they butted heads so often. He didn't feel like making Leah another reason for them to test their skills in pissing each other off all over again. "She was busy. It's all good. And now, I have to go. Songs to write and all that sort of stuff. Thanks for the doughnut." He moved past her, stopping to drop a quick kiss on her cheek—half surprised when she stood still and let him—and escaped through the door before she could interrogate him any more.

As it turned out, he had the perfect reason to stick to Grey's studio and the guesthouse for the next two days. Because when he woke on Thursday morning, it was to the annoying buzz of his phone. The stream of notifications drowning his screen was enough to make it clear that the news about Ryder had gotten out.

He flopped back on the bed, shoving the phone under one of the pillows. He'd known this was coming. He'd thought he was ready.

But apparently he'd been wrong. Because it felt like being punched in the gut all over again.

Still, he knew how to ride out a media storm and he was in the perfect place to do it. No one would get onto the Harper grounds to stick a camera or a microphone in his face.

Hopefully the press would be more focused on Ryder anyway.

He could turn his phone off and focus on his songs.

But he probably should give Faith and Mina a heads-up first. If the press did decide to come hunting for him on Cloud Bay, they might just try to ambush his sisters if they couldn't get to him.

He dragged the phone back out, scrolled briefly through the screen. Saw that he'd missed several calls from Jay. And a series of texts. Which could be summed up as "we need to put out a statement, so fucking call me already." There was a similar series of messages from Hal, who managed Fringe Dweller, as well. Austin and Ian had added to the barrage.

He fired back a series of texts. He didn't really care what the statement said. It would be some version of "we support Ryder, whatever he needs, bros before bands, yada yada."

He definitely wouldn't be making any statement in person. Not until he was less pissed with Ryder and could say that shit and not be lying through his teeth. Because sure, the dude's life was more important than the music, but the way Ryder had handled it sucked.

Much like the way Zach had handled Leah.

There was too much suck all around.

He sent two final texts—one each to Faith and

Mina—then turned the phone off, tossing it into the drawer in his bedside table for good measure.

So. Plan for the next few days. Play guitar. Write music. Hang out with Eli. Stay out of sight.

Figure shit out.

Easier said than done maybe but there was no time like the present to at least give it a shot.

But no sooner had he gone back downstairs to grab his guitar than the house phone started ringing. He stared at it warily. Faith calling to check on him? Or had some scum-sucking paparazzi somehow managed to get the number? He was tempted to ignore it but if it was Faith, she'd just come on over to check on him. Easier to have the conversation. He could hang up if it was anybody he didn't know.

"Hello?" he growled, lifting the phone.

"Zach?" Lou's voice sounded a little surprised.

He felt his shoulders relax. "Oh. Hey, Lou."

"Honey, I just saw the news. Are you okay?"

The concern in her voice made him smile. Lou, at least, would always be the one person guaranteed to stand by him. He'd known that since the first time she'd met him when Grey had brought her home to Lansing. He'd still been pretty young but he remembered the feel of her arms and the sense of safety. She'd never left any of them since that day.

"I'm fine," he said gently. "But thank you for calling."

"Of course I'm calling," she said, sounding indignant. He could picture her face, all bright blue eyes and cropped silver hair. "You just keep your head down and ignore the press. They'll lose interest."

"That's my plan."

"Good. Can I bring you anything?"

He hesitated. Part of him didn't want her to go to any trouble, but there was a bigger part of him that knew that one of Lou's pies would help his mood right now. Along with some of her common sense. He'd seen her at Faith's for dinner the night he'd arrived but she hadn't pushed to find out more about his plans since then. "How about you bring me a hug?" He knew the hug would come with baked goods. Added bonus but if he had to choose between pie and a hug from the tiny whirlwind that was his stepmom, he'd pick the hug.

"I'll be right there," Lou said.

Two days later he was leaving the studio in a mood—turned out the good effects of Lou's hugs and pie didn't last forever——after wrestling with a song that just wouldn't play ball for four solid hours, when he met Faith coming the other way along the path.

"Oh good, you're alive," she said.

"Yep."

She eyed him up and down. "Or maybe you're the start of the zombie apocalypse. You need a shave."

"It's my designer stubble," he said, scratching a hand over his chin. He'd never liked designer stubble. It itched. He usually shaved daily.

"Nope. Designer stubble looks cool." She squinted at him. "You look like Shaggy from *Scooby Doo*. On a bender."

He looked down at his clothes. Ancient tattered board shorts and a scruffy T-shirt that had several holes in it. He'd shoved his feet into flip-flops, intending to head down to the beach and work off some frustration on some waves. Okay, so maybe Faith had a point.

"I'm going surfing."

"Well, that's better than stewing in the studio, I guess," Faith said. "I was beginning to think you were never going to emerge." She pulled a folded stack of papers out of her back pocket. "I was bringing you these messages. Every man and his dog has been calling for you at Harper Inc. Including Jay. What happened to your phone?"

"I turned it off," he said. "Seemed like the sensible thing to do while Ryder is the media sensation of the moment."

"No, the sensible thing to do is switch to a phone that only a few people know about," Faith said.

"Two phones is a hassle." Grey had always had two. Or more, as he'd constantly lost them.

"If your other one is switched off, then it's really still only one phone," Faith pointed out. She waved the stack of papers at him. "Here, take these and I'll leave you alone. At least I can report back to Mina that you're still alive."

"Given I saw her walking Stewie past the studio this morning, she probably knows that already." It had been kind of nice to think Mina was checking up on him. Especially when he knew she wouldn't come up and disturb him. Mina was a painter. She knew all about holing up to work.

"She worries." Faith's mouth quirked and he wasn't entirely sure if Mina was the only one who worried.

He took the messages, trying not to feel too pleased that Faith had brought them to him. "What about you?"

"I worry that my entire phone system might be going to melt down," she said. But then she looked up at him, biting her lip. "Are you okay?"

"I'm good," he said. "Just don't want to get caught up

in the circus. Makes more sense to keep moving on with the plan, you know? I'm sorry you're getting hassled." They'd grown up with fame, knew the downsides of it. But he'd chosen to stay in the spotlight, and she'd stepped a few degrees sideways. She didn't actively avoid it in the way Mina did, but even so, she shouldn't have to deal with his fallout.

She nodded. "Okay. But you don't have to be a hermit. Come up for dinner tonight."

Another olive branch. Which meant he had to take it. "Thanks. I didn't stock up on enough groceries to keep hiding out here much longer."

"The grocery store delivers. Lou said there were press in Cloud Bay today. Hopefully they get bored soon. But we won't let you starve." She hesitated. "How's the writing going?"

"I'm going surfing."

She grimaced. "That good, huh?"

"Early days. Need to shake some cobwebs off, I think." Faith would understand that. And it seemed she did because she nodded at him.

"Whatever works. Enjoy the surf. Dinner's at seven."


When Zach walked through the open patio doors into Faith's kitchen, Leah almost spilled the wine she was pouring.

Crap. What was he doing here? What was this, national-Zach-Harper-darkening-her-doorstep-out-of-the-blue week?

"Leah," he said, coming to a halt just inside, looking just as surprised as she felt. "Hi."

She finished pouring the wine. Took a large swig of it. "Hi," she said brightly. "Wine?" She held up the bottle, still too caught out by his appearance to think of anything else to say. She tried not to look at the stairs. Faith was upstairs, changing her T-shirt because she'd spilled red sauce on it. She needed to change faster.

Zach shook his head, walked past her, and stopped at the fridge a couple of feet away. "Ah. Beer. I knew Caleb would have some." He cracked a bottle, took a swallow. Then another.

Was he nervous? What did he have to be nervous about? He'd turned her down. End of story.

"Bad day?" she asked. Dammit. When would she learn not to poke the bear? She was supposed to be ignoring Zach Harper. Consigning his far-too-pretty ass to the depths of whatever fiery hell would take him, burning the memories she had of him—past and present—and getting on with her life. That didn't involve asking the man how his day had been.

Zach grimaced. "Wrestling with a song." He didn't offer more. She didn't ask. Song writing was way too close to the subject of producing. She definitely wasn't going to be asking him who he'd found to work with. She might be dumb enough to poke the bear, but she wasn't going to hand it a stick to whack her back with.

Wine. That would be good. She drank again, hoping like hell Faith would reappear before she put too much wine in her currently empty stomach. The pasta sauce simmering on the big stove smelled amazing. Having spent the week eating at the studio, while she worked with Nessa and her band, she was looking forward to a meal that didn't come in takeout cartons or pizza boxes.

She eyed Zach. What the hell did you talk about with a musician when you were determined to avoid the subject of music? Did he like sports? She wracked her brain but it stalled, too busy cataloguing just how good he looked in the dark green shirt he wore loose over dark jeans. He'd rolled the cuffs up, putting his arms and tattoos on display. Dammit. It was like he knew her secret weakness. A very stupid part of her wanted to walk over to him, run her hands up his arms, peel off his shirt, and bite one of his tattoos.

She'd done that once. When he'd been deep inside her and she'd—

Nope. Stop. *Not* thinking about that. She dragged her eyes up to his face. His hair looked kind of windswept. Like maybe he'd been—

"Surfing!" she exclaimed. God. Had she said that aloud?

"Pardon?" Zach said.

"Er, have you been surfing since you got back? You used to like that, right?" Wow. She sounded like an idiot.

He looked amused. "Right. And, yes, actually. I went this afternoon. 'Round to Shane's place."

"Any good?" Cloud Bay didn't have world-class surf but the beaches on the farthest end of the island where Shane King's house stood on the top of high cliffs, got some good waves. She'd surfed there herself. Not yet this season though. That would require remembering what free time was. Since the divorce she'd been throwing herself into the studio. Easier than sitting around at home alone. Apart from the odd girl's movie night with Faith and Ivy and, occasionally, Mina, which was about as wild as the four of them got now that the other three were all hooked up, it was all work, work, work.

"Not bad. Been a few months since I've had time to

swim in anything other than a hotel pool." He grinned. "Salt water is way better than chlorine."

That smile. Pure delight. She remembered it. Had seen him grin like that when surfing. And when doing other things. Naked things. There was a sudden throb between her legs as she remembered.

Oh, God. Her girl parts were dumb. So very very dumb.

She reached for the wine to refill her glass. Zach lifted an eyebrow.

"What?" she said. "Some of us have been working all day, not surfing."

He held up his hands. "No judgment."

"Who's not judging who?" Faith said, appearing at the top of the stairs. She started down. "Zach, are you annoying Leah?"

Leah avoided wincing. Focus on the wine. Act normal. Faith did not need to know anything about Leah's unfortunate weakness for Zach. Leah had kept it a secret for a long time now and she didn't intend to change that any time soon.

"Not on purpose," Zach said. "I'm just drinking beer."

"Trust me, you can annoy people accidentally," Faith said, but she smiled at her brother. "Go find Caleb. Talk boy stuff. Leah's going to play me some stuff from Nessa's session today while I cook."

Zach tilted his head. "Nessa's stuff? Can I listen?"

"No. Because I haven't asked her if that would be okay with her," Faith said. She flapped a dishtowel at him. "Shoo. Boy things. Go. Do. Soon to be brother-in-law bonding and all that stuff."

"But—" Zach started to say, but shut up when Faith just pointed at the kitchen door. He picked up his beer, then stopped and grabbed another out of the fridge, before he retreated toward the living room.

As the door closed behind him, Leah felt relief for about five seconds. Until she realized that she actually wished he was still here in the same room with her.

Good grief. She really was stupid when it came to Zach. And there was probably not enough wine in the universe to cure her.

# chapter six

Leah didn't stay long after dinner was done, and Zach took her departure as an excuse to head out as well.

She'd seemed a little nervous around him, but maybe she was just still getting over him turning her down.

Hopefully. He didn't want things to be weird. Which was why he'd spent most of dinner pretending not to notice how good she looked in the red tank top and jeans she wore.

Because there was one sure way to fuck things up while he was home and that would be to tangle with Leah in a whole different way.

The evening air had turned cooler, clearing his head as he walked the short path through the garden to the guesthouse.

In another few weeks it would be warm late into the evening, making evening swims and cold beers the order of the day. He needed to check that the air-conditioning in Grey's studio was working or else he'd sweat himself to death trying to make this album.

He added that to his mental to-do list as he opened his front door and headed to the kitchen to open the French doors—smaller versions of the ones that graced Faith's kitchen—to let the air in.

The breeze ruffled the stack of messages he'd pinned down on the table under a bottle of whiskey he'd found in the pantry.

Salt Devil whiskey. Will's distillery. Mina had told him they were releasing their first batch soon. Maybe this was an advance sample. Not that he was in the mood for whiskey. Or the messages beneath the bottle.

But ignoring them wasn't going to make them go away and he had just enough of a buzz on from the three beers he'd had with dinner to make reading them bearable. Maybe.

He set the whiskey to one side and picked up the stack of papers. Press. Press. Press. Jay. One of the execs from Fringe Dweller's label. Press. Press. Press.

Nothing of any interest until the very last piece, which read only CHEN followed by CHECK YOUR E-MAIL.

Holy mother of—Chen Li was one of the two producers he was chasing.

He wondered where he'd left his laptop because there was no way he was turning his phone back on yet.

Then remembered it was lying on the table in the tiny galley kitchen in Grey's studio.

Tempting to leave it until morning, but he didn't want to miss a message from Chen. And it was early. He could get in a few more hours work once he was there.

When he reached the studio, the laptop was right where he'd left it and he turned it on and watched impatiently as it started up and connected to the Wi-Fi.

He found the e-mail from Chen, which, luckily, was

only from midday, not two days ago. Apparently he
was interested. Asked Zach to send a demo to let him
play around with and see if he could come up with a
sound.

Zach sent him one of his favorite songs from the current batch he was working on. It was simple and spare.
A good blank canvas.

Chen had a reputation for having an ear for finding
new directions to push musicians toward. He did the sort
of innovative stuff that Zach needed to make his album
stand out.

After he'd sent the track he scrolled through the rest
of the e-mails. There was a message from Davis Lewis's
manager saying that Davis had no availability. "No
availability" was producer speak for "not interested."
Damn. He'd tried to ignore the sting in his gut. Davis—
the other producer he'd gone after—had been a long
shot. The man was a legend. And these days he mostly
worked with artists who'd already hit the heights. Back
in the day he'd been a star-maker, though. But apparently
he wasn't going to be making a star out of Zach.

But Chen had been his top pick, so he was less worried about Davis now. Grey had always said you
shouldn't chase a producer who didn't like your sound.
Said it never ended well. After two Fringe Dweller
albums during which he'd seen the studio pushing to
mold the band's sound into a more radio-friendly version of the grungy indie rock they'd started with, he'd
learned that was true.

He didn't hate the music Fringe Dweller played—he
wouldn't have stuck around if he did—but he did think
Ryder, as self-appointed bandleader—was too quick to
agree to bend when the studio asked.

But they were doing okay—or had been until two weeks ago—so what did he know?

But for this album, even though he would use the marketing might of a studio if the right one was interested, he was in the fortunate position of not needing their money to fund the recording. Which meant he was going to get the sound he wanted and then find it a home. Present the studios with a done deal.

And if they didn't bite, well then, he hadn't ever spent much of his trust fund. He'd release the damn thing himself, sink some money into promotion, and see what the hell happened.

But to do that, he needed to have songs to put on the album.

Which meant he needed to stop worrying about what happened after they were written and focus instead on getting the job done.

"What the hell is that?" Zach turned on his heel to see Faith standing at the studio door. He hit pause, glad for the excuse to turn the disaster off. He'd listened to the song five times already since he'd opened his e-mail this morning to find it waiting for him—apparently Chen worked fast—and every time it sounded worse. It was a hell of a start to his Saturday.

"That is the mix of my song Chen Li sent me." He tried not to sound as gutted as he felt. Chen had worked fast but, in this case, fast wasn't good.

"Oh hell, no," Faith said. She marched over to the computer. Hit play. Then winced as the jangly electronic beats blasted into the air again. "Please tell me this isn't the direction you were thinking of."

Zach shook his head. "No." He didn't trust himself

to say anything more. He'd been so sure Chen would have the right vision for him. But the mix he'd sent him was so far from what Zach wanted, it wasn't even funny. In fact, it felt like someone was hazing him. Bubblegum dance music had its place. But it wasn't what he wanted to do. "Maybe he just wanted to make sure it was nothing like Blacklight or Fringe Dweller," he said as his voice—made weirdly tinny through whatever process Chen had applied—kicked in on the track.

"Maybe he's insane," Faith retorted. She paused the music. "You can't work with him."

"He's a hit-maker."

"He's not going to make you a hit with that." She scowled down at the laptop, hands on hips. "Play me your version of the song."

He frowned, surprised by the request. "The track I sent him?"

"How about you pick up that guitar and just play it?"

Faith in CEO mode. He looked at her, standing there in running shorts, an ancient CloudFest Sex and Sand and Rock 'n' Roll T-shirt, hair wild and looking completely sure of herself. Being in charge looked good on her. He grinned.

"What?" she demanded.

"You're cute when you're running the world," he said.

She stuck her tongue out at him. "I'm cute all the time, big brother. So pick up the guitar."

He did. Settled himself on the stool, feeling weirdly nervous. It had been a long time since he'd last played for Faith. And the song—about a guy trying to apologize to a girl—seemed a little close to the bone. So. Maybe he would sing it for her. It was a love song—weren't all songs love songs?—but maybe this once it could be a "hey sis, I'm sorry" song.

He let his fingers settle on the strings and began to play, losing himself in the music, letting it take him to that place where nothing else mattered and nothing could get to him.

When he finished, the echoes of the last notes fading as he came back down to earth, Faith was looking at him a little . . . weirdly.

"Do you hate it?" he asked.

"What, no?" She sniffed, and then smiled. "It's great, Zach."

That pleased him more than he expected. "You like it?"

"Yes." She shook her head. "Did you think I wouldn't?"

"Well, you don't seem to be that happy with me lately."

"Thinking you're behaving like a dick and thinking your music sucks are two different things, brother of mine. Luckily for you." She grabbed the laptop, sank to the floor cross-legged. Started tapping away at the keyboard.

"Are you posting rude things as me on Facebook?"

"That would be easier if you had a Facebook account that you actually used." She didn't look up. "Put the guitar down for a minute and come listen to something."

What was she up to now? He had no idea, but for the moment things seemed easy between them so he didn't want to mess that up again.

The guitar went back on its stand and he eased

himself down onto the floor beside her. "Can't we sit on chairs like normal people?"

"Nope. You need a different perspective."

"Is Caleb turning you into a hippie?"

That made her laugh. "Caleb is pretty far from a hippie. No. Dad used to sit like this sometimes in here. Said the music sounded different."

"Well, it's a theory." No one could accuse Grey of having a dud ear for music, no matter what his other faults had been. "Okay, play whatever it is before my back seizes up."

"Poor old man," Faith mocked softly. "We can get you a burly assistant to help you up and down."

"If I ever get an assistant, I don't think 'burly' will be high on my list of criteria. Probably because most people don't even know what the word means."

"You need to read more books." Her attention was back on the laptop.

"What kind of books are you reading where the word 'burly' is thrown around?"

"Good books. Historical romance."

"Girl books."

"*Good* books," she repeated sternly. "You can learn things from those books. Things the women in your life might thank you for."

He waggled his eyebrows at her. "The women in my life are plenty thankful, little sis."

"Oh? Are you dating someone?" she asked, still tapping on the keyboard.

Damn. He'd walked right into that one. "Not right now."

Her head turned toward him, face quizzical. "It's been a while."

"We're not here to talk about my love life, Faith. I do okay." He did, when he wanted to. But touring relentlessly didn't leave much time for actual relationships. And he wasn't into endless one-night stands. "New subject."

"Okay," she said. She put the laptop down between them. Then clicked play.

The voice that spilled out through the speakers was one he recognized. "That's Nessa," he said. "Great voice." Faith must have connected to the house network and pulled up the song from her system.

"Yes," Faith agreed. "She's the real deal."

He focused back on the music. Nessa's voice powering effortlessly through a song that was a little bluesy, a little rock, the guitars and drums providing a solid structure for Nessa's vocals to set on fire. "Nice."

Faith nodded but didn't say anything as the music played on. The song ended and he opened his mouth, but she held up a finger to stop him before he could speak. The next song was different in mood. Slower. Sexier. More . . . wistful. The band had been moved to the background, leaving Nessa and a single guitar and someone on keyboard chasing each other around with a stripped-down melody that somehow still packed a punch.

It was a great song.

When it was done, he kind of wanted to hear it again but Faith clicked a few keys, then closed the laptop.

"What did you think?" she asked.

"It's great. They're great." He almost envied Nessa. That first-album fearlessness that everything would be perfect. He'd had that once. So had Faith. He reached for the computer, and Faith handed it over without a protest.

"*Leah's* great," Faith said. "She's the one producing them. Nessa's got talent but she and her band were still really raw when I chose her. Leah's the one working the magic here." She tilted her head up at him. "Maybe you should ask her to work with you."

He froze in the middle of opening the computer.

"What?" Faith demanded.

*Busted.* "Nothing"

"Oh no, I know that look. And I thought Leah was acting weird around you. What did you do?"

No way he was getting out of telling her. "She came to see me, the day after I got back. She asked if I'd consider using her to produce a couple of songs."

Faith scowled. "And you said no. Dumbass."

"I was looking at other options."

"Like the guy who came up with that poptastic nightmare?" she said nodding at the computer. She sounded disgusted. "Did you even listen to any of Leah's stuff?"

"No."

"Well, now you know better. So apologize for screwing up, grovel abjectly, and ask her to work with you."

"Grovel abjectly?"

She nodded emphatically. "It's what men who've been so dumb should do. Women too." She grinned at him. "Though, in my experience we don't do things that require groveling quite so often."

He got the feeling they weren't only talking about Leah any more. But she was the more immediate issue. Groveling to Faith and Mina might take a bit longer. "I—"

"Don't go all weird and male and stubborn. Apologizing is a key part of any relationship."

"Leah and I don't have a relationship," he said, the

words spilling out a little too fast. Best to cut that line of thought off in Faith's head before she sniffed out any of his and Leah's history. He didn't think Leah had ever told Faith about it. Faith would, for sure, have had words to say on the subject of him sleeping with her best friend. And she'd never mentioned it. So, he didn't want her finding out. Or noticing anything like the weird moment there'd been in the kitchen last night when he could have sworn Leah had been giving him "take me now" eyes. Unlikely. But unlikely or not, he didn't want Faith getting anywhere near it.

"You're friends, you big dope. Or you used to be. That's a relationship," Faith pointed out.

"It's also what makes working with her kind of complicated."

"You've worked with friends before. You work with Eli. So what's the problem? Is it because she's a girl? Friends with boobs are still friends, Zach." She narrowed her eyes at him. "Unless her boobs are a different kind of problem?"

"No!" It came out too loud. "Not a problem." He bent his head to the laptop, hoping Faith wouldn't notice that he wasn't exactly telling the whole truth.

"Good. Because she's just divorced."

He looked up. "Wasn't that final like a year ago?"

"Who told you that?"

"Lou," he said. Faith's mom, who was also more of a mom to him than his own had ever been, had kept up her usual steady stream of information about what was happening on Lansing via e-mail and the occasional phone call. He didn't always pay attention to all of it, but he kept up with the big picture. Somehow that had always included filing away the stuff she told him about what was happening in Leah's life. "She also said it was amicable."

Faith sat up a little, toying with the honking big diamond on her left hand. "It was. That doesn't mean Leah feels nothing. She's a little singed around the edges, I'd say. She doesn't need to be messed around."

She took a breath and he thought she was going to say more, but she didn't. So he just nodded and tried to ignore the fact that he had a sudden urge to find Joey Nelson and punch him in the face. It didn't mean anything. He'd do the same if someone screwed over Faith or Mina, though it looked like he wouldn't have to do that any time soon. Will and Caleb were good guys. So his desire to squash Joey like a bug was purely because he'd grown up with Leah. One hundred percent.

Nothing to do with Leah's fierce eyes or the way her body curved or the way his memories of the night they'd spent together had been popping into his head at all the wrong moments since she'd showed up on his doorstep and asked him for a job. Letting it have anything to do with any of that could only be insanity. And a whole lot of trouble he didn't want.

"No messing, I swear," he said.

"Good. And don't screw with her about this producing thing. If you ask her, you need to give her a decent shot. Take her seriously."

"I always take music seriously."

"Yeah but sometimes you're not so good at remembering that the people involved have feelings too, Zach."

She said it gently but it still felt like a slap. A slap he deserved. "I know," he said. "I was an ass last year. I'm sorry. I know I need to make it up to you. I want to."

"Well, start by being more careful with my best

friend," Faith said, leaning over to shoulder-bump him. He caught her as she made contact, curled his arm around her shoulders to pull her into a half hug, and pressed a kiss to the top of her head. Damn. He'd forgotten how much he liked being with his sisters. Between Grey's erratic parenting style and his and Mina's moms bailing, the three of them had been the three musketeers. Their own little tight unit. Always there for one another. Until, of course, he'd left. Then proceeded to do his best to screw up the relationship he had with Faith completely.

He nodded. "I can do that." He let Faith go, but she stayed where she was, leaning against him. He angled his head so he could see her better. "So if you had to grovel to Leah, how would you start?"

"Probably with the biggest box of doughnuts Stella will sell you. Leah likes the custard ones." Faith peered up at him. "Stella doesn't deliver though. You'll have to go into town."

"Well, it wouldn't be a good grovel if I didn't have to run the paparazzi gauntlet, would it?"

Leah hesitated outside the screen door to Grey's studio, wondering what exactly she was doing here. Zach had called her just after five and asked her to come over.

Why, she had no idea. A wiser woman would have asked but the sound of his voice on the other end of the line had been so unexpected that she'd gone blank. She'd already been wrapping things up in the studio when he'd called but she'd messed around longer than she needed to, trying to psych herself up to seeing him again. After last night's awkward moments before dinner, her hormones needed a bit of a lecture about what constituted acceptable behavior around Zach before she saw him again.

But eventually she couldn't stretch things out any longer. She didn't even have the excuse of needing to keep working. Faith had managed to book Nessa a gig for a few nights in L.A., so she and her band had packed up and left after lunch. The studio's other clients had left two days ago.

All she needed to do now was lift her hand and knock. She wiped her palms against her jeans, feeling nervous and sweaty, but couldn't actually make herself do it. Maybe she should just go.

Before she could make herself leave, the inner door swung open, and Zach was staring at her through the screen.

There was an awkward moment of silence before he reached for the screen door. "Leah, hi."

She stepped back so he could open the door, distracted by the sudden heavy thump of her pulse in her ears. Dammit. Why did he do this to her?

He was Zach. Just Zach. The guy she'd known her entire life. She'd seen him gangly and awkward as a teenager, heard him tell a thousand terrible jokes, and watched him play baseball really badly. He should have no effect on her whatsoever. Yet there he was, hotter than the sun, making her forget how to talk again.

"I didn't hear you," he continued, as though he hadn't noticed that she hadn't replied to his greeting. "Did you knock?"

"I just got here," she said. "Just this second," she added. No way did she want Zach knowing that she'd been standing outside the door, hesitating like a weirdo.

"Good." He held the door open with one arm, angling

himself sideways so there was room for her to squeeze past. "Come in.

She managed to pass him without actually touching him by practically sliding her butt against the door-frame. She held her breath as she did so, not wanting to get a noseful of that familiar delicious Zach smell and lose her cool.

Once inside, she kept moving, heading into the rehearsal room without waiting for him. It was messier than the day she'd asked Zach to hire her. There were three guitar cases propped against the wall, not just one, though it was still Grey's old Martin cradled carefully in the stand nearest the mic and stool set up in the middle of the room. A pair of high-tech sneakers and a backpack lay on the floor behind the stool, and a tangle of cables and pedals curled around them. A laptop, a water bottle, and a yellow legal pad covered in Zach's familiar black scrawl sat on the small table along with packets of M&M's and pretzels. Classic Zach supplies.

He'd always loved M&M's, though he insisted that the green ones tasted weird.

*Just Zach*, she reminded herself again. The boy whose taste in M&M's she knew. The boy who never liked wearing shoes inside unless it was officially freezing. The boy who'd been mad for guitars as long as she'd known him.

The man who'd given her one of the best nights of her life and then left her behind.

*No.*

Not going to think about that.

Behind her came the sound of the screen door creaking shut, and then footsteps across the floorboards.

Right. Time to get a grip.

"Looks like you've been busy," she said, turning to face him.

Zach. The right-here, right-now Zach, who looked so damn good despite all her intentions not to notice. His inky blue T-shirt somehow made his eyes look extra green.

She took a breath.

"Well, I've been working," he said. "Not much to show for it yet." His mouth twisted. She knew that expression. The face of a musician wrestling with a cranky song.

"It's only been a couple of days." She did soothing-the-musician voice on autopilot. It was part of her job, talking nervous artists off the ledge, getting them to take the leap of faith necessary to make something magical out of nothing.

He hitched a shoulder. "I know."

"So what did you want to talk to me about?" Her voice sounded overly cheery, but hopefully he wouldn't notice.

"I wanted to say, um . . . crap, wait here." He disappeared into the back room where there was a tiny kitchen beyond the recording booth.

He reappeared fairly quickly, before she had time to wonder what the hell he was doing.

In his hands he had a familiar pink-and-white striped bakery box.

He held it out toward her. "Here."

She took it. The familiar yeasty smell of fried dough wafted up to her. "Doughnuts? From The Last Crumb?" Why was he buying her doughnuts?

"Faith said they're your favorite."

And why, exactly, was Faith discussing Leah's pastry preferences with Zach? She frowned at the box, trying to ignore how good the doughnuts smelled.

"I wanted to apologize for the other day," Zach continued. "I was a jerk."

"Yes," she agreed. "You were." He was apologizing? What was going on?

"So, um, sorry. I shouldn't have been rude. I could say I've had a bad couple of weeks, but that's not an excuse."

"No, it's not." She took a breath. Which only gave her another lungful of doughnut-scented air. Her stomach rumbled, reminding her that lunch had been six hours ago.

"So I hoped you'd accept the doughnuts and my apology," he said.

"Well, the doughnuts are a no-brainer," she said, keeping her face straight. He'd said "sorry." She was mostly willing to take that in the spirit intended. Especially when he'd had the sense to sweeten the deal with pastry. But it wouldn't hurt to tease him a little first. "I love Stella's doughnuts."

His expression turned worried. "And the apology?"

"Why's it so important that I accept?" she said. "All your big-shot producers turn you down?" She grinned at him, hoping he'd find the joke funny.

His expression didn't change.

Did that mean . . .

"Actually"—Zach took a breath, blew it out—"the answer to that is yes."

That shouldn't make her happy. But it kind of did. Did that make her a terrible person?

"Go ahead," Zach said. "You can gloat if you want to."

Dammit. She'd forgotten that her knowing him well meant that he had a pretty good handle on how her mind worked too. "Who said I wanted to gloat?"

"Human nature," he said. "Pride goeth before a fall and all that crap."

"Who did you ask?" she said. Gloating would be petty. She would rise above.

Zach reeled off a couple of names, including Davis Lewis—not exactly a surprise that he'd said "no" given how notoriously picky the man was these days—and Chen Freakin' Li.

"Chen Li turned you down?" Interesting. She would have thought Zach had just the right kind package of talent and platform to interest Chen.

"No," Zach said. He folded his arms. "Actually he was interested."

"You turned Chen Li down? Seriously?" No one turned Chen down, did they? The guy had a string of Grammy-winning artists and albums to his credit that was too long to list.

"I sent him a demo," Zach said. "He did a mix."

"And?"

His expression changed to a scowl so fast she almost flinched. "Let's just say he had a different vision than I did."

"Different?"

Zach didn't answer. Instead he flipped open the laptop and then hit a button. The song that came out of the speakers was electronic and poppy. Catchy in a way but hardly what she'd envisioned Zach playing. She could barely make out the acoustic guitar buried deep in the mix.

"*That's* the song?"

Zach shut the laptop, killing the music. "Yep." His frown as he stared down at the computer could only be classified as disgusted. "At least it used to be."

"So you said no?" She couldn't imagine it was the direction Zach wanted to take.

"Yup."

"Good decision," she said. "I don't know what sound you're going for exactly but that's not it."

"You know better than Chen Li?"

She hitched a shoulder. "I know you. Look, I'm sure Chen can make songs that will be hits for you. The question would be, will they be songs you'd want to play for the next twenty years?"

"Based on a sample of one, I'd say no," Zach said. He scowled. "Which kind of sucks. I loved what he did for The Scavengers."

"Yeah, that was cool." The Scavengers were another indie-edged rock band like Fringe Dweller. Their album with Chen had gone platinum. Which only made the mix he'd done for Zach even weirder. "But their sound is too much like Fringe Dweller. You need you."

"And you know what my sound should be?" He sounded hopeful.

She shook her head. "Not yet. But I think I could help you find out."

He smiled then. One hundred percent pure happy Zach. Happy with her. It shot through her like a lightning bolt. She blinked, but the image of him just floated in front of her closed eyes like it was burned there.

"I'd like that," he said.

Three little words. They shouldn't feel like a caress

over her skin, should they? She fought the urge to rub her hands over her arms where the hairs were prickling with awareness.

Maybe this wasn't such a good idea. But it was too good a chance career-wise to pass up. She just needed to control the situation.

"Right. So how about you send me that song and then I can try some ideas. See if you like mine better than Chen's."

"How long do you need?"

To be ready for working with him? More time than they had. Maybe forever. But she was going to suck that up and ignore it. "A day or two." She wasn't going to rush this. Wasn't going to screw it up. But she couldn't take too long. Zach needed to hear what she could do working fast if he was looking to have songs ready for CloudFest. That was a tight deadline to finish songs, get them recorded, and rehearse a set. Not to mention finding the other musicians he'd need. He needed to know that she could get the job done. "You've only just started writing, right? So you have plenty to do in the meantime."

Zach glanced around. "Yeah, I'm just settling in. Okay. A day or two sounds good."

She looked around too. The sky outside was just starting to fade into sunset, the light around them warm and gold and growing darker. It made the studio feel even smaller. Like the walls were wrapping around the two of them, pulling them into a tiny private world. Too intimate.

"You know," she said in that overly cheerful voice that kept surfacing around Zach, "I think we should work in the big studio for the first few days. When I'm done with the song, I mean."

"Aren't you busy with Nessa?"

"Faith got them a two-weekend gig in L.A. They're leaving Wednesday and won't be back until the following week. So, perfect timing really." Timing that might just save her butt. They would still be mostly alone in the big studio, no one else was due in this week, but the studio building was close to the Harper offices and Faith and Theo and the other Harper staff wandered in and out during the day to check out what was happening. Not to mention that the place was just bigger. Less intimate.

Zach looked unconvinced.

"The equipment there is better. You have to let me put my best foot forward here."

He considered that a moment, then nodded. "Okay. That's fair. So. That's settled. I'll send you the track and you'll get back to me?"

She nodded. "Deal." She tried not to let the grin spreading across her face get too wide. Fist pumps and happy dancing would have to wait until she was safely alone. She was going to produce Zach's album. Or some of it. She needed to keep her cool around him.

"Deal," Zach agreed. He held out his hand.

Did he seriously want to shake hands? That sounded like a bad idea. She didn't need to be touching Zach. Not when she wanted to keep her head. But she could hardly refuse to take the man's hand.

So she did. And tried to ignore the tingle of delight that passed through her when his skin met hers. She kept the handshake as brief as she could without being weird. Then stepped back. "Right. I should get out of your hair."

"All right. But I have one more question."

"Yes?"

He grinned at her and this time it was all kinds of wicked. As was the sudden glint in his eye. "Are you going to share your doughnuts with me?"

"Hell, no," she retorted and beat a retreat with the striped box firmly in her grasp.

# chapter seven

"What happened to you?" Faith asked at lunch the next day.

"Too many doughnuts," Leah groaned. "Sugar is the devil's work." Though really it was excitement and terror at the thought of working with Zach that had kept her awake last night, not the sugar high. She'd listened to the track he'd sent her—a song called "Falling Through"—about one hundred times already. It was good. But she could make it great.

"Tasty though," Faith said. She frowned as the breeze coming through the open French doors in her kitchen blew one of her long curls in her face and pushed it out of the way. Then her face brightened. "Who gave you the devil doughnuts? Was it Zach? Please say it was Zach."

Leah nodded. "It was Zach." She looked down at her plate, speared a piece of salmon out of the salad Faith had made them, so there'd be no chance Faith could read her expression when she said Zach's name.

Faith clapped her hands like a toddler who'd just spotted all four Wiggles. "He asked you, didn't he? To work with him? That's awesome."

"I though you were mad at him?"

"I am. Kind of. But that doesn't mean I can't approve when he does something non-jerkish."

"I don't think that's even a word."

Faith stuck out her tongue. "Sometimes big brothers require a whole new vocabulary to deal with. But he did ask you, right?"

"Yes. Sort of."

"Sort of?" Faith said indignantly. "He should jump at the chance."

"No, he shouldn't," Leah said. "Not sight unseen. He's given me one of his songs and I'm doing a mix. A try-out, I guess."

"Well you can't do worse than Chen Li. That track was so very wrong."

"He played that for you?"

Faith shuddered. "Yes."

"It wasn't bad," Leah said. "What I heard had some interesting stuff going on." She forked up more salad. Surely if she ate enough vegetables she could reverse the sugar overdose?

"It wasn't Zach though," Faith said.

"No. I agree with you about that. Zach is not the electro-pop kind. He could pull it off but he'd hate it."

"It would be kind of fun to see him in a video trying to do some choreography with a bunch of backup dancers," Faith said, then burst into laughter.

Leah laughed too. Zach as boy-band heartthrob trying to shake it was a mental image that was arresting for all the wrong reasons. "Yes, but it wouldn't be worth the pouting that would accompany it."

"No. I guess not," Faith agreed, looking sad for a moment. "Well, there's an opportunity for torturing my brother lost. So electro-pop isn't what you're planning?"

"Not at this stage. Not unless he gets annoying. Then it might be worth it, just to see his face. But that's kind of what I wanted to talk to you about."

"Oh?" Faith looked intrigued.

"I have a piano part for his track. I was hoping maybe you'd play it for me."

"Play it or record it?" Faith said, looking wary.

"Let's start with playing it for this try-out."

Faith glanced over her shoulder at the bright red upright against the kitchen wall. "You can play the piano just as well as me."

"That's not true and you know it," Leah said. "I can play but you give it that something more." She knew her limitations. She'd taken years of piano lessons, just like Faith. Hell, she'd started because Faith had already been able to play by the time they'd started elementary school together and she wanted to play too. She could play well enough to work out a melody or to keep herself entertained or to accompany someone at a jam session or to demonstrate something in the studio, but she couldn't turn it into art. Not the way Faith could. When she let herself.

"I'm out of practice," Faith said.

"Liar, I've heard you playing recently," Leah said. "Unless Caleb has secret piano-fu that I don't know about. Sound carries around here, you know. So if you're trying to keep it quiet, then you need somewhere more soundproof to hide your piano."

"That's just for fun."

Leah shrugged. "And that's just fine with me. But I really want this track to sound good. It's really stripped down. Just the piano and a touch of drums and the guitar. I can fake the drums on my computer but I don't want to fake the piano if I don't have to."

Faith looked torn. "Zach might not want me involved. He wants to do his own thing."

"I'm not asking you to join his band, just give me a decent piano part for my mix." Leah pulled out her laptop, opened it up. "Here, just listen this. I did a version earlier. You can make it better." She walked over to the piano, lifted the lid. There wasn't a speck of dust on it, which made it even more obvious that Faith hadn't exactly been telling the truth when she'd said she hadn't been playing. Her cleaners might dust the outside of the piano but they weren't going to bother making sure the inside gleamed. She touched middle C lightly and the note rang out, pure and true. So Faith had kept it in tune. Given that a beachfront location wasn't the most piano-friendly environment, that also took effort.

Turning, she pulled one of the kitchen chairs up next to the piano stool. "Come on, Faith. I'm not going to leave until you do. Don't make me invoke the best-friend-assistance clause."

Faith rolled her eyes. "You won't need to do that. I'll play the darn thing." She came to join Leah at the piano, making a show of reluctance. But as her hands touched the keys, she smiled.

Yeah. That was good. Even if Faith didn't want to perform, she still needed music. To play, not just to listen to. She'd cut herself off from that for too long. There had been quite a few years when Leah could have wandered into this kitchen and the piano would have been, well, if not out of tune because Faith wasn't going to neglect a Steinway—Grey had had the thing lacquered red but it was still a Steinway—but at least dusty inside.

"Okay, here it is." Leah hit play on the laptop. She waited while Faith listened to Zach's track with the piano part she'd inserted last night.

When the song ended, Faith nodded. "It's good, isn't it?"

"Yes," Leah said. "And it will be better."

She studied Faith a moment, searching her face. "Are you really okay with this? I don't want to bring up bad memories."

It seemed to take a long time for Faith to answer. "It's okay. It's not like the stuff Zach and I played together. And that was a long time ago." She played a chord. "It's ten years, when you think about." She blinked at Leah. "How the hell did that happen? We're getting old."

"Thirty is the new twenty," Leah retorted. "And we're only twenty-nine. Or almost twenty-nine in my case." Her birthday was more than a month away. Faith had turned twenty-nine in April. "So I still have my youth."

"It's just as well I don't have sheet music or I'd be swatting you right now. So. That's the song. Now play me the piano part on its own."

Leah pulled up the file. "This is still rough." She hit play, then watched as Faith listened, her fingers moving above the keys as she followed along. She'd have it memorized after she'd heard it once or twice, an ability Leah still envied. She could puzzle out something by ear eventually but she didn't have Faith's speed at picking up a song so fast. Zach had that gift too. But then, neither of them knew how to finesse a soundboard like Leah did, so things evened out, she guessed.

The track came to an end, and Faith flexed her fingers then began to play. The tempo was a little slower than what Leah had just played her but she had the melody right. She ran through it once, nearly perfectly and then stopped. "Okay, let me hear it again."

"Freak," Leah said with a grin, but obliged.

The second time Faith ran through the part it was perfect. Then she did it again, adding a couple of variations while she did so. It sounded even better.

"Okay, remember that," Leah said. "That was awesome. *You're* awesome."

"You wrote it," Faith said. "I just played."

"Then *we're* awesome," Leah said. "And now, you need to come down to the studio and let me record that."

If she held her breath any longer, she was going to pass out. But Zach was standing in the middle of Grey's studio, listening to the mix she'd made for his song, and she couldn't quite remember how to breathe.

Nerves. That was all it is. Nerves and the fact she'd spent almost all her spare time for the last two days working on his song. Sleep hadn't featured much.

She forced herself to relax. Opened her mouth and let out her breath noisily. Zach slanted a glance at her, then turned his attention back to the laptop. Four minutes. The damn song was only four freaking minutes long. Who knew four minutes was eternity?

She always got nervous waiting to see what someone she was working with thought about a mix, but this was ridiculous. She twined her fingers together. Then loosened them and sat on her hands instead, sliding her palms under her thighs where they pressed against the wooden top of the stool she occupied. She picked the stool over a chair because she couldn't curl up and assume the fetal position on a stool while she waited.

Being this nervous was one thing, but letting Zach see it was another. He needed to think she was one-hundred percent confident in her work. He needed to trust her. Or they'd never be able to work together. Producing an artist's work was an intimate thing. A producer had to be a cheer squad, a critic, an inspiration, a hand-holder, a sounding board, a taskmaster, or any of a myriad of other things the particular musician or band needed. Every collaboration was unique and, while she hadn't done a ton of producing on her own, she'd watched enough producers work their magic over the years to know that the key to all of it was trust. If the artist didn't trust the producer, the relationship would never work.

She waited impatiently as the song went into the last chorus.

Silence descended. Zach stood there staring down at the laptop, hands shoved into his pockets.

*God.*

Was he going to say something? Did he like it? Did he hate it? Hell. She bit down on her lip—hard—to keep from asking.

She should give him time to reflect, to process his reaction but . . . hell, he was a guy. How much thinking time did he need? If he hated it, couldn't he just put her out of her misery?

"Nice piano," Zach said, turning to face her.

"Thanks." It didn't seem like the time to mention it was Faith playing. Zach probably knew anyway. He'd grown up listening to Faith play. Surely he would recognize her style. And anyway, she wanted to know what he thought about the whole song, not just the piano. It was just as well she was already sitting on her hands or she'd be gnawing her fingernails down to stubs.

Zach looked back at the laptop. Oh God. Was he going to play it again? She wasn't sure she could survive another four minutes of limbo.

"Just tell me whether or not you like it already," she blurted out and then wished she could sink through the floor. So much for professional.

He turned back to her, eyebrows lifting. "You know I did."

"How exactly am I supposed to know that?" she said, indignant. "I forgot to turn my psychic powers on tonight and you were giving pretty good poker face while you listened."

"I was concentrating. That was my concentrating face."

"When you concentrate, you kind of frown and bite your lip," she retorted and then wished for the second time for a great big hole to open up so she could climb inside and be done with it. She did not want Zach Harper getting the idea that she paid any kind of attention to his facial expressions. "I mean, when you play, that's how you look. At least, from what I remember."

"I do?"

"Yep. But don't sweat it, most musicians have something they do when they play that they don't know they're doing. I used to wriggle my eyebrows when I was playing the piano, when I first learned. Used to drive old Mrs. Anthony mad. She threatened to tape them in place at one point."

He laughed. "That would be a look."

"I don't think she actually would have done it," Leah said hastily. "She was a softie underneath it all. But she had definite ideas about appropriate ways to address the piano. But enough about my childhood music traumas, we were talking about the song."

"Which I like."

"Just like?" she prompted. She slid off the stool. "Don't make me come over there. I might be shorter than you but I can take you."

"Is this how you woo all your potential clients?" he asked, looking amused.

"Only when they're all manly and annoyingly non-verbal.

"I'd be verbal if you'd shut up for a second and let me talk." He shook his head. "You always did talk a lot when you were nervous. Some things don't change. But you can relax. It's great. So yes, let's try this thing. Make a little music together."

She refrained from jumping up and down like a lunatic. But she couldn't stop herself indulging in a fist pump. "*Yes.*"

Zach snorted.

"I mean, great," she said, wrestling the grin threatening to spread across her face into a more-sedate expression. "I look forward to working with you, Mr. Harper."

He rolled his eyes. "Likewise, Ms. Santelli. You can talk money with Jay. He handles all that stuff."

Money. Right. She hadn't even thought about the money. She'd been too focused on getting the job. "It's your studio," she pointed out.

"I'm hiring you as producer, not studio manager. If I

was hiring the studio it would cover your fee as engineer, not producer. So you need to work out a fee."

"I'd—"

He held up a hand. "Do not say you'd do it for free. You're good, if that track is anything to go by. Don't sell yourself short. You wouldn't tell anyone asking you for advice to work for free, would you?"

No. The working-for-exposure thing so many artists and musicians started out getting fobbed off with was bullshit. "Right." She stuck her chin out. "You'd better hope you can afford me, now that you want me so bad."

Her words floated out into the air and there was a long shimmering moment where they just stared at each other, neither of them breathing.

*You want me so bad.*

Her cheeks felt hot. Say something. Anything. Anything that couldn't be interpreted as flirting like that last sentence to fall out of her mouth. "Jay. Fee. Right. I'll get on that."

"And you're good with Eli still working on a couple of songs?"

"Sure." She hadn't expected Zach to change his plans entirely. "We can do some planning and scheduling once you know what songs you have. Two producers might even help with your timetable if you want stuff ready for CloudFest. In the meantime, when did you want to start? Like I said, the studio is free this week."

His brow wrinkled. "Studio?"

"That's what we agreed, remember?" Please say he remembered. The studio was safer than here. Less chance for more awkward moments like the one they'd just shared.

"I've been liking the sound in here."

Dammit. "This is nice, Zach, but I'm not sure it's the best plan for you."

"What does that mean?"

She swept her arm at the room. "I mean, I know that you want to tap into the Blacklight mythos a bit—or at least the marketing machine will want that—but I think when it comes to your music, you need to be yourself."

"I am being myself. I'm writing the songs and doing the vocal and playing lead guitar. Not sure how much more "myself" it can get."

Awkward. But if she was going to be his producer, it seemed like she was going to have to get used to some awkward moments. And tell him the truth when he needed to hear it. Yes, she would be more comfortable working in the big studio but now, as she thought about what she was trying to convince him of, she knew there was a bigger argument. A less selfish one. "It's just that this is Grey's studio"—she nodded at the Martin on the guitar stand—"Grey's guitar. And, if you want to break out, then I think you have to let Zach be Zach. In a place where there aren't quite so many ghosts for you."

"I have just as many memories of Dad at the studio as here," Zach said, folding his arms, mouth set in a stubborn line.

"Maybe. But 'here' is the place where you used to sit outside the window and listen to him. The place you weren't allowed into unless he asked you. Grey's famous man cave. It's all his. I mean, until you came back, I doubt anyone else had dared to come in here for years. At the studio, you could always walk right in and watch him. It was never exclusively his." Blacklight's recording sessions had been fairly open affairs unless the band was trying to work on something that wasn't going well. Then Grey would get cranky and ban everyone from hanging around, but otherwise there'd been wives and girlfriends and kids and friends coming and going at all hours. She should know, she'd been one of them, just like Zach had been. "This place is . . ." she trailed off, not knowing exactly how to explain it. But this place was Grey's. And maybe Zach could make it his own in time, but he was on a deadline. So why put himself at a disadvantage?

She changed tack. "At least come and try the big studio for a couple of days. You can always work here writing, if you like. But the big studio is easier all around. Better gear. More space when you get the rest of your band in."

"When did you get so practical?" he said. But he smiled as he said it, and she knew she was winning him over.

"I've been running the studio for a few years now. I know what I'm doing. So, trust me. That's what you're going to pay me the big bucks for, after all." Well, semi-big, maybe. She didn't know how much she should ask for. Zach wouldn't care—he'd never had to worry about money in his life. Never would. She'd have to talk to Sal. Or maybe Eli. He'd done some producing, and explaining to him that she was working with Zach might be easier than telling her dad. After all, her parents liked having her here on Lansing. If she started producing, not all the musicians she worked with would want to trek to the island. Her parents had always been supportive, but she knew damn well they were happy she'd never moved away.

Zach went over and picked up the guitar, running a

hand over its curves, expression serious. Was he thinking about Grey?

He looked back at Leah and smiled lopsidedly. "All right, we'll try it your way."

Morning came eventually. Actually she knew exactly when it came because she was already up and walking along the harbor front, having given up on the concept of sleep sometime around four a.m. So she had the perfect view of the sky lightening slowly over the water.

"Just another day," she muttered as she reached the end of the marina and stopped to breathe for a moment as the sky painted itself gold and pink and deep blue, the light making the sleeping boats shine gold and the water below them shimmer while they waited for the day to begin.

A new day. Just like any other. Yeah and if she believed *that*, she could probably convince herself that pigs could grow wings and fly her to the mainland. It wasn't just another day. It was day one of the season of Zach Harper. A season she'd never expected would return. But here it was. She'd be spending a lot of time with him until these songs were finished.

She just needed to make sure that her heart survived the experience.

Five hours later she was sitting outside the booth, no longer worried about her heart, but starting to wonder if it was possible to die from terminal awkwardness. Zach had arrived about an hour ago, by which time she'd practically scrubbed the studio from top to bottom as well as changed her *set up* for the song they would be working on today about five times.

It hadn't done much to calm all the nervous energy that was making her feel as though her veins were full of tiny spiky balls bouncing around. She'd almost spilled coffee on herself when she'd offered to make Zach a cup as a way to break the ice.

He'd almost spilled coffee on himself when he'd taken it from her.

Then he'd retreated inside the booth after making the bare minimum of small talk, leaving her to go back to her seat in front of the board and try to summon the nerve to get started.

While she hesitated, she still watched him. Sitting there, looking nervous or something close to it. His fingers drummed the side of the guitar as he shifted on the stool.

She hit the intercom. One of them had to act like the adult in this situation. It was just first-day jitters. Lots of bands had those when they came into a studio. So it was her job as producer to make Zach feel comfortable so they could stop being weird and get to work. "Everything okay? You need to change something?"

He shook his head. "No. It's good."

"All right." She stared at him through the glass. If it had been Nessa, she might have gone in there and made chitchat until she relaxed. But she wasn't really sure that would work with Zach. "So why don't you just run through the first song a few times so I can get a feel for it and then we can try for a take?"

Maybe they should have kept this to Grey's studio. It was smaller, more familiar to him. But she was more at home with the set-up here, and she wanted to give him her best.

Zach nodded, closed his fingers around the guitar's

neck, and adjusted the angle it rested at on his thigh. Then he began to play.

It sounded great. He was good. More than good. She'd spent half the night listening to Fringe Dweller's two albums and the couple of demos Zach had e-mailed her, plus a few old recordings of him and Faith playing that she found buried in the depths of the studio server, but none of them were quite the same as listening to him play live.

Seeing him curving slightly over the guitar, fingers moving surely, she felt like she was seventeen again, trying to listen to him on the sly and wanting him more than she had imagined it was possible to want someone.

*No. No-oooooo.*

Not going to happen. She crossed her legs, leaning forward. She was here to listen. To hear the music and decide how to bring it to life, not to crush on the guy playing it.

She was a professional. She'd had famous guys on the other side of her glass before. *Hot* famous guys.

And she'd done her damn job.

So that was what she was going to do now.

No stupid crush allowed.

No sirree. All hormones would be maintained under strict control.

And then Zach began to sing.

God. His voice. Lower than Grey's famous tenor, but it shared some of the honeyed quality that had made his father's voice so compelling. And despite that touch of familiarity, it was somehow all Zach. Grey had been known for the hint of rasp under the power of his vocals. Zach's voice was clearer, even when he dropped to a low note. Stronger than she remembered. He'd been working on it, it seemed, and something told her if he

ever decided to let fly on one of the power-rock ballads
that Grey had been the master of, he might just be able
to blow Grey out of the water.

But that wasn't how he was singing now. No, this tune
was low and intimate and a little dirty. A song of longing and of trying to win back a woman wronged. And
seemingly every note he sang was perfectly pitched to
set all her nerve endings on fire, heat springing to life
in every female part she possessed.

She sat frozen, trying not to melt into a puddle as she
listened. She had no idea what words he was singing any
more, just that right that second she'd do just about anything to keep him singing them.

*Fu-u-uck.*

She was screwed.

Because she pretty much wanted to bolt into the studio, yank that guitar from his hands, and do him right
there on the no-nonsense studio carpet.

She dug her fingers into the edges of her chair to stop
herself doing exactly that and tried to remember how to
breathe as he sang. It took a few moments after he finished the song before she realized he'd stopped singing.

And that he was staring at her through the glass.

*Crap.* Was her face as hot as it felt?

"So?" Zach asked.

Her brain still hadn't kicked back into gear. Her
fingers closed around her water bottle and she drank, trying to regroup. Music. Producing. All that stuff.

"Leah?" Zach said. "Something wrong?"

"Um. No." She shook her head, hoping she sounded
less scrambled than she felt. "All good. Sounded great."

"Want me to run it again?"

*Absolutely not.* But there was no way she could say

that. Listening to him play and sing to her was precisely the job she'd just signed up for. Okay. So she just needed a quick break so she could regain her grip on her stupid hormones and then get back to work.

So what if the guy sounded like the devil had sent him up specifically to entice her into a sexual frenzy? That was just her stupid nostalgia talking. She just needed to give herself a chance to get used to the sound of him again. Get over the shock of him being right there just a few feet away from her again. Then the impact would wear off. Disappear.

Immersion therapy. Or something. That was the thing where they made you confront the thing you were scared of to make you lose your fear of it, wasn't it? She just had to spend enough time with him so she could re-accustom herself to Zach, then her hormones would calm down and reality would be restored.

But first, she needed a break. "Why don't you grab a water or something? I just want to move some of the mics around. Maybe switch one or two out. That guitar has such a great sound, I want to make sure we're getting all of it."

Zach's brows rose slightly. Understandable. It was early to be changing the set-up, but what the hell. It was the best excuse she could come up with right now.

"I promise I won't take long," she said.

To her relief, he put the guitar down and stood. She did too, heading for the booth door. Zach opened it as she reached it and she almost walked straight into him.

He caught her arm to steady her, and the shock of his hand against her bare skin was like fire. She stepped back in reflex and they did an awkward little dance around each other, while she tried not to breathe too deeply so that the smell of him couldn't make things worse. Not easy when her heart was thumping so hard she felt like she'd been running a marathon. She made it into the studio, and then fussed with the microphones for about five minutes so Zach wouldn't think she'd gone completely crazy.

He wandered back in from the kitchen just as she was finishing up.

"Hey, are you about ready to get going?" he said, passing her a fresh bottle of water.

"I just need another minute," Leah said. She bent back down and fiddled with the microphone stand. She was definitely stalling now. So ridiculous. Why was she being such a dork around him? It was just Zach. Time to put on her big-girl panties and get this done.

She straightened. "There, that should be better."

Zach was standing way too close, the smell of him surrounding her. Warm man. Fresh soap. The spicy scent that was all him. She'd never quite figured out if it was cologne or aftershave or deodorant. It didn't matter. All that mattered was that it was brain-meltingly delicious. It made her want to lean in, press her nose into the curve of his neck. Taste his skin. Gah. She straightened, picked up the water, and beat a hasty retreat back to the soundboard.

"Ready when you are," she said, pasting on a fake-cheerful smile. She was going to get this done if it killed her. She held the smile, cheeks aching, while Zach settled back into his spot. All about the work. Right. She could do this.

A few hours later, she wasn't sure either of them were going to survive the day. The music part was fine. But the part in between, when they had to talk to each other, well that was horrible. Long pauses. Stilted attempts at chat between takes. As long as she concentrated on the music, she could fake it for a while. But if the concentration lapsed, then she started noticing Zach. And her stupid traitorous body turned brain to mush. Stammering hot mess was not a look she was comfortable with.

And, as for Zach, well he wasn't doing much better. He'd knocked over a microphone stand, almost blown up the microwave, and somehow managed to delete a song from his laptop. Luckily, he had an online backup. He'd seemed just as tongue-tied as she was.

For two people who'd had some smoking chemistry in the past, not to mention an easy friendship, they were both doing a good impression of really dorky teenagers trying to talk to someone they liked for the very first time.

When five o'clock rolled 'round, she suggested they call it a day. Zach looked at her like she was a little nuts—most musicians didn't keep to a nine-to-five schedule—but the speed with which he packed up and headed for the door suggested she wasn't the only one feeling the weird vibe.

After he left she did her usual end-of-day tasks—backing up files, taking notes for tomorrow, making sure all the equipment needing to be stowed was stowed. All the while wondering how the hell they were going to get past this. Surely there had to be a magic bullet? A way for them to become comfortable with each other again?

That couldn't be so hard, could it? They'd been friends once and, heck, she'd managed to talk happily

enough with Zach at various Harper events on his infrequent visits home. When she'd been safely married
to Joey and any attraction she'd once felt for Zach had
been buried deep in the recesses of her brain. Surely
they could get back there again?

Perhaps she should invite Zach over for dinner or
something? Sure, the dinner at Faith's had been awkward too but she hadn't had any time to prepare for
that. No time to steel herself against his charms. But
with enough notice, surely she could do it? To be safe,
she could even invite Eli as well. After all, it would be
nice to see him too. She couldn't even remember the last
time Eli had been to Lansing.

That could do it. Maybe even round up a few other
friends. Have the sort of big-raucous, shooting-the-
breeze-and-ragging-on-each-other dinner she and Joey
used to host. That was one of the things she'd missed
since the divorce. Most of their friends had chosen Joey.
She couldn't entirely blame them. Most of them were
townies, and well, technically she was a townie too, but
her dad had always worked for the Harpers.

Which put the Santellis, in the eyes of most of Cloud
Bay's residents, firmly in the music-people camp. Rich
people, in other words. Which wasn't even remotely
true. Even though Sal had made a very nice living doing
what he did here at the studio, her family had nothing
like the sort of wealth the Harpers had. But still, their
friends had reverted back to being Joey's friends. Since
she had Faith and Ivy, she hadn't thought about it much
at first, too focused on surviving the divorce and trying
to sort out the messy tangle of feelings she had about it
to notice what was happening. But as she had emerged
from the divorce-crazy, she'd realized there were quite

a few people she hadn't heard from in a while. So, yeah, maybe dinner with Zach and Eli could be fun. She could ask Ivy and Matt as well.

Have a dinner party like a freaking adult.

Show her hormones who was boss.

She coiled the last of the cables into a neat roll and tucked it back into its place. Then turned back to see if there was anything else she'd missed in the studio. Her gaze hit the stool where Zach had been sitting all day and stuck there, as though glued. The memory of his voice, low and crooning, hit her all over again, and a rush of heated want snaked down her spine and spread through her body. Her hands curled into fists as she tried to will the feeling away. But it did no good. Zach was back in her head.

And she knew, deep in her gut, that it was going to take more than a damn dinner party to exorcise him.

The alternative—at least the only one that spring to mind right now as she stood there hungry for him—was to seize the bull by the horns so to speak.

The thought made her break out in a cold sweat, which at least cleared the fog of lust. Seizing the bull by the horns meant asking Zach to sleep with her, pure and simple. The nuclear approach. Burn off the awkwardness with some good old-fashioned sex. Though, if memory served her, sex with Zach had been anything than old fashioned.

*No, don't think about that.* Thinking about sex with Zach would only make things worse. Not that she was sure that anything could actually make the situation worse. They might grow more comfortable with each other over time, but, if she was honest with herself, she couldn't see this inconvenient lust going away any time soon. After all, it seemed to have stuck around for over ten years now. So she was either going to be horny the entire time Zach was on the island, or eventually lose her head and proposition him. If it was going to happen anyway, what was the point in waiting?

They were working together, yes, but Zach wasn't the kind to kiss and tell. This didn't have to have anything to do with that.

All that waiting could achieve was them wasting time that could be better spent working on achieving some mutual satisfaction, as well as—hopefully—improving their ability to focus in the studio. After all, Zach was only going to be here for a few months at most. Then he'd be gone again. Just like last time. Just like every time. She wasn't dumb enough to let herself fall in love with the man. She knew too much about how he was built for that. So a few months fling could be exactly what the doctor ordered. Kill the weird and burn out this stupid crush once and for all. So that when he left, she would be cured and able to get on with the rest of her life.

The only question was whether she could actually do it. March on over to Zach's guesthouse and talk him into bed. Her hands clenched tighter, fingernails digging into her palm as she contemplated the thought.

"What the hell?" she muttered and turned to leave the studio before she lost her nerve.

# chapter eight

Zach was standing at the fridge, trying to decide if he had something he could turn into dinner or whether he would be throwing himself on Faith's or Eli's mercy again, when someone knocked on his door, rattling the screen.

What the hell? He wasn't expecting anybody. Barely anyone knew where he was, for a start. But maybe it was Faith or Mina or even Eli, come to see him. Or, in Eli's case, come to make Zach come up with dinner for a change.

But when he got to the door, the person facing him on the other side of the screen was Leah. Wearing the same clothes she'd had on at the studio, with her dark hair pulled back into a ponytail and those damn silver hoops that had been drawing his attention to the sweet curve of her neck all day dancing at her ears.

She held up a six-pack of longnecks. "I thought our first day deserved some sort of celebration. I went with beer. Hope that's okay with you?"

"Sure," he said. He opened the door and stepped out. It was too nice a day to sit inside when they could hang out on the porch. Besides, after the way he'd kept finding himself watching Leah all day at the studio, tracking her moves like a teenage boy following the head cheerleader around like a puppy, outside might just be wiser than inside. It had been weird between them. So some extra space couldn't hurt. He lowered himself onto the top step, deliberately sticking close to the stair rail so that there was plenty of space for them both.

Leah sat beside him, not as far away as he would have liked, and handed him a longneck. "Bottom's up." She took a long swallow, and he found himself focusing way too hard on her mouth.

And on how close she was to him on the stairs.

He stood abruptly. Walked back down to the grass, then turned back to face her. She was watching him with an odd expression. As though she was trying to make up her mind about something.

"So, that was not the greatest first day ever," she said eventually.

"Can't argue with that," he said, glad he wasn't the only one who'd noticed. "But it was the first day. We'll find our rhythm."

Leah took another swig of beer and then pushed to her feet too, came down the stairs, stopping on the bottom one. Which put her eyes almost level with his.

He'd forgotten there were tiny golden flecks among the green. Kind of made you want to lean in and look closer. An impulse he wasn't giving into.

Those eyes narrowed slightly, her expression turning serious. "I'm not so sure."

He tensed. "What does that mean?"

She pursed her lips. "I don't think the problem is that we're not used to working together."

He was suddenly gripping the beer too tightly. Partly because he was staring at that lush mouth again. But mostly because he agreed with her. Work wasn't the problem. But he was just going to stay silent on that subject because opening that particular can of worms sounded like a really dumb idea. Pleasurable as hell, maybe, but destined for disaster.

Leah waited for a beat—giving him space to answer, presumably—then tilted her head slightly, the expression in those fascinating eyes suddenly all challenge. "So I guess the question is, are we going to deal with the problem or pretend it doesn't exist?"

In the interests of sanity, he had to vote for the latter. "What problem?"

She sighed. "Seriously? That's how you want to play it?" She set her beer on the step. The big hoops in her ears were dancing when she straightened again and put her hands on her hips, staring at him.

She'd liked it when he'd kissed her just behind her ears. Had trembled and sighed when his tongue had touched her skin. Soft. It had tasted of salt and warmth and something that was all Leah. His mouth dried.

Her eyes were locked on his. She licked her lips. He swayed toward her, unable to resist the lure of that mouth any longer.

"There!" she said.

He almost dropped his beer as he jerked back. "What?"

"That look."

"I have no idea what you're talking about." Total lie.

"I hope you're not one of those celebrities who likes poker," she said. "Because you are a terrible liar."

He took another step back, hoping space might equal sanity. "Did you hit your head on the way over?"

"Nope. And neither did you, so why don't we talk about it?"

She wasn't going to give up. Wasn't going to go away. Trouble was, he was fairly certain his inappropriate memories weren't going anywhere either. He sighed. "Do you think that's a good idea?"

"It's a better one than continuing to act like morons around each other in the studio."

He shrugged. "Maybe we'll just get used to it. It might fade away."

If there'd been a picture in the dictionary next to the word "skeptical," it would have shown Leah's face.

"So you're suggesting I ignore the fact that every time you come close to me, I remember that I know what you look like naked. How you taste? How it felt when you—"

"Leah, don't." *God.* She was going to kill him.

"You know, I believe in just dealing with things," she said. "Get it all out on the table."

They'd done it on the table. He'd laid her down and spread her legs and—

He swallowed. Looked up. She was blushing. She remembered too. Fuck.

"Okay, bad choice of words," she said, and her voice was ever so slightly too high and breathless. But she didn't falter. "I believe in being honest. So, yes, I remember those things."

Her gaze dropped to his crotch. Where there was no

hiding just how right she was about the clarity of his memories. "Looks like you do too."

If he gripped the beer any tighter, the damn bottle was going to shatter. He should put it down. But that would mean bending closer to Leah. He didn't want to get any closer. That would be stupid. Suicidal even. "What if I do?"

"Well, then, we need to do something about it."

"I hear cold showers are good."

"Overrated."

"The ocean is cold. Early morning swims?"

"You turn into a morning person? I find that hard to believe."

"No," he admitted. And she hadn't changed all that much either. She'd never been good at letting go of an idea. He'd learned that lesson the night of her eighteenth birthday when she'd made him an offer his younger self hadn't been able to refuse.

"Do you have any better ideas?" Leah asked, arching one eyebrow at him.

He drank. It was something to do that didn't involve thinking too hard about the topic of their conversation. The fact that Leah had the hots for him. The fact that the feeling was apparently mutual. The fact that he was an idiot of massive proportions.

"I'll take silence as 'no,' Leah said. "Well, I have one."

"Please don't tell me," he said, voice rasping. He didn't know what he'd do if she said what he thought she was about to say.

"Sorry, that's just dumb." She paused. Took a deep breath, which only drew his eyes to the curve of her breasts under her tank top. "There's always no-strings-attached hot-sweaty sex until you leave town again."

He almost choked on his beer. Had to put it down and stay bent over for a moment, as he tried to remember how to breathe. How to breathe and how to ignore the fact he was now hard as a rock.

Leah snorted. "Sorry, did I upset your delicate male sensibilities?"

He straightened slowly. Shit, she was determined to talk about this. "No, but you did surprise me."

"Really? I would have thought that a big rock star would be used to being propositioned by now."

Well, he couldn't deny that women made passes. But women whose names he didn't know asking him to sleep with them apparently wasn't half as . . . unsettling? . . . intriguing? . . . downright tantalizing? . . . as Leah doing it. "I think you're overestimating my fame."

That earned him an eye-roll.

"Hello, have you seen you?" Leah said.

"I don't stand around admiring my reflection, if that's what you're asking."

"I don't think you're Narcissus, Zach. I think you're a hot guy who would have to be an idiot not to know he was hot. Especially since you've been hot for quite some time."

"Oh, really?" He wasn't an idiot. But he had to admit, there was something about Leah standing there telling him she thought he was that was . . . pleasing.

"Stop fishing for compliments. I'm the woman who propositioned you at eighteen. You already know I think you're hot."

He shook his head, trying to quell the heat rising through his body and tame the hard-on that was making him very glad his T-shirt was long. Apparently part of him was very happy with Leah's announcement. "I didn't know you still felt that way." Not entirely true. There'd been too many little moments of chemistry since he'd come home to ignore that there was something there between them. But he hadn't imagined she'd want to actually do anything about it. "Or that you wanted to do something about it."

That part was true. It hadn't crossed his mind she'd even think about sleeping with him again. He'd known, at least some part of him had, that when he'd said "yes" to her all those years ago that he was going to hurt her. That part of her didn't think he'd really leave and had spun teenage girl dreams about what would happen next. But he hadn't said "no." Maybe that made him an asshole, but he'd been young and Leah, at eighteen, had been gorgeous. And she'd asked.

She shrugged. He couldn't help noticing that that did very nice things to her breasts in the scoop-neck tank she wore.

"To be fair, neither did I. But from the way you're staring at my boobs, I'm not alone in my lack of judgment. So, once again, why don't we lack some judgment together?"

*Yes, please.* No. Wait. He needed to think about that. Put the brakes on his cock, which was trying hard to take over all the thinking right now. Re-engage the brain. It was difficult. Very difficult. There were reasons he couldn't sleep with her. He just couldn't remember what they were right this second. "I just don't think it's that simple." As much as certain body parts really, really wanted it to be.

"Why not?"

It was a reasonable question. If you looked at it from her perspective. The perspective of someone who'd decided they should start having sex.

But someone was going to have to be sensible about this. It was clear Leah wasn't going to be taking that role so, fuck it, it was going to have to be him. Right. Reasons why he shouldn't do exactly what she—and his body—were suggesting. It was an effort to think of any. He had to wrestle with himself to get his brain back in control.

"Well, the most important reason is that we're working together."

"I think today proved that things can only improve in that department. And will only improve if we get this out of our systems."

"That's not what I meant. It's not just about us getting comfortable with working together. Sex complicates things. Sex with someone you're working with never seems to end well."

"It only gets complicated if someone gets all mushy and emotional. Like, I said, I'm talking strictly no-strings here."

"There's also the fact that you're my sister's best friend."

She shrugged. "Faith doesn't need to know."

It was his turn to raise his eyebrows. "You and Faith tell each other everything."

"Not when it comes to me sleeping with you, we don't." Leah made a little "go on" gesture. "Next."

"Wait, you never told Faith? About before?"

She pulled a horrified face. "No-ooooooo."

"Why not?"

"Because you were gone. And she went with you. By

the time she came back, I didn't think there was much to tell. You were clearly not coming back. She had enough to deal with." She hitched a shoulder. "Besides, I was fine. Back then I knew what I was asking for. Just like I do now."

She sounded so certain. And there wasn't even a trace of doubt in her eyes. But for some reason he didn't quite believe her. Which meant the only choice he had was to say "no."

"I'm sorry. I think we need to keep this simple, so no."

He thought she'd flinch. Maybe get mad. But instead her eyes just widened briefly, then narrowed. Her chin came up.

"If that's what you want," she said and then moved around him to walk away.

On Sunday night, Leah sat on the Harpers' beach, staring at the sinking sun and the path of gold the light painted over the water, and wondered if maybe she could just start swimming toward the horizon and find a boat out there to carry her off somewhere exotic. Exotic and one hundred percent free of Zach Harper.

She dug her fingers into the sand, curling them hard to dig in. She'd just spent the best part of an hour swimming in the surf and the breeze was enough to chill her as she sat there, wrapped in a towel, hair still wet but her stupid stupid body still burned with a heat that would probably give the sun a run for its money.

It was downright embarrassing. Or horrifying might be the better word. The past three days had been both those things. She had no one to blame but herself for that, of course. She'd been the one who'd marched right on up to Zach and propositioned him. It appeared to be a habit of hers. One she was never *ever* going to indulge again. The first time she'd done it, she'd half-expected him to say "no," and he'd surprised her with "yes." This time, it hadn't really crossed her mind that the reverse might happen, but it had. He'd said "no" and she'd left.

And then because she wasn't going to compound her mistake by letting it ruin the other thing she wanted from him—a big fat producing credit—she'd spent fifteen hours a day with him, doing her best to convince him, and herself, that she'd never asked and that nothing had changed. She'd been so goddamn friendly and professional that it made her teeth ache.

The trouble was that her teeth weren't the only things aching. Her body, it seemed, didn't care about humiliating rejections. It still wanted him. A little bit more every time he opened his damn mouth and sang. He wasn't singing to her. But her body didn't give a damn about that either. He opened his mouth and that voice rolled over her and all she wanted to do was roll over for him. Gah.

So much for his stupid theory that whatever it was between them would wear off. It wasn't. It was getting worse. At least, for her it was. And, if she was honest, she thought it might be for him too. She'd caught him looking at her more than once. Caught him being careful to leave a little more space than a man who was completely indifferent to her might leave, stepping away if he noticed he'd gotten too close. Which seemed to happen quite often. They drifted toward each other without thinking. Then one of them would notice and pull away, and they'd both go back to pretending everything was perfectly normal until they drifted in again. It was a ridiculous dance that had wound her tighter and tighter with every repeat of its steps. Until she'd been driven here to the beach to try and work off some of the excess energy driving her crazy. It hadn't worked.

But he'd turned her down and she wasn't going to be the one to ask again.

She'd rather die of frustration. Or you know, flee the island. Whatever worked.

The sun was slipping lower and her stomach rumbled suddenly. If she couldn't have Zach, then maybe the answer was to do some good old-fashioned comfort eating.

She dropped the towel briefly to reach for her big-ass bag and then performed some gymnastics after wrapping the towel bag around herself to ditch her bikini and put her underwear, bra, and dress back on. There was no view of this particular part of the beach from the big house and there was no light on at Mina's cottage, which meant Mina was probably with Will, but she was damned if she was going to risk Zach suddenly strolling down the beach path to find her half naked.

Armor—or clothes at least—back in place, she marched back up the path. When she reached the edge of the gardens, she hesitated. The most direct route to the spot on the long drive where she'd left her bike earlier went past Zach's guesthouse. She'd been a wimp and gone the long way around earlier after she biked over from the studio an hour after Zach had left for the day. But now she was hungry and well, screw it. If she was supposed to be acting like she was perfectly fine with how things were between her and Zach, then there was no reason to avoid walking past the damn guesthouse.

Except, when she got there, Zach was sitting on the front step, a beer in his hand. His brows shot up when he saw her.

"Been for a swim?" he called.

She nodded, tightening her grip on her bag, determined to just keep walking. But then he held out a beer.

"How about a beer?" he asked. He reached down beside his feet and drew a bottle out from a pack she hadn't noticed before at his feet. Held it out to her.

It was a perfectly casual question. No reason why she wouldn't have a beer with him at the end of a long few days of hard work. Unless she had a problem with him. Which she did. But she couldn't let him see that.

She bit back the curses that rose on her tongue and walked over, taking the proffered beer then retreating a few steps back. She dumped her bag on the ground and opened the beer, trying not to think about how they were now standing in almost exactly the same position as they had been a few days ago.

"How was the water?" Zach said, after a moment.

She shrugged. "Nice. No swell though, if you were thinking of going down later."

He twisted a little to look at the sky, now turning orange and pink and red. "Bit late for that."

She sipped the beer. It was cold and tangy and good but didn't offer much distraction from the fact she'd rather be anywhere but here. She'd just have to drink fast and leave. She tipped the bottle—and her head—back and drank some more.

"Thirsty?" Zach asked, looking somewhat amused when she lowered the bottle again.

"Too much salt water," she said. "You know how it is." As excuses went, it wasn't her greatest effort ever but it was better than admitting she felt terminally awkward.

Zach blinked slowly, his eyes steady on her. "Yes, I do know how it is."

Something rumbled through his words. Something low and raspy and not quite casual. Something that made her think he wasn't talking about salt water and beer. The thought made her freeze and she couldn't think of anything to say. She was imagining things. Her overactive hormones were making her read something that couldn't possibly be there into what he'd said. And she wasn't going to make a fool of herself again.

"So are you happy with how things are going?" Zach asked after a long pause. He put his beer down on the step.

She made herself smile. Made herself take a breath before she answered, so that her voice would be normal and calm. "Yes. I am." She hesitated. "Why? Aren't you?" Now there was a thought that hadn't occurred to her. She'd been so busy being the perfect "nothing to see here, move right along" professional producer over the last few days that she hadn't stopped to really talk to him about the results they were getting. Of course, it was early days and if he'd hated it, surely he would have—

"Yes," he said, cutting off her rapidly spiraling thoughts. "We work well together."

She avoided sighing in relief only with an effort of will. "Yes, we do," she said, a little too cheerfully.

"But—"

"There is a but?" she squeaked, unable to stop herself. Crap, was he going to fire her?

Zach stood, walked down the stairs toward her. "Maybe," he said.

That was hardly reassuring. "What—"

He moved a step closer, stepping inside the boundaries of what would be considered by any sane person to be personal space, and the words died in her throat. Her heart began to thump. Zach. So close. Why was he so close?

"There's still our other problem," he said, staring down at her. In the sunset light, he was outlined in gold like a painting of some ancient god. As if she needed anything to make him look any better to her.

" 'Other problem?' " she managed.

He nodded. "The one you brought up the other night."

"The one you said would go away?" she asked. She should step back from him. Out of reach. It was what a smart person would do. Yet, she couldn't have moved if she tried. She stayed right where she was, every inch of her waiting for his answer.

"Yes. That one." One side of his mouth quirked suddenly. "It seems I was wrong about that."

Wait, what? Was he saying what she thought he was saying? She stared up at him, suddenly dizzy. Maybe she'd fallen down on the beach and bumped her head and she was dreaming this whole conversation. There was a pulse throbbing between her legs now in time with the too hard beat of her heart. "What exactly are you saying, Zach?" He needed to say it this time. He needed to be the one who asked.

"I was wondering if you might let me change my answer? In relation to the whole hot and sweaty sex thing."

*Yes.* She wanted to scream it. But no, she was going to hold onto some last shred of sanity. "I believe my proposal was hot and sweaty and no-strings sex," she said.

She wanted him. She wanted him more than she wanted to breath right now, but she wasn't going to give in to anything more than wanting him.

He nodded. "Yes, that. Yes to whatever you want. Just, yes, Leah."

She could feel the tension in him, feel the heat of him standing so close. Could feel that he was holding himself back. That he wouldn't touch her unless she said so. The sensation made her giddy. Giddier. "A sensible woman would, at this point, make you grovel a little."

He smiled at that. Then his face turned serious again. "I'll grovel. I'm more than happy to kneel at your feet. Whatever it takes. Whatever you want."

The mental image set her alight. He had shown her he was good with his tongue on that long ago night. And the memory meant she couldn't answer with anything other than the truth. "I want you," she said.

"Thank God for that," he said, voice full of naked relief that only made her burn hotter. His hands landed on her waist, tugging her a little closer.

She stared up at him. "We're really doing this?"

He nodded. "Yes. Even though it's probably still a bad idea." His fingers tightened on her waist.

"You keep saying that. But here we are," Leah said. "And I don't care." Damn. He was even prettier up so close. She remembered the last time she'd been this close to him. That night had ended in heartbreak, but there'd been some truly excellent orgasms before that point. And she was older and wiser now and determined to be heartbreak-proof. She knew exactly what she was getting into and exactly what she wanted. Which was Zach. And some more of those excellent orgasms. As many as she could get while he was here. Starting right now, or her lady parts were going to explode from frustration.

She ran her tongue over her bottom lip, watched his eyes shift and focus on her mouth. Yeah, he didn't care either. "Are you still leaving once this album is done?"

"Yes." His voice was low, but it was certain.

So she had to remember exactly how he sounded when he said it. Keep it on repeat in the back of her head in case her emotions tried to get stupid. He was leaving. But he was here right now. And he wanted her.

"Good," she said, rising on her toes and putting her arms around his neck. "Then this is the same deal as last time. I want you. I know it's temporary. We don't have a problem."

"Easy for you to say," he said as she tilted her hips forward.

Oh yeah. Right there. Hot, hard, Zach. This is what she wanted.

"New rule," she said. "Less with the talking. This is simply sex. The only talking we need is to ask for instruction." She didn't want to talk. Talking came with thinking. There was nothing to think about. She wanted him. She was going to have him. Consequences be damned.

"What makes you think I need instruction?" Zach said. "I don't remember you having issues last time." He grinned down at her, the curve of his mouth making her water. She wanted to sink her teeth into that lip, wanted to taste him. "And I've learned stuff since then."

"So have I," she said. "So maybe we won't need to talk at all."

"You know, this is not exactly what I expected to be doing tonight," he said.

"Me neither. But you're still talking. Maybe I need to try harder to distract you?" She swayed her hips again, grinding a little against him and batted her eyelashes.

"If you try much harder, I may just spontaneously combust," Zach said. His right hand splayed over her back, yanking her closer. "God, Leah."

"*Still* talking," she said, feeling a little breathless herself. "Here, I'll make it easy for you." And she closed the gap between him. Hip to hip. Chest to chest. Mouth to perfect mouth.

Ah. She nearly purred with satisfaction as he kissed her back, began to work some of that Zach Harper magic.

She opened her mouth to him, let him in. His tongue touched hers, the taste of him, flooding her tongue, so startlingly familiar that she gasped.

Zach.

She'd dreamed about these kisses over the years. Now there was a guilty little secret. That sometimes she woke sweaty and aching—or worse sweaty and actually coming—from the tangled memories of her night with Zach. Why couldn't she have normal weird sex dreams about some celebrity that she didn't even like in real life? But no, she had Zach in her head. It had even happened a few times during her marriage, though she'd never have told Joey. Not in a million, billion years.

So. She had the man of her dirty dreams back in her arms. Kissing her wildly. She could feel the ache burning fiercer between her legs, feel how hot he was making her with just his kisses. So there was only one thing left to do. And that was have sex with him as many times as possible until this stupid annoying crush died from sheer exhaustion. Or boredom. Whatever. As long as it died so that when Zach left the island again, she was free to move on to whoever actually *was* Mr. Right.

They were moving now as they kissed, Zach half-steering them. Up the stairs. Through the front door. Partway down the hall. At first she thought he might be aiming for his bedroom but then her back hit the wall with a thud and she smiled through their kisses. Oh yes. Hot wild crazy sex. That was what she wanted.

She didn't wait for any encouragement, just hooked one leg around his hip and started pushing his T-shirt up. Zach helped her out, pulling it over his head. Which left her hands free to deal with his buttons instead. Who even wore button-fly jeans anymore? Such a rock star cliché.

But, she had to admit, they did make things easier, and presumably were less hazardous to sensitive male anatomy if one was about to have crazy wall sex while still partially clothed.

She'd also never been quite so thankful that she'd worn a dress today.

She took care of the last of the buttons, and Zach helped her by pulling his underwear out of her way. When her hand closed around his cock, he groaned.

The noise went straight to her loins, every part of her that wasn't already ready and waiting melting with lust.

"Condom?" she managed and he nodded. It took a minute to unhook her leg and wriggle free of her own underwear while he rummaged in his pocket. The pleasing sound of foil ripping reached her ears. She'd barely straightened again when Zach was lifting her, coaxing her legs back around his hips. Hands locked around his shoulders as she felt him nudging at her entrance.

"Leah?"

She wasn't exactly sure what the question would be, but any that she could think of had only one answer.

"Yes," she said, and he pushed into her.

"Oh *God*, yes," she added. So good. So full of him.

They kissed again, hungry and searching, mouths nipping and teasing, adding to the sensations flooding through her.

She clenched around him. Zach groaned against her mouth and began to move.

Her fingers dug into his shoulders as she held on and moved with him. The man was relentless, his rhythm sure and strong and fierce.

*Maybe this was the benefit of sex with a musician*, she thought hazily. *They knew how to keep time.*

Though how he knew the exact tempo designed to drive her crazy, she had no idea. But he did, and it was perfect.

It was Zach and it was madness and dumb and he was leaving but she could care less about anything but the slide of her body against his and his mouth at her neck and the ache in her breasts and the need that was rapidly turning her liquid.

"More," she said to him, voice raspy. "More, Zach."

He obliged and everything blurred and shimmered around her as the world went away. Zach drove into her, pressing her into the wall until she was suspended in pleasure, unable to do anything but give in to him, let him have her. Let each move he made inside her drive her higher and higher until finally there was nowhere else to go and she broke and came around him, half-sobbing his name as he muttered hers like a prayer and came with her.

Wall sex was awesome, Leah decided when her brain

had cleared enough to function again. Somewhere in there after that amazing brain-melting orgasm, Zach had lowered her to the ground, and they'd were standing now, her forehead resting against his chest, his arms braced on the wall to either side of her. The smell of Zach and sweat and sex surrounded her. Someone should bottle that. Not a scent you might want to wear all the time, but it was heady stuff. It was making her knees feel wobbly all over again and she could feel the little sparks of hunger starting to simmer and burn, even as the aftershocks of what they'd just done shimmered through her.

She wanted to do it again.

Which was perfectly in keeping with her plan.

She lifted her head and found herself staring at his chest. Which was currently heaving up and down. Which only served to emphasize how spectacular it was. Better than you got from just playing the guitar five zillion hours a day. He'd been a surfer when they'd been kids. That couldn't be an easy habit to maintain traveling the world. What did he do now? Run? Work out? Yoga?

He'd be a damn pretty sight in those tight-fitting bike-short yoga-pants things, all hot and sweaty . . . and damn, there were definitely more than just sparks of hunger now. A smart woman would leave now. But hell. This was their first night. And it had been a while since she'd had an orgasm that had involved another person. Zach was right here, all big and tall and willing.

At least she hoped he was still willing. She leaned forward, and swiped her tongue over his nipple. The groan that rumbled through him was a positive sign.

"Are you trying to kill me, woman?"

"Dude, you're a rock star. You're supposed to be a sex god."

This time the sound that rumbled through him was laughter. "Not sure there's anything I can say to that. If I say 'yes,' I sound like a conceited jackass, and if I say I'm not a sex god, well, that will get my man card revoked."

She tipped her head back, grinned up at him. "Well, then, how about we go with less talk, more action. If I'm remembering correctly, there's a perfectly good bedroom back there." She flapped a hand vaguely in the direction of the door they hadn't quite made it through.

"There is," he agreed. "With a nice big bed."

"Good." She pushed at his chest lightly. "Let's go show it what a sex god can do."

# chapter nine

Turned out that a sex god could do pretty amazing things. And that she could keep up with him. Maybe she'd turned into a sex god herself. Or was that goddess? Leah smiled, thinking that post-sex thoughts got pretty random when her brain was this scrambled. She lay on her back, staring up at the ceiling. All her limbs felt distant and floaty, lost in a sea of satisfaction. She might eventually be able to move in a day or so. But right now she wasn't sure she'd get more than an inch or two, no matter how hard she tried.

Her shoulder was pressed to Zach's. Who also lay, breathing heavily, on the well-rumpled bed. She leaned into him a little harder—all the movement she was capable of. "You okay over there?"

"Just trying to remember how to talk," he said.

"Oh good, I like it when I disrupt a man's brain functions." She turned her head toward him to find those ever-changeable Harper eyes were watching her from just a few inches a way. The look of sleepy satisfaction in them made her smile widen.

"You seem to be talking okay," Zach said.

"My mouth is moving, but not sure about the rest of me, if that makes you feel any better."

"You always did like to talk. Which is fine with me, by the way. I like a girl who can use her mouth."

She snorted at that.

He rolled his eyes. "Mind out of the gutter, Santelli. That's not what I meant. I'm a songwriter. I like words."

"Nice save," she said dryly.

"I noticed you like words too, just now," he said, wriggling his eyebrows at her.

"Shut up." She was blushing. No idea why. She hadn't blushed when he'd said all those dirty things in her ear. No, she'd dug her nails into his back and egged him on.

"No blushing. We're just getting started. I intend to find out all the things you like, Leah."

God. If it was going to get better than this, then she would probably just spontaneously combust. But what a way to go.

"I like your thinking," she said. "And I have to say it's good to know that you sex gods are pretty good in bed after all."

He laughed. "I was just thinking the same thing about sound engineers."

"What, you've never slept with a sound engineer before?"

He shook his head. "Most of the sound engineers I know are male. So, no. And I've definitely never slept with my producer."

Leah laughed. "Well, that's what you get for working in a male-dominated industry."

"I'm regretting my life choices as we speak."

"So you should," Leah said. "Look what you've been missing out on all these years."

He blinked, and for a moment she thought she saw something like—wistfulness?—float over his face. That couldn't be right. Zach Harper didn't do "wistful." He'd always been a charge-at-life, head-down, no-holds-barred kind of guy. Besides, what did he have to be wistful about? He was finally getting to do what he'd always intended. Joining Fringe Dweller had sidetracked him, even if it'd been a successful sidetrack. As far as she knew, he'd always intended to be a solo artist. Or at least the front man of his own band. Or his and Faith's band. And now he was back on Cloud Bay, and back in her bed, knowing neither of them held any strings for him. What more could a man want?

*Nothing*, she told herself firmly. There was nothing more he wanted and therefore nothing for him to be wistful about. Which was good, because the thought that Zach might be wistful about anything in their past was kind of freakin' terrifying.

He would be leaving at the end of this. That was what she wanted. That was what she was counting on to stop her doing anything stupid. Like letting her heart get involved.

So what was really needed here was a way to distract him if his brain was going down any sort of nostalgia track. And she had a pretty good idea how to do that. In fact she was pretty keen on the thought. Which was kind of crazy, they'd already done it twice. And those two times had involved three, maybe four, orgasms. She was already losing count and it was only their first night. The man really was a sex god. A fact she fully intended to take advantage of.

Starting right now.

She rolled toward him, and threw her leg over his thighs.

"Leah?" he said, sounding startled.

She kept her voice light. "If you think I'm wasting any of this, you need to think again."

"I think we've created a monster," Zach said with a grin.

She reached out and put her hand on his cock, delighted to feel it start to stir to life again under her palm. Apparently sex gods had divine powers of recovery too. "Not yet," she said grinning down at him, "but I'm working on it."

The next time she got to pause for breath was when she was wrapping her wet hair in a towel after a bone-melting session of shower sex. It had been awesome, but her stomach was starting to suggest that it was long past dinner time and, judging by the way her legs were trembling, there was no way she would survive another bout with Zach without refueling.

"You got any food in this place?"

Zach paused in the act of wrapping a towel around his waist. She was tempted to yank it off him again so that she could keep admiring the long lean lines of his body. But that would have to wait. She was still getting used to the sight of him. He was different now. More muscled. All man. And she needed to adjust her mental image. Let reality override memory.

"I have the basics," Zach said.

"Right now, I'll take anything," she said. "I don't know about you, but I'm starving."

"Worked up an appetite, have you?" Zach said, tucking the towel into place.

"I calculate that we've burned about eleventy zillion calories between us. I think we've earned a snack." She wrapped the towel turban style around her wet hair and left the bathroom to find her clothes. It was late now, and she doubted anyone was going to come to the guesthouse, but you never knew. After all, Eli and Billy were on the island. And Billy, like most of the Blacklight guys, was a night owl. It would be just like him to turn up on Zach's doorstep wanting to chew the fat about old times. And while she might be able to come up with a feasible excuse for why she'd used Zach's shower after a long day of recording in the studio, she doubted she could justify being found wearing only a towel while eating a meal with Zach. So, clothes were necessary.

By the time she dressed and finished drying her hair, Zach had relocated to the kitchen. She found him rummaging in the fridge, looking at the shelves, and pulling random stuff out.

"What did you find? Anything good?"

"Eggs, bacon, cheese, leftover Chinese from the other night. I think there's chips and salsa and stuff in the pantry," he said. "I got groceries a few days ago, but supplies are getting low again. There's bread and shit. You know, peanut butter, jelly."

"You still like peanut butter and jelly sandwiches?" she asked, delighted. "Some things really never change."

"Hey, you have a thing about doughnuts, I have a thing about PBJ. Everyone's gotta have a vice."

"I'm pretty sure that rock star sex gods are supposed

to have vices other than peanut butter and jelly sandwiches," she said. "It would ruin your street cred if that ever got out."

"I think you overestimate how much street cred I might have," Zach said, bending to take plates out of the cabinet. "And peanut butter and jelly is always pretty easy to find when you're on the road. It's my version of comfort food. Dad used to make peanut butter and jelly sandwiches at midnight and sneak them up to me in my room when Lou wasn't looking."

"That definitely sounds like Grey," Leah said with a smile. "Okay you can have a sandwich, but I think I'm going to make bacon and eggs. Assuming this place has a frying pan of some kind."

"This place has just about everything," Zach said. "Dad went all out stocking the guesthouses when he built them. He wanted his friends to be able to do whatever they wanted. Including cooking. Not that I'm sure many of them ever did." He moved to another cabinet, extracted a frying pan. "If I make toast, do I get some of those bacon and eggs as well?"

"Deal."

The cooking went fast enough—it wasn't like bacon and eggs was anything too complicated. And she and Zach moved easily together around the kitchen, passing plates and utensils and ingredients without the need to talk much. Almost as though they had been cooking together for years. Maybe it was all that time they'd spent watching Lou cook in the Harper kitchen as kids, or the time Zach had spent hanging around the Santelli house, angling to get his hands on some of Leah's mom's lasagna. Whatever the reason, it was kind of nice.

The bacon and eggs eased some of the rumblings in

her belly, and by the time she was finishing her third piece of toast, this one smeared with some of Zach's peanut butter, she was starting to feel human again. And starting to think a little harder about what they had just done.

Sleeping with Zach. Which, from the point of view of her very satisfied body, was undeniably awesome. But from the point of view of the rest of her life, it also had the potential to be undeniably complicated.

She put down the toast, suddenly not so hungry. "You know, we left the rest of those beers outside."

"I don't think a few hours in the open air is going to hurt them," Zach said, pushing his own plate away. "But I can grab them if you feel like one. They might still be cool."

She shook her head. "No, it's a bit late for me. And we have to work tomorrow." She shifted on the chair.

"Something on your mind?" Zach said, watching her.

"I was thinking that we need to talk about how we can handle this," she said, waving her hand back and forth between them. "I mean, if this is something you want to keep doing, of course."

Zach nodded without hesitating. "You're not getting rid of me that easily."

She tried not to feel too pleased about that, but it made her feel ridiculously happy. She smooshed that part of her back under control. "Okay, then we need to talk about it. I mean, do you want everyone to know?"

"Do you?" he parried.

Part of her wanted to shout it from the rooftops. But luckily that wasn't the part that was in charge. She took a breath. She'd started this whole thing by being honest. No point changing that approach now. "You're leaving. It seems kind of mean to let everyone get excited about the two of us being together if it's only a short-term thing."

"So you don't want to tell anyone?" Zach asked. He pushed back his chair, expression not quite a frown, but definitely not entirely happy.

"I just think it's going to cause more trouble than it's worth," Leah said. "For one thing, I don't want to be the 'got the gig because she was screwing the talent' girl. And for another, well, you know what your family's like. Mine's probably worse. If they think we are seeing each other, they're going to start spinning all sorts of fantasies in their heads."

"I think they're all pretty distracted by Faith and Caleb's wedding, don't you?" Zach said.

"In my experience, wedding fever spreads very easily," Leah said. "I'm not sure why this idea bothers you. I mean, you're leaving, right? This is temporary. Why make it more complicated than it has to be?"

He shrugged. Then picked up his plate and carried it over to the counter, dropping the silverware into the sink with a little more force than seemed strictly necessary

"Zach?" she said. Lou had raised all her kids to be helpful—they didn't get out of doing chores around the house just because they were Grey Harper's kids. But Zach had never struck her as the kind of guy who got up and started doing the dishes straightaway after dinner. The fact he was doing so now meant that he was either pissed off or trying to avoid the rest of this conversation. Well, she wasn't gonna let that happen. This was something that needed to be sorted out before they went any further. Otherwise someone was going to get hurt. And she didn't want that someone to be her.

"Where do you keep the dish towels?" she asked, joining him at the sink.

"I was just going to put everything in the dishwasher," Zach said.

That only confirmed her suspicions. After all, no one who regularly washed dishes would put a cast-iron skillet in the dishwasher. "How about we just finish this conversation? Then we'll know where we stand."

"Not big on beating around the bush, are you?" Zach said.

She shook her head. "Generally I find it just saves a lot of time to ask the question up front."

"If you want to keep this secret, that's fine with me," Zach said.

He sounded casual enough, but she wasn't entirely convinced he was telling the truth. Though, she couldn't really figure out why he wasn't perfectly happy to be agreeing to sneak around. Wasn't that what guys wanted—hot sex with no commitments? No needy females demanding their attention all the time? She shook her head. She really hoped Zach wasn't one of those guys. The rock star cliché. She didn't want him to be the cliché. But then, why was it throwing her that he wasn't behaving like one?

Maybe she was the one who was odd. But she couldn't see any other way that this would work. Leaving aside the fact that Zach was Faith's brother—and that was kind of awkward—Cloud Bay was too small a town to not expect everyone to get very interested very fast if Zach and Leah started dating in the open.

"Good," she said eventually. "Then we're agreed."

Zach hitched a shoulder. Not exactly a full-blooded nod of agreement. But it would have to do.

"So how do you see this working?" he asked. "I mean, Faith and Mina both live right here, so it's not exactly going to be easy to fly under the radar. Are you thinking we do this at your place?"

"God, no. My parents live only a few blocks away. And you know what Cloud Bay is like. You'd only have to drive your car up and park out front of my house once and the entire island would have us engaged in about five seconds flat."

"Well, what then? I mean, I guess there's always the studio. But sex on the carpet gets old pretty quick." He grinned at her. "And it's kind of hard to explain why you have carpet burns in awkward places."

She considered the problem. She had to confess she hadn't thought this part through. Because she hadn't expected Zach to change his mind. Apparently she was a slow learner. "We going to be working pretty long hours, so that explains us hanging out. I mean, making music isn't all about recording time. Faith is busy with Cloud-Fest, and with the wedding, and Mina's house could practically burn down around her ears when she's painting. She's got a show coming up soon. So I think, as long as we're careful, it shouldn't be a problem. We'll figure something out. We seem to have gotten away with it tonight, anyway. Neither of your sisters have come knocking at your door, demanding to know if my intentions are honorable."

"And if one of them did appear?"

"Then I guess we'll deal with that when it happens," she said. "But I'm a big believer in not borrowing trouble before you have to."

"Okay, but if we get caught, then I'm telling them this was all your idea. After all, Faith is your best friend, so you get to be the one to deal with her."

"She's your sister," Leah protested. "Why don't *you* have to deal with her?"

"For one thing, I'm trying to mend fences with her. So I don't think I need her getting mad at me for banging her best friend. If she asks, this was all your idea. You're the one who's the evil seducer in this scenario."

Leah snorted. "Leaving aside how gross the term 'banging' is for a moment, I'm happy to tell Faith what happened. But let's just make one thing clear—you're the one who made the move *this* time." She moved a little closer to him, stared up into his face, and lifted a hand to run her finger along the line of his six-pack under his T-shirt. The shiver that ran through him was pleasing, and it made her want to take things further. Which was a little unnerving, since she could already feel that she'd be sore in the morning. Sore in places that hadn't been sore for quite some time. But here she was, wanting to get down and dirty with Zach all over again.

"Yeah," he said smiling down at her. "I remember."

"Me too," she said. "So why don't you take me back to bed?"

# chapter ten

Apparently when you mixed hours of hard work at the studio and hot nights with Leah, time sped by. Zach felt like he'd blinked, and a week had passed. Apparently Leah's theory had been right on the money. Things were easier between them while they were working—no more awkward pauses. But now he had a new problem, namely, that he had to work pretty damn hard to keep his hands off her. Which was a whole other kind of distraction.

They worked hard, but his attention still wandered. He found himself watching her, caught by the spill of dark hair down her shoulders or the curve of her mouth as she laughed or the way her hands cut through the air excitedly when she talked. But he wasn't the only one who had more than just music on his mind. He caught Leah watching him too, and then their eyes would meet and the air would go thick and hot and still around them while color rose in her cheeks.

So far they'd managed to keep their hands off each

other while they were working. Leah had put her foot down about fooling around in the studio, saying it was too risky—too easy for someone to come in and catch them. And lust was a lot easier to deal with when he knew that he'd have her in his bed again when they were done for the day. So he'd contented himself with hot looks and just enjoying being with her, and then waited for her to appear at the door of the guesthouse each night.

But on Thursday night Leah, having spent almost every night or part of it with him since they'd first gotten together, had left him to his own devices. She had to go home for a family dinner for her parents' anniversary. Not an event that Zach could easily muscle in on without raising the sorts of questions from Leah's folks that neither of them wanted to answer.

So he found himself at loose ends. And, naturally enough, ended up drifting back around to Billy's house to hang out with Eli. He'd sort of fallen off the face of the earth for the last week, and hoped Eli and Billy wouldn't have been wondering too hard about why.

But neither of them seemed particularly surprised to see him when he strolled out onto Billy's deck to join them sometime around seven. Eli simply passed him a beer and pointed to the pizza boxes on the table. "Grab some if you haven't eaten."

"Thanks," Zach said, scooping up a piece. He'd eaten lunch at some point, but the afternoon had sped by while he and Leah had wrestled the bridge of his current song into submission. He devoured the pizza in about five bites and reached for another slice.

"I was wondering when you were going to emerge from the depths of that studio," Eli said with a grin. "I was starting to think that Leah must be a total slave driver."

Zach shook his head, taking a seat on the lounge beside Eli and staring out over the ocean as he finished the second slice. Then he picked up the beer. "She's damn good at her job, that's what she is. But no, she is letting me set the pace."

"But the recording's going well?" Eli asked.

Zach nodded. "Yes, it's good." He didn't offer anything more. Eli knew he didn't really like to talk about music while he was in the middle of making it.

"Tricky thing," Billy said.

Zach looked over to where Billy was standing by the rail of the deck, a bottle of San Pellegrino in his hand. He looked tanned and healthy, his short graying hair sticking up in spikes. But he didn't look entirely relaxed, his dark eyes focused on Zach.

"What's tricky?" Zach asked.

Billy flipped his free hand at him, the gesture somehow dismissive, as though Zach should've known what the hell he was talking about. "Making a comeback. Comebacks are a bitch."

Zach frowned. "I wouldn't call this making a comeback exactly. It's not like I've done a solo album before. This is more like adding another option."

Billy raised his eyebrows, but he only grunted in response and then turned to stare out at the ocean. Zach studied his back for a moment, wondering if he was going to add anything more to his pearl of wisdom. Or what exactly he'd been trying to say. After all, after Grey had died, Billy had seemed to transition smoothly into his new role with Erroneous. The band was doing very well and Billy always looked like he was having a good time playing with them, sitting up at the back of the stage, behind his drums, pounding away.

Of course, "very well" for Erroneous was nowhere near the heights that Blacklight had reached. Did Billy miss that, that being on-top-of-the-world feeling? It had to be hard to give it up once you'd had it. The adrenaline buzz of the crowd could be an addiction, no matter who you were or how well you were doing.

As the crowds got bigger, the buzz did too. Zach knew that as well as anybody. Though for him, it was the music that gave him the buzz, not necessarily the crowd. He couldn't deny that hearing hundreds or thousands of people singing along and cheering while he played wasn't satisfying, but it was riding the music itself that he loved.

But maybe he just hadn't hit the level where the crowd would take over as the source of the fix. Fringe Dweller were doing okay, but they weren't making a meteoric rise by any means. More like a slow build, and maybe that was better. Blacklight had catapulted to the heights early in their careers. And while that had brought money and financial security, it also caused all four of them problems over the years. Drugs, alcohol, family pressures from grueling touring and recording schedules. Along with the stress of always having to top your last effort, though that was the same for any musician. Hell, it was what he was trying to do now.

"Any tips for changing paths?" he said.

Billy turned back to him, shrugged. "Make great music. The rest doesn't mean shit." He straightened his shoulders. "Right, I've got crap to do. You two have fun." He walked off the deck and disappeared into the house.

Zach looked at Eli. "He's in a mood."

Eli shrugged. "He always starts getting antsy a month or two before a tour."

"Isn't being here supposed to be distracting him from that?" Billy had always been the most tightly wound of the four Blacklight guys. Grey and Danny had been wild, and Shane was quiet in comparison to the other three. But Billy had been . . . well, the one who'd seemed to take the weight of the world on his shoulders. He'd used his share of drugs and booze to take the edge off, just like the others had, but it had always seemed to Zach that Billy had been the one to start fights.

"He'll be fine," Eli said, glancing back over his shoulder in the direction Billy had gone.

Zach hitched a shoulder. "If you say so." He picked up his beer. It was still early. He didn't really feel like going back to the guesthouse. What he really wanted to do was swim, but with Eli still bandaged and braced, it would be kind of a dick move to suggest that. Lansing wasn't exactly known for its wild nightlife. So the options were limited. But there was one place they could go. "If Billy's in a mood, why don't we go to Salt Devil? Get out of his hair for a while?"

Eli hadn't objected to his proposal, so twenty minutes later, Zach found himself sitting on the deck of Will's bar, beer in hand and fries and onions rings on their way. Two slices of pizza hadn't exactly cut it as dinner. He looked out at the ocean, tilted his glass at the view in appreciation. In all the time he'd spent away from Lansing, he'd forgotten how chilled life could be here. And how much he missed the ocean never being far away.

"You look happy," Eli said. "I take your sessions really are going well?"

Zach nodded, propping his feet up on the deck rail. "Yeah, we've made a good start on three songs this week."

Eli swung his own chair around to stretch his booted foot out on another chair opposite Zach and then sampled his own beer. "It's working out with Leah then?"

"Yeah, she knows her shit. She's killing it, actually." Zach said. "But don't worry, I still want you to work on those two songs with me. Just let me and Leah get through this first week, find our groove or whatever."

Eli was still watching him with an odd expression in his brown eyes.

"Unless you don't want to do that anymore?" Zach said. Was that the reason that Eli was looking so weird? He'd changed his mind?

Eli shook his head, face clearing. "Nah, I'm still happy to do it."

"Then why are you looking at me like I just grew a second head or something?"

"Just trying to remember if I've ever seen you look this happy over a couple of songs before."

Zach narrowed his eyes. "What's that supposed to mean?"

Eli shrugged. "Just that things must be going *really* well."

His jaw tightened. Where the hell was this going? "They are."

"You sure that's all it is?" Eli asked.

Zach froze, beer bottle halfway to his lips. "What else would it be?"

"Oh, I don't know. Usually when you get that goofy look there's a girl involved."

"Have I told you lately you're full of shit?" Zach said. He brought the bottle to his lips, sipped slowly and deliberately, as though Eli's words hadn't bothered him at all. But crap, his brain was racing. Had Eli caught on to what was happening between him and Leah? Not good. She'd been pretty clear that she wanted to keep this thing quiet. He wasn't entirely sure he didn't agree with her. It would make things simpler. But he didn't like their chances of trying to sneak around for the next few months in a place as small as Lansing without anyone busting them. But being busted was one thing. Him outing them was another altogether. Leah would not be happy with him if he did that.

"I may be full of shit," Eli said. "But that doesn't mean I'm wrong."

Zach shook his head, trying to keep a neutral expression. "Maybe we need to start working on those songs sooner rather than later. You've obviously got far too much time on your hands. Otherwise you wouldn't be making up weird-ass theories about my good mood."

Eli laughed, not looking convinced. "You keep telling yourself that, buddy."

Zach shook his head. Right. Time to change the subject. "I meant it about the getting-to-work thing, though," he said. "We should get into that. I'd like at least six songs ready for the CloudFest set. Which means having them down in the studio and having time to rehearse. Leah said something about maybe having another chunk of studio time free next week. I can check with her and book it, if you want."

Eli's expression changed from amused to focused. "Sounds good to me. It beats listening to Dad talk about his boat all day. When did you want to get started?"

Good. Eli had taken the bait. Subject safely changed. "Let me talk to Leah, double-check the timing. Like I said, I want to finish off this week with her, then those two songs I showed you are the closest to finished, so it makes sense to work on those next. We just need the studio time. I mean, we can use Grey's studio for a while if we need to, but I'd prefer to keep things consistent. Leah is getting a great sound up at the main studio."

"Whatever you want. Just let me know."

Surprising Zach naked in bed had seemed like a good idea. But now Leah wasn't so sure. She'd been sitting on his bed for nearly thirty minutes now and she had absolutely no idea where he was. It wasn't like there were many options—particularly at this time of night. She'd checked Grey's studio on her way to the guesthouse, just in case he'd been there. He definitely wasn't at the Harper studio. There'd been no lights on in the building when her cab had dropped her off there. Given she knew all of the cab drivers on the island, she'd figured that was the safest option—it was plausible for her to be wanting to get some work done late at night after all. Less likely for her to be visiting Caleb and Faith at midnight on a Thursday. So she'd gone to the studio and then walked over to the guesthouse in the moonlight, not entirely sure why she was there at all.

But she'd spent the night with her parents and her family and their friends, watching everyone congratulate her parents for thirty-three years of marriage. She wasn't blind. She'd seen the looks thrown in her direction. The "poor Leah, she couldn't make her marriage last even ten years" looks. And by the end of it, she'd just wanted out.

Marriage. She'd tried it. It hadn't stuck. And maybe one day she might try it again but not any time soon. After all, she knew her parents' marriage hadn't been all parties and champagne toasts. They'd had their share of tough times and fights and tensions. Particularly early on when Blacklight had been at the height of their fame and her dad Sal had been one of the crowd who partied with them on the island. And sometimes off it too.

Marriage was hard work and compromise and a lot of other things. Right now, she just wanted fun. The good bits. The screaming orgasms and the thrill of that giddy stage where your blood bubbled and fizzed and ran hot just thinking about the other person. The easy part. All the wanting and none of the hard work.

And so she'd come to Zach. Who could give her all that. And wouldn't ask for more.

Who could strip her down and lay her on his bed and make her forget about pitying looks and the tiny doubt-ful voice in her head that said maybe those looks were right. Who could make her feel like Leah again. Make her feel strong and confident and happy.

One thing that getting divorced had taught her was that "happy" was pretty damn important.

She wanted some happy now.

The only problem was that the source of her happy fix wasn't here.

And there was only so long she could wait before it became obvious coming here was a bad idea. Question was when to call it and leave?

She and Zach were just casual. So the right thing to

do would be to cut her losses for the night and go home, right? Lying here waiting for him might just be moving into territory that was a little more serious than she wanted.

Right. She climbed out of bed, pulled on her clothes, grabbed her purse and phone. Straightened the bed so there was no sign she'd been there. She'd go back to the studio, call a cab and go home. Alone.

But she reached the front door just as it opened and Zach stepped though. He started when he saw her, then hit the light switch by the door.

"Leah? You nearly gave me a heart attack."

Yeah, she hadn't thought about that part. About what someone who'd grown up living with security like Zach had might feel about coming home to find someone in his house when he hadn't been expecting her. Even though he'd given her the code to the guesthouse. "Sorry," she said. "I thought I'd swing by. I should have called."

He raised an eyebrow. When she'd left the studio she'd told him she'd see him tomorrow, so she couldn't exactly blame him for being surprised to find her here now. "Don't worry about calling. I was only at Salt Devil with Eli." He smiled then. "In fact, don't ever worry about calling. I'm always going to be happy to see you."

She stared at him for a moment, not sure how to take that. Then decided to ignore it. "Male bonding time?" It came out crankier than she'd intended. She had no right to be annoyed. He didn't have to tell her where he was at all times. That wasn't what they were, no matter what Zach had to say about always being happy to see her.

"Something like that." He closed the door, punched

in the alarm code, and turned back to her, offering no further explanation.

She wondered if he'd been talking to Eli about the songs they planned to work on together. And ignored the sharp sting of jealousy that twisted briefly inside her. She'd known that Zach wanted to work with Eli. He wasn't hers exclusively in any sense of the word— least of all when it came to his music—and she needed to remember that. "And how is Eli?"

"Good," Zach said. "We talked about starting work on the songs he's producing."

The sting intensified. But she ignored it. "I'll check the schedule. I'm sure there'll be something we can squeeze in later next week. Faith was talking about looking for another weekend gig for Nessa and the guys."

"Thanks."

His smile almost made her feel better about the prospect of letting Eli take the reins on some songs. Almost. Her hand curled into a fist and she made herself relax.

Zach, at least, didn't seem to notice. "But you didn't come here to talk shop. How was dinner? Did Sal and Caterina have a good time?"

"They did." She forced a smile. She wasn't going to explain her evening to him. That was her own personal mess to deal with. She and Zach weren't at the dealing-with-each-other's-baggage stage. They were never going to be. "Dinner was great."

"You sure about that?"

"Absolutely," she said.

"Yet you're back here with me?" His tone was almost . . . concerned. And she'd had enough concern for one night.

"What can I say? It's that sex god thing you've got going on." She moved a little closer, toeing off her shoes. She'd come here to forget, not to talk. So she was going to have to move things along.

"Can't resist me, huh?" Zach said, eyes following the path of her hands as she toyed with the buttons at the front of her dress.

"Something like that," she said. "Want to remind me why?"

# chapter eleven

Leah watched Eli and Zach laughing in the recording booth and tried not to grit her teeth. The two of them had been horsing around for nearly ten minutes, since Zach had finished his first run-through of "Air and Breath" and Eli had left the board, supposedly to talk to Zach about the setup. Instead they'd been trading inside jokes like a pair of fourteen-year-olds, leaving Leah twiddling her thumbs at the board, awaiting instructions.

After the last week with Zach, knowing the producer's seat was all hers, for some reason, sitting meekly at the soundboard now, waiting for Eli to call the shots, wasn't sitting well.

She leaned forward and pressed the intercom button. "You guys about ready? We only have two days here." The studio was becoming busier in the lead-up to CloudFest. Every year some of the acts performing at the festival decided to try out the studio Blacklight had made famous. They'd come for a few days, then release a version of an old song—or a whole new song—recorded on the island to go with their appearance. She'd managed to block out chunks of time here and there in the schedule for her and Zach to keep working over the next six weeks or so, but this was going to be the longest continuous block they'd have for some time. And it was Eli who was getting to use it instead of her.

Eli turned to face her. "Hang on a second," he said, and then leaned in and said something to Zach too low for Leah to catch. Zach laughed in response and Eli turned back to face the booth window. "Okay, got it. I'm going to change the set up in here a little." He started to reel off a list of gear he wanted.

Leah's jaw tightened again. Zach was using the same guitar he'd been using for the songs she'd worked on with him. The studio was perfectly set up for it.

"Got that?" Eli said.

"Yes." She turned the intercom off. Neither Zach nor Eli had made any move to leave the booth. So apparently she was the one who was expected to go get all the stuff Eli wanted.

Normally that wouldn't bother her. After all, it was part of her job. But Zach and Eli both knew the Harper studio well. They'd spent chunks of their childhood here just as she had. They knew where the damn storage cabinets were.

*But they don't know how everything is organized.* She tried to push down her irritation as she walked into the gear room and started pulling things out of cabinets, working methodically. She might be irritated, but there was no point taking it out on expensive equipment. She lifted out the last mic and then made herself take three deep breaths, still feeling twitchy. Stupid, really. She'd known that Eli was going to be at the studio eventually. Zach hadn't pretended otherwise. He'd told her from the beginning he still wanted Eli to work on a couple of songs. So why was it bugging her that today was the first of those days? After all, they were on the same team. Trying to make Zach's album as good as it could possibly be.

And she had no place getting possessive.

The deep breaths didn't help much, not even when she took three more and then stretched, taking a final three. Still didn't help. She glared at the pile of gear as though it was the cause of all her troubles. Maybe that was it. She was just being territorial about the studio. After all, she and Zach had been working with the set up she'd worked out for almost a week now, and it was sounding great. But Eli, almost as soon as he walked through the door, had started wanting to change things. She didn't know if he'd even heard what she and Zach had done. Maybe Zach had played him the tapes, but if he had, he hadn't told Leah.

Or maybe it was the way that Eli just kept asking her to do things for him, as though she was some little helper monkey at his beck and call. Not so easy to just slip back into the sound engineer role, perhaps. Not after a week of being producer.

The sensible thing to do, of course, would be to march back in there and tell Eli, ever so politely, that he didn't get to order her around. The guy was only a couple of years older than her after all. Sure he had a few more producing credits under his belt than she did. But she'd known him when he'd been a scruffy kid and then a scrawny pimply teenager. So he didn't get to lord it over her.

In fact, maybe she should just take an extended coffee break now. Let Lord Eli do some of the work. She got that he was used to having his orders obeyed. He traveled with Billy on the road, sometimes stepping in as tour manager, so he was used to being a boss. But this was her studio, and really this was partly her album too now, so Eli needed to give her some respect.

She gathered the mics and other bits and pieces, carried them back into the booth, and shoved them into Eli's hands. "Here, all yours." She turned on her heel, and marched back out toward the kitchen. She was halfway through making a cup of coffee before it hit her that the thing that was really bugging her was that Zach wasn't stepping in to call Eli on any of his bullshit.

When they had been working alone, he'd been polite and considerate. Sure they had a few clashes about particular sections of the song, but that was part of the biz. But now, with Eli here, he seemed to have reverted into some weird dude-bro mode that set her teeth on edge.

And while, yes, it was his album, and ultimately he got to call the shots about how things were done. That didn't mean that she needed to take any crap. It was, after all, *her* studio. She knew what she was doing, and Zach bloody well knew it after the time they'd spent on his songs. As for Eli, well, she didn't remember him having this kind of attitude before. Maybe he'd been running around the world with his dad a little too long.

She poured milk into her coffee and looked around the small kitchen. Dammit. No doughnuts today. The least Zach could have done, if he was going to bring Eli full-of-himself Lawler to work with him, was replenish the doughnut supply. She opened a couple of cabinets, scrounging around to see what snacks might be lurking in their depths. She usually kept the kitchen fairly well stocked, but she had been pretty distracted with Zach lately and had forgotten to stop by the grocery store. Or even notice that supplies were running low. Apparently sex gods scrambled her brain.

That thought only made her more annoyed, and she sped up her search. The only thing she could find was a half-empty packet of Oreos. She didn't even like Oreos, but they were going to have to do.

As she pulled the first cookie out of the package, Zach's voice said, "Everything okay?"

She turned and saw him standing in the doorway, one brow quirked. "Why wouldn't everything be all right?"

"Well, for a start, you look at those Oreos like you think they deserve complete obliteration."

"Maybe I just don't like Oreos," she said.

"I know you don't like Oreos, you never did. But still, it seems a little harsh to look at them as though they've killed a puppy." He crossed the small room and lifted the Oreos, taking one for himself. "So, how about you tell me what's bugging you?"

"What's bugging me is that Eli is talking to me like I'm a gopher, not the studio manager *and* his bloody coproducer," she ground out. "And you're just letting him."

Zach's brows shot up. "What?"

"You heard me."

"He just asked you to get some gear," Zach said.

"He could have come to help me." She pitched the Oreo toward the garbage can in the corner of the kitchen. "So could you for that matter."

"Eli and I were talking about the songs."

"You can talk while carrying stuff."

He held up his hands. "Okay. Right. Sorry." He studied her for a moment. "This is only for a couple of days. Just these two songs. Then it's back to you and me. I'm not ditching you for him."

Was she being that obvious? Ugh. She really needed to suck it up. "I know," she said. "Sorry, I'm just . . ." She wasn't sure what to say, because she wasn't sure exactly why she was so annoyed.

"Don't take this the wrong way," Zach said, "but I know this time of year is crazy here. You have a lot on your plate with CloudFest coming up and Nessa and everything. I could get another engineer in to work with Eli if you don't have enough—"

"No." She cut him off. "No, I want to do this." She didn't want any more hands on the album than was strictly necessary. She took a breath. "You're right. It's busy. But I'm fine." She might be fine if it were just the two of them. Then she could jump him and work off some of this bad mood. But with Eli hanging around, there would be no jumping Zach. Not unless she was ready for everyone to know about them. And that would be just another layer of pressure she didn't want to deal with.

"Two days," Zach said. He cast a quick glance over his shoulder then reached out and tangled his hand briefly with hers. "Forty-eight hours. Or a bit less even. Time will fly."

Time hadn't flown. In fact she'd never felt two days move so slowly. It wasn't the music. *That* had gone smoothly. Zach worked his magic with guitar and voice—and at least those moments hadn't been a struggle. Eli knew what he was doing and, to her relief, what he was doing wasn't a million miles from what she'd been doing with the other songs. One was a little more raucous, heavier, and electric, but it suited the song. The other, "Air and Breath," fit right in with the style she'd established.

So no, the music was fine and Eli had relaxed after the first couple of hours and stopped giving orders—which had made her think that maybe he was just as nervous as she had been—and the three of them had worked seamlessly after that. The parts that made the time drag were the parts where there were three of them. Where it wasn't just her and Zach anymore, and she couldn't touch him whenever she wanted. They'd recorded late into the night on Thursday—late enough that Zach had invited Eli to crash at the guesthouse rather than drive back to Billy's place, which ruined any plans she'd had for her and Zach's time. And now it was after two a.m. on Saturday, and Zach was just walking Eli to the door while she dawdled in the studio, tidying up a little.

They'd finished recording close to midnight after so many takes of "Air and Breath," a song about how the singer wanted a girl like oxygen that was so stupidly sexy when Zach sang it that she'd been ready to crawl out of her skin with need. Eli, instead of going home like a sensible person, had sat around as he and Zach tossed around ideas for Zach's backing band for CloudFest and drank a couple of beers. Leah had joined in the conversation at first but then had started to reset the recording booth, hoping Eli might take the hint and leave.

It had taken two hours for him to get the idea. And now she was trying not to pace with impatience as she waited for Zach to come back in. He'd gone outside with Eli to wait for his cab almost ten minutes ago.

She'd tidied away everything that could possibly be tidied away. Well, almost everything. She'd leave Zach's guitars for him. She opened the piano, sat down on the bench, and started playing the melody from "Air and Breath" softly, checking the sound. The studio pianos were due to be tuned next week, something she arranged maybe more often than necessary, but the sea air was hard on them. This one, her favorite, still sounded sweet, the notes ringing true under her fingers.

She caught a glimpse of headlight reflection through one of the windows and took her hands off the keys. The last thing she needed was for Zach to come in and find her playing. Playing for Faith was one thing, as was sitting down at the piano to demonstrate how she thought something might go, but her skills were just that—skills. Not the kind of talent that Zach and Faith had that turned their music into that something more that stopped people in their tracks and made them pay attention.

As Zach came back into the studio, she was closing the door to the booth behind her.

"All set?"

"I left the guitars for you," she said. "Didn't want to mess with your babies."

"I trust you," he said with an easy smile that turned into a yawn.

"Yeah, but does your insurance company?"

"If I put them away, can we get out of here? Back to my place?" Zach said, suddenly sounding more awake.

Nice to know she wasn't the only one who'd been suffering. She smiled at him. "I was counting on it." She tipped her chin toward the door. "Go pack up your stuff."

"Yes ma'am," Zach said. He headed into the booth, humming just loud enough to be heard. It wasn't a melody Leah recognized—a new song maybe?—and she hit the record button on the board, in case Zach might want to remember it, then went to take the empty beer bottles and dirty coffee mugs to the kitchen.

When she came back, Zach was still in the booth, sitting on the stool, guitar in hand, picking out a series of chords, face intent as he watched his fingers

"You're hopeless," Leah said from the doorway.

Zach looked up, those long tanned fingers stilling. Which only made her wish they were touching her, not the guitar.

"Just passing time. You could come over here and distract me," he said.

"Oh yeah?" It was tempting. He was tired and rumpled and kind of irresistible. Especially when she hadn't had her hands on that body for over forty-eight hours. She reached out an arm and hit the button to kill the recording without looking.

"Yeah," he said. He put the guitar down and crooked a finger at her. Her legs moved of their own volition, crossing the width of floor between them before she knew what she was doing.

Zach rose to meet her, his hands catching her waist as she reached him, pulling her tight against him. He groaned, a satisfied kind of sound that caught her in all the right places.

"God," he said fervently. "This has been a *long* two days."

"Very," she agreed, pushing her hips against him.

"Want to fool around?" Zach said, hand sliding down to her butt.

More than anything. But this was the studio.

"I locked the door," he added. "It's late. No one's

coming to check on us at this hour." He lowered his head to her neck, pressing his lips to the place where he had to be able to feel the thud of her pulse—which was racing way too fast now that she was close to him again.

"I—" It was hard to remember why the studio was a bad idea. He was right. It was the middle of the night. No one was coming anywhere near the place. And right now, the guesthouse seemed way too far way. "We shouldn't," she said, but she knew it was only a token protest as heat spread through her.

"I disagree," Zach said. He pushed his hips into her, and the feel of him, hot and hard behind his jeans, was hard to argue with.

"Oh, what the hell," she said and pulled him down to the floor.

It was nearly midday Saturday before Leah made it back to the studio. She hadn't had enough sleep but she didn't mind. She'd dragged Zach back to the guesthouse after their initial round in the studio. His bed was far more comfortable than carpet, and great sex was worth a little missed sleep. Hopefully it wasn't going to take her long to get things set up for Sienna Reese, who was arriving on Sunday. Then she could sneak in a nap this afternoon.

But when she scanned herself in, the lights were already on.

"Hello?" she called.

"In here," Faith yelled back. It sounded like she was in the main studio.

Leah tried to summon an I'm-wide-awake-from-plenty-of-sleep-all-alone-in-my-bed face as she headed in that direction. "What are you doing here? Checking up on Nessa's stuff?" she asked as she reached the studio and found Faith sitting at the board. "Did you find the recordings okay?"

Faith knew her way around the studio nearly as well as Leah. She couldn't work the soundboard with the same skill but she knew how to play back a session.

"Actually, I was snooping on Zach," Faith said. "He won't tell me anything about how it's going."

"Maybe that's because he thinks you're still mad at him."

Faith's nose wrinkled. "I'm not mad. But that doesn't mean he's forgiven. He has ground to make up."

"Tough crowd, huh?"

"Well, you know Zach—give him an inch and he'll take a mile."

"He's not that bad," Leah said, then cursed herself mentally. Defending Zach to Faith wasn't going to make the situation any better. She smiled at Faith, aiming for happy and innocent. "Did you find his tapes?"

"Not all of them."

"Yeah, he has been a bit protective of them. Wanted to keep them on his own hard drive." It wasn't entirely unusual. They were just laying down acoustic guitar after all and Zach's vocals, which they'd probably do again when they got time with the full band. Once Zach decided who he wanted to use as his band. And whether or he wanted to go analog for some of the album. Until then, he wanted to keep everything under wraps, so she'd been happy for him to copy the recordings once he'd assured her he had a decent backup service.

"There was one tape though," Faith said. "A song called 'Air and Breath'?"

The one they'd been recording yesterday. "Yeah,

that's what we've been working on this week with Eli. It's shaping up."

Faith nodded toward the computer monitor where, now that she looked, Leah could see the file name. "I thought so. Interesting bridge though." She pressed play and Leah heard Zach's voice say, "Want to fool around?"

Her gut clenched and her skin went cold as though Faith had dumped ice water on her heat. Holy crap. *No.* She'd turned off the recording last night. She was sure of it. Had she hit the wrong button? Left the recording going? For how long? She slapped pause on the keyboard without thinking. "How much of that did you listen to?" She dropped her bag and leaned against the desk, feeling ill.

"I hit pause right about when you did," Faith said. "So, you're sleeping with my brother?" She sounded kind of incredulous.

"Er—" Leah wasn't sure there was a good way to answer that question.

Faith shook her head. "So that's a yes? What were you thinking?"

That your brother is smoking hot? No. That would be the dumb thing to say in this situation. "It's . . . complicated," Leah said.

"You know, he's leaving, right? He's not going to stick around."

"Oh yeah, that part is crystal," Leah said. "That's the only reason I'm sleeping with him."

Faith blinked. "Excuse me?"

"I'm not clueless, Faith. I know Zach."

"Apparently so. Better than I thought." Those Harper eyes, so like her brother's, narrowed. "You know, I always thought you had a crush on Zach when we were in high school."

"I kind of did," Leah said. Understatement of the year.

"Is that why it's complicated?"

Leah hesitated. Faith was her best friend. They didn't have many secrets they didn't share. But she'd kept this one a long time. And maybe it was time to tell her best friend. So she could keep her from doing the same stupid thing all over again. If she told Faith this was just a fling, then Faith could make sure she didn't lose her head. Maybe she could say she was just using Zach to finally have a rebound fling.

Which was also true. Just not totally true.

"That's not the only part that's complicated."

"Why?" Faith asked. "Forget that I'm his sister." One side of her mouth quirked. "I'll try to do the same—that might make the rest of this conversation easier."

Leah smiled. This was why she loved Faith. Because she was always there, no matter what. Always *had* been there. She had a lot of Grey in her but it was well tempered with a lot of Lou. "Okay, deal." She took a breath. If she was busted, she might as well come clean about everything. "Well, it's like this. I slept with Zach at my eighteenth birthday party."

Faith looked startled. Then enlightened. "Is *that* where you disappeared to that night? I always thought you'd snuck off with Kyle, and were too embarrassed to tell me you'd caved."

Leah snorted. "No. I would have had to drink a lot more champagne that night to do that."

"How much champagne *did* you have to drink?" Faith asked curiously.

"Two glasses," Leah said. "Zach isn't a saint but he isn't the kind of guy who sleeps with women who are drunk."

"I didn't think he was the kind of guy who'd hit on my best friend either."

"He's not. I hit on him."

"You sure it was only two glasses of champagne?" Faith said.

"Yes. I can plead temporary insanity, but not drunkenness." Leah shrugged at her. "You were right about the crush. And I figured he was leaving and it was worth a shot. Otherwise I was just going to spend my life wondering. Haven't you ever had a crush like that? Wild and mad and entirely a bad idea? One that destroys your common sense?"

"Not until I met Caleb," Faith said, with a smile.

"That was love, not a crush," Leah objected. "You just didn't realize it at first. Anyway, I took a chance. Zach obliged. Then he left. And yes, it hurt at the time but I was eighteen. I got over it."

"And then you married Joey."

"Joey was years later," Leah said. "I'm not blaming Joey on Zach. Come to think of it though, there was a lot of champagne the night I first got together with Joey too."

"Okay, in the future we're finding you a different drink," Faith said.

Leah laughed. "Sure."

"So eighteen-year-old Leah had a crush on my brother. One she acted on. That still doesn't explain what twenty-eight-year-old Leah is doing compounding her mistake."

"I'm not sure I can explain it—though if you weren't

his sister you would appreciate that your brother is pretty hot . . ."

Faith made a face that suggested this was not an appealing concept.

"Hey, you said you were going to pretend you weren't his sister," Leah said. "And you started this whole conversation."

"Ugh. Okay," Faith flapped a hand at Leah, looking pained. "Go on. Zach is hot."

"And, well, we get along. We always did. So I figured, he's here and he's hot and he's leaving, so why not enjoy myself?" She shrugged. "It's not like this island has been brimming with single men beating down my door since the divorce."

That was the problem with growing up in a small community. You had pretty much worked out which of the local guys you had any chemistry with by the end of high school and then you weeded out the rest by your early twenties if you had any sense. Probably explained why people tended to marry young if they stuck around. After that, well, maybe you had to be like Mina and hope some hot strangers arrived in town.

Faith's solution to this problem had been to sleep with guys off-island. But she got to travel a lot more than Leah did for Harper Inc. There were always tourists, but again, that was kind of tricky. All that dancing around trying to figure out if a guy was single—really single, not just island-holiday single, because she drew a hard line at sleeping with married men—and if he liked you, and then getting awkward first-night sex over with to get to the good stuff all within a week or two at most was a level of sexual wizardry that she just didn't think she was up to any more.

Zach might be a tourist for all intents and purposes, but the rest of it was already established. She knew him. Knew they were good together. And knew he was leaving.

Faith was chewing a nail. So, she was worried.

Leah patted Faith's knee. "Trust me, I'm doing this with eyes wide open. Zach and I have chemistry, but it's not the lasting kind."

"If you say so."

"I know so," Leah said. "So don't worry. I won't tell Zach you snooped around his tapes. And I'll erase the offending portion. We'll keep things discreet."

Faith lifted an eyebrow. "Last time I checked, having sex in the recording booth probably didn't fall under the category of discreet."

"You're ruining all my rock'n'roll fantasies," Leah said. "And I'm sure these walls have plenty of stories to tell."

"Yeah but most of them involve my dad or his best friends. So I don't want to think about them. Just like I don't want to think about Zach."

"All right. I'll save all the good gossip for Ivy." Leah grinned.

"Thanks," Faith said drily. "And now, I think we can declare this subject closed. Preferably forever."

"Do you want me to tell Zach that you know?" Leah asked. Part of her wanted Faith to say no. Telling Zach she'd accidentally made a sex tape of them wasn't going to be fun. But by the time he found out, the tape would be dead and buried.

"Do you think he'd want me to know?" Faith asked.

She could lie and say that Zach had been the one who'd wanted to keep it quiet. That would be easier.

Faith wouldn't be surprised. But Faith was her best friend. And Zach wasn't the bad guy in this situation. "He wanted to tell you from the start. Didn't want to sneak around you."

"And you did?"

"I didn't want you to get mad at him when he left," Leah said.

"You really thought you could keep it a secret for a few months? Here on Lansing?" Faith shook her head.

"I hoped. Call it temporary madness. I hoped you'd be distracted by CloudFest and wedding planning. Guess I shot myself in the foot." She hesitated. "I'd still prefer it didn't become everyone's business."

"Don't want your folks to know?"

Leah spread her hands. "Not sure they'd understand."

"Okay. I'm not going to tell anyone." Faith said. "Do your worst." She paused. "What about Mina?"

Leah shrugged. "I'll leave that one to Zach. So don't you tell her until he can."

Faith nodded. "Trust me, I intend to think about this as little as possible."

"Good," Leah said. "So how about we change the subject and I find you Nessa's recordings?"

"Deal," Faith said. "And while we're on the subject of wedding planning—or somewhere near the vicinity of the subject—I had a call from Elise Ng's salon last night."

"About your dress?" Leah asked. She and Ivy were Faith's bridesmaids. Mina was going to be maid of honor. The four of them had had a few crazy days in New York in March visiting so many bridal salons and designers that Leah had lost count.

"Yes. Apparently Elise can come to Lansing next

weekend for a fitting. Which is good because my schedule is getting too jammed for me to get back to New York before CloudFest."

"You're the one who wanted to have a summer wedding," Leah said. "So your pain is self-inflicted."

Faith shrugged. "Maybe. But one of the functions bridesmaids fulfill is to support me in my hours of need. So, one girls' afternoon at my place next Saturday for dress fittings." Faith smiled goofily. "You three need fittings too, after all."

"I'll be there," Leah said and tried to think about weddings rather than the conversation she was going to have with Zach.

# chapter twelve

"So, busted, huh?" Zach said, looking at Leah across the kitchen table at the guesthouse. She'd arrived on his doorstep mid-afternoon bearing pizza for what she claimed could be a late lunch. Then she'd told him about Faith and the tape at the studio.

She pushed her piece of pizza around on her plate. She'd hardly eaten anything yet. Was she upset that Faith knew? Or about the way she'd found out? Ignoring the fact that it was his sister who'd heard them—that part was bad—he thought the way the recording had happened was funny. But he couldn't tell yet how Leah felt, so he kept that to himself.

"Yes. Sorry," she said.

"It was bound to happen sooner or later." After all, he'd told her that from the beginning. No point her feeling guilty about the inevitable. "How did Faith take it?" Zach asked.

"Surprisingly well," Leah said.

He wondered if the answer would be different if he'd

been the one talking to Faith. After all, Faith wasn't going to yell at Leah. But he hadn't wanted to keep it from his sisters in the first place, so he wasn't sorry the news was out, even if Faith did read him the riot act. Maybe. He refilled Leah's water glass and studied her a moment, still trying to figure out what she was thinking. "So what happens now?"

She stabbed at the pizza some more but still didn't eat any of it. "What do you mean?"

"Is Faith the only one we're going to tell?" Faith would keep a secret if Leah asked her to. Well, she might tell Caleb, perhaps, but he wasn't going to tell the whole island.

"Faith said if you want Mina to know, you have to tell her," Leah said.

*What did that mean?* "Do you want Mina to know?"

A shrug.

"Can I get something more definite? We need to be on the same page here."

"I don't know." She didn't look at him. Okay, definitely not happy.

"Well, for what it's worth, I think Faith has proved my point. You can't keep secrets in a place this size. Maybe we should just accept the inevitable." He'd understood why she'd wanted to try to keep it a secret. He just hadn't thought it would work. But maybe Leah had? Question was, how upset was she now that it turned out he'd been right about that? Upset enough to call the whole thing off? His gut clenched as his whole body tensed at that thought. Having Leah in his bed was something he wasn't anywhere near ready to give up.

"Easy for you to say," she said, frowning. "You're not the one who has to live here afterward."

"What's that supposed to mean?"

"Just that you're not the one getting all the pitying looks. Can't keep a husband. Can't keep a boyfriend." Leah pushed back from the table.

"Hey," he said. "Talk to me." He didn't like seeing her like this—tense and quiet. His Leah was laughter and movement and guts and brilliance. Seeing her shut down was almost . . . painful. He needed her to be okay.

Leah shook her head. "It's just that it's easier for you. I'm the one who'll have to deal with my parents and everyone else."

"Your folks are cool," Zach said. He hoped he was right. Sal Santelli was like an uncle to him, along with the Blacklight guys. He'd always been around, ready to give advice or to crack bad jokes. But Zach had never really paid much attention to how he was with Leah and her boyfriends.

"Less cool when you scratch the surface," Leah said. "At least when it comes to their kids. Sal tries to hide it most of the time but he's still got a big chunk of traditional Italian dad in there somewhere."

"You have been married," Zach pointed out. "It's not like he can think you're a virgin."

Leah winced. "Maybe not, but I'm sure he'd rather not think about my love life at all. He took the Joey thing pretty hard. I don't want to disappoint him again."

"You can't live your life twisting yourself into shapes to please other people."

"Maybe *you* can't," she said, voice sharp. "You've proven that much. It's not that simple for the rest of us."

O-kay. Wrong approach. He held up his hands. "I don't want to fight with you. If you don't want me to tell Mina, I won't."

"Then I'm the reason you're lying to your sister. No." Leah sighed. "Maybe you're right. Tell her."

"And everyone else?"

"Let's play that one by ear." She managed a smile.

At least that wasn't "Hell, no." An improvement. Maybe. "Okay." He nodded toward the table. "How about you sit back down and actually eat something. Tell me about the rest of your day." He sat, hoping she'd follow suit.

She did. And he was happy to see her reach for the slice and actually take a bite. Then another. He watched as she ate the whole piece.

"Your day?" he prompted when she'd finished.

"Not much to tell. I set up the studio. Did some admin." She pulled the pizza box over and put another slice on her plate. "I checked the schedule. I think we can probably squeeze in some time Wednesday night. The same on Thursday. Maybe Friday afternoon. There's a slot on Saturday afternoon as well, but I'm busy. Maybe you can ask Eli, keep playing around with his songs."

She sounded more normal now. Good. "What's on Saturday?"

"Girl bonding time. Faith's having a dress fitting. Bridesmaids too. So I kind of have to be there." She smiled again, and this time it was an all-the-way smile. He smiled back.

"Definitely girl time." Faith was getting married. It still seemed kind of not real to him. She'd always said she wasn't the marrying kind. Yet, here she was, throwing the dice. And this time, unlike when Mina had gotten married, he was going to be around for a lot of the hoopla that went into the lead-up to a wedding.

"Caleb doing anything during your girlfest?" he

asked. He thought Eli had said something about sailing with Billy on Saturday. Maybe he should try and hang out with his future brother-in-law.

"Faith didn't say," Leah said. "But if I had to guess, I'd say he'll likely be hanging out with Will and Stefan. Maybe you should tag along. Do some future-brother-in-law bonding."

"That's what I was thinking," he said. He had some ground to make up with Caleb, who was definitely on Faith's side when it came to Faith versus Zach. And the same went for Will Fraser. Sure, Mina had never been as mad at Zach as Faith had been, but things were still cool. He'd known Adam for a few years by the time he and Mina had gotten hitched. And he still missed the guy—Adam had had a very dry sense of humor and a love of surf as well as the boats he'd built that had made him easy to get along with. Besides, it couldn't hurt to restore the gender balance in the Harper world a little. Brothers-in-law could only be a good thing. "Manly activities coming right up," he said. "Though hanging out with you would be more fun."

"We can do that after my girl stuff and your manly activities," she pointed out. "Especially if you tell Mina between now and then. I won't even have to sneak over here."

When the doorbell rang, Faith was still hidden behind the temporary screen that the designer had erected in the family room on her arrival. Leah thought the whole screen thing was kind of overkill—after all, anyone in the room was there because Faith had asked them to be—but who was she to argue with a woman who commanded tens of thousands of dollars for her dresses?

Maybe adding a bit of theater to the experience was part of how she justified her prices.

"I'll get it," Leah said. She figured her job as bridesmaid was to do whatever Faith wanted her to do to make things run smoothly. Just like Faith had done for Leah's wedding.

"Thanks," Faith called from behind the screen. Leah left Mina and Lou to do whatever Faith might need them to and headed for the front door, expecting it to be Ivy—her fellow bridesmaid—who still hadn't arrived for this bit of female bonding. But instead of Ivy, Stella stood on the doorstep, her arms full of a giant bakery box in her trademark pink and white stripes. Behind her stood Anna Leighson, who ran one of the spas on the island.

"Hi," Stella said brightly. She lifted the bakery box. "I've got a delivery."

"Was Faith expecting you?" Leah asked. Faith hadn't said anything about more food arriving. After all, Lou had brought a mountain of food, and Faith had drinks covered. They had very nice French Champagne along with equally fancy sodas and sparkling water for Mina, who didn't drink, and canapés and fruit platters and cookies enough for a whole squad of bridesmaids.

Stella shook her head. "This is a surprise."

"A surprise?" Leah asked. "Organized by who?" She'd hung out with the Harpers long enough over the years to know that sometimes Blacklight fans came in the less-than-desirable variety. Every so often one of them decided to play a prank or send a parcel that was kind of creepy. The letters and parcels were almost always stopped by the security team before they got anywhere near the Harper house, but deliveries from people on-island had made it through a couple of times before. Like the time a hundred pizzas had been ordered for the house. Leo at the pizzeria hadn't questioned it, and to be fair to him, Grey had been known to throw parties that would need a hundred pizzas. It wasn't until he had driven all the way out to the Harper house to deliver them that everyone had figured out it was a prank. Faith had sent the pizzas down to the search-and-rescue team and the doctor at the clinic and the fire station and the police department, so they hadn't gone to waste. And she'd paid Leo. But that didn't mean she had forgotten. Neither had Leah. She lifted an eyebrow at Stella—who also knew the score.

"He wanted it to be a surprise," Stella said, looking defensive.

"He? Caleb?" Leah asked. It would be just like Caleb to want to surprise Faith like this. He'd been banished to hang out with Will and Stefan down at Salt Devil for the afternoon with firm instructions not to return until summoned. Zach and Eli were supposed to join them. Presumably they'd do whatever the male equivalent of pre-wedding bonding was. Only with far less tulle and satin and intimidating dress designers. Probably watch baseball, shoot pool, and drink beer. Guys had it easy.

Stella shook her head. "No, Zach."

Zach? Leah couldn't help a stab of surprise. Zach was sending Faith goodies for her wedding-dress fitting? She wasn't quite sure why she was so surprised. Except, somehow, it didn't quite seem like him. Though, maybe she was being unfair. Since he'd been back on the island, he'd been on his best behavior when it came to his sisters. "You sure about that?" she asked.

Stella nodded. "He came into the store himself. He was very particular about the order." She looked over her shoulder at Anna, who nodded agreement.

"Me too," Anna said. "He came to the spa as well."

Now *there* was something she'd never pictured. Zach Harper in the spa? She pictured him wearing only a towel . . . then lying naked on a massage table, all oiled up and gleaming. Then she wrenched her thoughts back to the present, trying not to blush. Okay. Zach had sent goodies. Who was she to argue? He was trying to do something nice for Faith and it would be nice if the two of them could get back to the kind of relationship they'd had before it had all gone wrong when Grey had gotten sick.

She stepped back out of the way. "Come on in," she said and gestured down the hallway. "Everyone's in the family room." Stella had been to the house before, but she couldn't remember if Anna had. "Down the hall then right then first door on the left.

Stella nodded. "I know the way. Here, you take this box." She held it out to Leah. "I've got a couple more in the car."

"I guess overcatering runs in the family," Leah said, accepting the box. She resisted the temptation to open it and see what Zach had sent. It was Faith's surprise, not hers.

"I tried to tell him he was ordering too much," Stella said. "But I couldn't talk him out of it." She turned and headed back outside.

Leah nodded at Anna. "Come on, let's go. What's Zach got you doing?"

Anna patted the big bag on her shoulder—some sort of complicated-looking black metal case that Leah would've guessed held some sort of music equipment, except that as far as she knew, Anna didn't have a musical bone in her body.

"Manicures for whoever wants one," Anna said. "I can do pedicures too."

"Cool," Leah said. "Sounds fun. But you'll probably have to hang around until Faith finishes with the whole dress bit."

Anna nodded. "Absolutely. Wedding dresses and nail polish definitely don't mix." They'd reached the back room. Faith hadn't emerged from behind the screen. Leah remembered her own wedding-dress fittings. They'd seemed to take forever. And her dress wasn't anywhere near as elaborate as the one Faith had chosen. They were going to be here a while.

"Zach sent goodies," she announced. "Anna is here to make us all gorgeous, and Stella is following with diabetes in a box."

Mina grinned at Anna. "Zach sent you?"

Anna nodded. "Is there somewhere I can set up?"

Lou stood, smiling at Anna. "Sure," she said. "We'll clear off one of the tables for you."

Mina jumped up and followed Lou over to one of the tables to clear the platters of food and pull up a couple of chairs. By the time everything was organized, Stella had ferried her other two bakery boxes into the room as well and started laying out platters of exquisitely decorated cupcakes and other goodies. She was almost done when Ivy came wandering down the hall as well.

"Sorry I'm late. Got held up with a client." She surveyed the room, taking in Stella and Anna, and then tilted her head at Leah. "Looks like quite the party." She straightened, her purple-streaked black bob falling neatly back into place. The streaks matched the color of the tiny aliens dotted over the fabric of her sundress.

"Courtesy of Zach," Leah said. "Apparently he thought we needed the full girly bonding experience."

"Well, I'm not going to argue with him. This week has been crazy. Some girl time sounds perfect to me," Ivy said. She flopped down onto one of the armchairs and started unlacing her Doc Martens. Then she looked around. "Faith? Where are you?"

"Behind the screen." Faith's voice drifted out. "Being tortured into underwear that I swear contravenes the Geneva convention."

Ivy snorted. "You're the one who wanted the full-disaster wedding. No complaining if your uber-frock needs scaffolding."

"I do not need scaffolding," Faith said indignantly. "And if I'm only going to do this marriage thing once, then I'm doing it right."

Ivy shrugged. "Whatever floats your boat." She pulled off her boots and then sat back into the armchair, sticking her legs out and wriggling her toes happily.

"You need a hand, honey?" Lou asked, pausing from her examination of Stella's platters to twist her head toward the screen. Stella, Leah thought, looked vaguely nervous at the scrutiny. Rightly so. Lou was one of the best bakers on the island.

"No, Mom," Faith said. "I think we've got it under control." She sounded kind of breathless. More sounds of rustling came from behind the screen, followed by a muffled "Ow!"

By the time the cupcakes were set out and Anna had set up rows of polishes and hand bowls and clippers and all the things that went into a manicure, Faith still hadn't emerged.

"Are you being sewn into that dress inch by inch?"

Leah called, good-naturedly. Stella's cupcakes, topped with little fondant decorations of hearts and tennis balls and guitars and tiny brides and grooms, looked delicious. But she could hardly eat one before Faith had seen them.

Instead she topped up her champagne.

"Just a few more minutes," came the serene voice of Elise Ng, the dress designer. There was more rustling. Leah remembered the dress as being spectacular, but from the amount of rustling going on, it sounded like it should be adorning a Disney princess, not Faith.

"There," Elise said, sounding approving. "You can go out and show off now."

"Finally," Ivy called and everyone laughed. But the laughter turned into "oohs" and "aahs" as Faith walked out from behind the screen.

"Oh, honey, you look beautiful." Lou pulled a Kleenex out of her pocket and started dabbing at her eyes.

"Mom!" Faith said. "Don't cry, you'll make me cry." She smiled at Lou, but the expression was a little wobbly. But tears or no tears, Lou was right. In yards of creamy white silk, set off by subtle hints of gold embroidery, Faith looked like a goddess.

"No tears," Elise said, from where she was smoothing the short train at the back of the dress. "Tears spoil silk." She straightened and studied Faith, dark eyes narrowed as though looking for any imperfections in her creation. Apparently there were none, because she smiled and faded back behind the screen.

"I'm allowed to cry," Lou said. "I cried when I saw Mina in her dress. And Leah. And I'm not going to stop now."

Leah exchanged a look with Mina, who simply tilted her glass of soda at her. Then Mina turned back to her sister and widened the smile on her face. Leah did the same. Faith looked beautiful and Leah was happy for her—over the moon for her—but with her standing there looking so happy it was hard not to think about her own wedding. And the aftermath. The sting of it was unexpected. And for Mina, even though she now had Will, it had to be even worse. Weddings. Tough sometimes. And, maybe, just maybe, she might contemplate doing it all over again. But it would take one hell of a guy to convince her.

"Who wants a cupcake?" she said brightly, then downed half her glass of champagne.

Faith turned to look at Stella's handiwork. "Oh." Her expression went even wobblier. "Oh, Stella, they're so adorable. Look at the little tennis balls. Zach did this?"

"He wanted them to have things to do with you and Caleb," Stella said, nodding. "He had a list."

"A list?" Faith bit her lip. "He made a list?" She looked at Lou. "I should have invited him."

"He's fine, hanging out with the guys," Leah said, then kicked herself as Mina lifted an eyebrow at her. Luckily Lou was too preoccupied with Faith to notice. Zach hadn't said he'd told Lou. Besides Mina, Ivy shook her head—Leah had told her about Zach last night—but didn't say anything.

"I want to show him my dress."

"We could Skype him. Or FaceTime him," Ivy offered. "What kind of phone does he have?"

Faith lost her wobbly look, a smile lighting her face. "Great idea!"

"He's with Caleb," Mina said. "Do you want Caleb to see the dress?"

Faith turned to Leah. "You call him. Tell him to leave the guys for a bit and then we'll show him."

This time Lou turned and give Leah a look. Damn. Busted again.

She went to grab her phone off the counter and called Zach as instructed. He picked up and she explained what was happening. He looked kind of surprised but pleased that Faith wanted to show him the dress, and Leah was treated to a lightning-fast view of the inside of Salt Devil as Zach walked off the deck where the guys were sitting and into the depths of the bar.

"All clear," he said. "No groom in sight."

He meant Caleb. She knew that. But she couldn't help thinking it was also a reminder. Zach wasn't hers. Not for long, at least. "Good," she said and handed the phone to Faith.

"This is good," Zach said when he and Leah were settled on the patio behind the guesthouse, watching the sun starting to set over the ocean. The big house had a view of part of the patio so up until now, they'd avoided sitting out. But now that Faith and Mina—courtesy of a slightly weird conversation he'd had with Mina a few days ago—knew about him and Leah there was no need to stay inside.

Leah smiled at him. "Yes, it is. And sorry I wasn't very hungry. I ate too many of Stella's cupcakes." Her smile widened. "That was very nice of you, by the way, sending those. And Anna." She lifted her leg and waggled her foot at him. "Don't my toes look nice?"

"Your toes always look nice," he said. Though he had

to admit the deep red color on her toes was hot. Especially displayed on the end of her long tanned legs clad in nothing but cut-offs. "And it was nothing."

"It wasn't nothing, it was thoughtful." Leah frowned at him. "Faith was really happy."

"I know, we FaceTimed, remember?" He wondered exactly how much champagne the girls had drunk over the afternoon. Leah didn't seem tipsy, but she was definitely . . . relaxed.

"Of course I do." She rolled her eyes at him. "But I wanted to make sure you knew."

"Thanks," he said. "I guess the next big get-together will be for you."

"Why?"

"Hello? Fourth of July in a couple of weeks, it's your birthday."

"Oh. That." She hitched a shoulder, turned her gaze back out to sea.

"Not 'Oh, that.' It's your *birthday*."

She looked back at him, looking faintly surprised, as though she didn't quite know why he was mentioning it. "It's not a big deal. It's not like I'm turning thirty. Not yet."

"Still, it's your birthday. Don't you want a party?" Leah and Faith had always loved their birthdays when they'd been teens. There'd been plenty of parties. And excitement about presents. And endless teen-girl talk about what to wear and who to invite. Birthdays had definitely been big. And Sal and Caterina had loved throwing parties for their kids. In the Santelli household, birthdays were definitely not something to be shrugged off. So what had happened? Had Joey Nelson somehow destroyed Leah's love of birthdays? Or was this a weird post-divorce thing? Screw that shit if it was. Leah deserved to be spoiled a little. Maybe he should ask Faith what was going on.

"I'll have a family lunch. It's Fourth of July. Everyone's busy with tourists that weekend and it's too much trouble to organize something. Plus there's pre-CloudFest craziness and the wedding as well this year. I only do parties for the big numbers."

"So, what, you haven't had a party since your twenty-first birthday?" That was just sad.

"Not a big one, no. Get-togethers with friends a few times. No big deal."

"And what if I want to spoil you?" he said.

"You can take me to watch the fireworks down at the harbor."

"I have a better idea," he said. "How about we take advantage of the fact that everyone else will be down there, and you come here and let me make you dinner. We could have a picnic. I'm sure Mina will be working at search and rescue and Faith and Caleb will go down to the harbor. We can have the place to ourselves. We could surf maybe—go 'round to Shane's maybe—then come back here for dinner."

"Will there be cake?"

"As much as you like."

"Surf and cake and you," she said, smiling at him. "It's a date."

"You want to throw Leah a surprise party?" Faith stared at Zach like he'd announced he just wanted to fly to the moon.

"Yes," he said. "I do." He'd been thinking about it all weekend. Couldn't quite shake the idea that something was off about Leah's lack of enthusiasm for her birthday. He'd even climbed out of bed early on a Monday morning to come talk to Faith at the Harper Inc. offices to talk about it.

Faith got up, came around her desk, and closed the office door. Leaned against it, still looking confused. "Leah said that you and she were just a short-term thing."

The bluntness of it stung a little. Faith didn't sound mad about it, just matter of fact. Like it was obvious that he could never be a long-term prospect. He squared his shoulders. "Don't see how that's got anything to do with throwing her a birthday party."

Faith came back to her desk and sat. "Throwing someone a party is a very boyfriend kind of thing to do."

"Leah and I are friends. We've known each other a long time."

Faith leaned back in her chair. "Does she even want a party?"

"She deserves one," Zach said. "I asked her what she was doing for her birthday and she kind of shrugged it off. Like she thought it wasn't a big deal. She used to love her birthday. What gives?"

For a moment he thought Faith wasn't going to answer, but then she leaned forward again. She reached for a pen, twirled it between her fingers. "She's been quieter the last couple of years, I'll admit."

"Since her divorce?"

"Since Joey left, yes."

"And when exactly did he leave?"

Faith shook her head. "I don't remember the exact date . . . late June though.

"So just before her birthday?" Jesus. From what he'd heard, the divorce had been a mutual thing but asking for a divorce just before your wife's birthday seemed stone cold.

"Yes." Faith pulled a face. "Joey never did have great timing."

"That's enough to take the shine off, I'd say," Zach said. His hand clenched briefly, picturing Joey Fucking Nelson. He shook out his fingers. It was doubtful that him punching Leah's ex was going to improve her views on her birthday. He needed to give her good memories, not more hassle.

"Yes," Faith said. "We had a girl's lunch last year . . . but I don't remember the year before."

"Which means maybe she did nothing."

Faith nodded, looking guilty.

"So it's time to change it up," Zach said.

"Do you want to have it at the house?"

He shook his head. "I want it to be a surprise. She might notice if we have caterers or whatever arriving at the house."

"Caterers? How big is this party going to be?"

"Not huge," Zach said. "But I don't cook. So I figured I'd buy the food."

"You might have trouble finding one of the island caterers free. Everyone will be booked up for the weekend. Lou would be happy to help," Faith said. "Me too."

"Lou does too much. So do you." He smiled at her. "If no one on the island can do it, then I'll get someone from the mainland."

"So where are you planning on holding this shindig?"

"I thought I'd ask Billy. I don't think he and Eli have anything planned for the Fourth. Eli said Nina was going to come over if she could but she's got some big case going on, so he didn't think it was likely she'd make it. If not, then I can ask Danny. Or Shane. It's not like we're lacking for houses around here."

Faith's nodded, her expression odd for a moment. "Danny's loaned his place out for the weekend."

Zach nodded. "Okay. Billy it is. I'm sure he'll be okay. Never one to turn down a party. And I get the feeling he's getting a bit antsy."

"He's touring after CloudFest, right? He always gets nervous before a tour. I'm surprised he came here." Faith said. "Normally he chooses somewhere with a bit more distraction."

"Pretty sure his main reason for choosing Lansing was trying to find a place where Eli will rest," Zach said.

"Which means Eli is bored out of his mind too?" Faith said.

"Heading in that direction," Zach admitted, with a grin. "I've distracted him for now, he's helping me chase down some guys for my band.

"You're going to have your set ready for CloudFest then?" Faith asked.

"Yes. Don't worry, I won't be pulling out."

"Good," Faith said. "Because if you did, I'd have to hunt you down and do things you won't enjoy."

"Which I would deserve," Zach said. "But you won't have to."

Faith grinned at him. "All right. You going to ask Sal and Caterina to this party?"

"I'd like to. Leah said she was having a family lunch but I'd like them to come to the party too. Only trouble is that Leah isn't so keen on them knowing about her and me."

"Ah," Faith said. "Well, maybe I can help you out a little with that. I can send the invites. Then as long as you play it cool on the night, then you and Leah can slide under the radar for a while longer."

"You think Sal would be weird about it?"

"About Leah seeing someone? No. About you. Maybe." She studied him a moment then made an apologetic face. "Sorry, but he's like the rest of us. He doesn't want to see her get hurt again. And you're not sticking around."

He didn't want to have this conversation again. So he just nodded. "All right. Quiet then. You send the invites, I'll do the rest. I'll talk to Billy today and we'll take it from there."

# chapter thirteen

When they came out of the ocean, Leah couldn't stop laughing as she wrung seawater out of her hair. She collapsed back onto the sand, trying to catch her breath. She and Zach had, as he'd promised, driven around to Shane's house, which fronted onto one of the smallest but best surf beaches on the island, and spent the afternoon surfing and fooling around. She'd be sore in the morning—she was out of practice with her board—but it would be worth it. Zach in lazy, relaxed, silly mode was irresistible.

"C'mon, lazybones," Zach said, when he caught up to her. "No lounging around on the beach all day." He leaned over and offered her a hand.

She pouted at him, ignoring the hand. "Why not? It kind of fun to have it all to ourselves. And it's my birthday, so shouldn't I get to decide what we do?" She twisted back to look back up at Shane's house. It had always been her favorite of the Blacklight houses.

Not as extravagant as the Harper house, not as cutting-edge *Architectural Digest*–darling as Danny's. It was stone and weathered wood and glass that curved around the land as if it had grown there. It was a pity it was empty most of the time. She couldn't remember the last time Shane or any of his family had been to Lansing. "It's nice here. Peaceful." No chance of being interrupted. Zach had been right about today. Mina was on duty at search and rescue—Fourth of July being one of the island's busiest times of year outside of CloudFest—and Faith and Caleb were spending the day with Lou and then going to the fireworks. She'd had a nice birthday lunch with her parents at Jin's diner and then headed out to see Zach. Nearly the perfect day, in her book. All that she needed to top it off was a couple of good orgasms, and she'd be one happy birthday girl.

"Exactly. It's your birthday." Zach said. "And I have things planned."

"What things?" she asked suspiciously. But she held out a hand so he could haul her to her feet.

"Things you'll like."

She grinned. "I would've thought we had plenty of time for those things later."

"*Other* things you'll like, woman. You have a one-track mind."

"You like the track my mind is on just fine, rock boy."

"True, but as you said, plenty of time for that track later on."

"Okay, then." She ran a hand through her hair, which was pretty much a mess of tangles and salt water even though she'd tied it back. "Do I get a chance to shower before we try these things?"

"I think that can be allowed," he said.

The shower, back at Zach's, turned out to involve some of the things her one-track mind had imagined. Well, he couldn't really blame her for that, could he? After all, he'd come into the bathroom in just his wet shorts to bring her some towels when she was just starting to run the water. Half-naked Zach and a shower was too promising a combination to resist. And he hadn't resisted too hard. Still, by the time they were done and then dried off and dressed it, was nearly six.

"Do your plans involve dinner?" she asked as she came back into the kitchen.

"I've known you a long time, Santelli. And I've seen you when you're hangry." He shuddered theatrically. "So yes, I planned on feeding you."

She stood on tiptoes to kiss his cheek. "I knew there was a reason I liked you."

"If you've been won over by my culinary skills then you're setting your standards too low," he said. He pulled a bandanna out of his pocket and waved it in front of her nose. "But before we get to the food, you need to put this on?"

"Dude, I thought you said the special things had to wait until tonight. And we just did it like thirty minutes ago." She was teasing. Mostly. She wasn't adverse to the idea of Zach and a few knots and a blindfold. Just hadn't expected it right this minute.

"Mind out of the gutter, Santelli. This is so you don't spoil the surprise."

"I bet you say that to all the girls." But she reached

for the bandanna, folded it into a strip, and tied it around her eyes.

"You've done that before," Zach said.

"Too many games of blind man's bluff as a kid."

"I don't remember those." He came 'round behind her to tug on the knot.

"We didn't play it with stinky boys," she said with a smile, trying to get used to the sensation of darkness. She could feel Zach behind her, the warmth and the scent of him. It was tempting to press herself back against him and see if she could distract him some more. But if he'd gone to all the trouble of actually making plans, it was kind of sweet, and it would be unfair to ruin them.

"I wasn't stinky." He pulled on the knot again. "Are you sure you can't see anything?"

She felt the air move in front of her face. He must have reached around to wave a hand in front of her face.

"Total darkness, I promise."

"Good." He moved away from her and she turned, trying to follow the sound of his footsteps. Too late she remembered he was barefoot. And that he could be awfully stealthy when he wanted to be.

"You had stinky phases," she said, hoping to provoke him into talking so she could figure out where he was from the sound of his voice. But apparently he was stealthy and sneaky because she heard nothing for a minute or so until there was the sound of something thumping onto either the kitchen table or the counter. "If you're filming me standing here looking like an idiot, I'm going to be pissed."

Zach laughed then, the sound closer than she'd expected. "Patience, grasshopper."

"You're not the one standing here blindfolded."

"Easily bored, are you?"

"When I'm blindfolded, yes."

He laughed again. There were a few more mysterious noises, and then his hand slipped into hers. "Ready?"

"As I'll ever be," she said, curiosity burning. "Just don't let me walk into anything."

"Trust me," he said, and she had to fight a shiver.

Trust him? It sounded easy. It sounded simple. She would love to trust him. Love to believe he'd always be there. But that would be beyond stupid. Because he was leaving. CloudFest was rapidly approaching. Then Zach would be gone. So she had to be smart. But still, that didn't mean she wasn't willing to let him take her by the hand and take her wherever he wanted to go. At least for tonight.

She'd half-expected Zach to lead her back toward the main house and put her in his car. But instead, they walked into the garden, Zach directing her carefully once they reached the grass. It made more sense, she supposed. Why leave when the whole purpose of this weekend was to hide away and enjoy the solitude.

After a few more minutes, her feet crunched back onto a gravel path, and she wondered if they were heading back to the beach. Unless she'd completely lost her sense of direction with the blindfold, they hadn't headed inland. The sound of the ocean, which was almost always a background noise on most of the Harper estate, was growing louder, which confirmed her theory.

But then they crossed onto grass again instead of continuing down to one of the beach paths.

"Almost there," Zach said encouragingly. He guided her for a couple more minutes, keeping her hand in his, fingers tangling together. It was foolish that his touch and the way he'd made sure she hadn't so much as stumbled warmed her heart. But she was going to live with foolish for now.

"Okay," Zach said. "Just stay here for a minute."

He let go of her hand and, for a second, she mourned its loss. But then she heard a rustle and curiosity won out again. She strained her ears, trying to hear. But apparently one rustle was all Zach was giving her. She gave up and stood still, focusing on enjoying the warmth of the early evening and the sea air ruffling her hair, knowing that Zach would be back with her soon enough. Apparently that was all she needed right now to be happy.

"Ready," Zach said, and she realized he was standing in front of her. His hands undid the knot of the blindfold and she opened her eyes cautiously, shielding them against the light.

At first all she could see was Zach, but then, as she caught a glimpse of white out of the corner of her eye, she knew where she was. On the small patch of grass behind—or in front of, maybe—Mina's lighthouse. With a view of nothing but the ocean rolling out in front of them in endless blue.

"Here?" she said.

Zach smiled. "Remember?"

"Oh, I remember." She stared at the spot. She hadn't been here for a long time. Possibly not since the night of her eighteenth birthday, in fact. A night that was hard to forget.

A night that she suddenly remembered . . .

*It had nearly been the perfect night. Leah surveyed the marquee from just inside the entrance. Her eighteenth birthday party. Or the tail end of it. An hour or so ago, just before midnight, her parents and the younger kids and the rest of the adults had all left, leaving the tent and the music to Leah and her friends. For anyone else it would totally have been the perfect night. A stack of presents taller than she was waited for her to open in the morning; the cake had been a wonder of cream and chocolate and sugar; her dad, Sal, had managed to make a speech that was funny without being completely humiliating, and everyone had had a great time.*

*Nearly perfect.*

*So close.*

*But not quite. Because there was just one more thing that Leah wanted for her birthday.*

*She scanned the tent again. On the dance floor, Faith was dancing with Eli, the two of them lost in the music. A few others were up and dancing too. The rest were talking in groups at the tables or, she suspected, had sneaked out to see what nooks and crannies could be found on the Harper property to make out in.*

*Ivy was sitting by the bar, talking to the bartender rather than drinking.*

*The one person she couldn't see was the only one she was looking for.*

*Zach.*

*Faith's older brother. The one boy—man, these days—she wasn't supposed to want.*

*The one man she really, really did.*

*Crap. Had he left? It didn't seem likely. Zach liked a party and really, this party was partly a farewell for him and Faith too. They were headed out on the road to play their first shows in one short week. Neither of them had wanted a going-away party, despite their dad wanting to throw them one. Leah suspected that might have been part of the reason that Grey had offered to let Leah throw her birthday party here on the Harper estate. Which was big and right on the beach. A far prettier location than her parent's backyard or the town hall. Not that she would have minded having her party there either. But it had been nice of Grey to offer—after all her dad had worked at the Harper Inc. recording studio here on the island for twenty years as the main sound engineer—working on all of Blacklight's albums over that time.*

*It was a pretty cool place to have a party. The Harper house was beautiful, as were the gardens, and the weather had cooperated and been spectacular. The day had been warm, but not too hot, and now the night was gorgeous, the sea breeze keeping everyone cool.*

*Of course, nowhere on Lansing was really far from the ocean, and even her house, in Cloud Bay, was only a ten-minute walk to the beaches that curved around the harbor. But the beaches up here on this part of the island, more private and a little wilder than those in town, were her favorite.*

*And, she realized, that she probably knew where Zach was. She closed her hand around the neck of the bottle of very nice champagne—well, she assumed it was nice, she wasn't much of a drinker and tonight she'd limited herself to one glass, wanting to keep her head—and tried to ignore the nervous energy sliding around her stomach.*

*Now or never.*

*A simple choice.*

*Leave the tent and go find Zach and tell him what*

*she had in mind, or stay here and be safe and watch him leave in a week's time and never know.*

*So. Brave or safe?*

*She was eighteen today. She'd spent almost all of her life on this small island. Who knew, maybe she'd spend most of the rest of it here too.*

*So screw safe.*

*There was going to be plenty of time for that. She swigged a mouthful of the champagne—a little extra courage couldn't hurt—and walked out into the night.*

*No one saw her go. And she didn't pass anyone on the path that led from the garden down to the old lighthouse that guarded the headland. The Harpers kept the building maintained and the light operational, but no one lived here.*

*But the view from the small yard in front of the light looking out over the ocean was amazing and it had always been one of Zach's favorite places.*

*Her steps slowed as she walked around the lighthouse. For the first time, it occurred to her that if Zach was here, he might not be alone. She stopped, listened. No voices. Then, as she waited, the sound of an acoustic guitar—very soft—floated into the air.*

*She recognized the song. One of Faith and Zach's.*

*Seemed like everywhere she'd turned for the last few months she'd heard it. Faith humming the melody or practicing the piano part. Or this sound. The sound of Zach's fingers bringing a guitar to life.*

*He was playing it slower now, so that the melody twined around the sound of the waves in the distance, the rhythmic whoosh of them forming an odd sort of backbeat. She paused to enjoy it, wondering idly how she'd mix it, if she could capture it in the studio. But that thought brought back reality a little too fiercely. In a week Faith and Zach would be gone, and then in another month she'd be going to live in L.A. for a year to do an intensive course in audio engineering before coming back to Lansing to work at the Harper studio with her dad. She'd been helping him unofficially for a long time and hanging around the studio since she could toddle, but he'd insisted that she go get an actual qualification.*

*Just in case, he kept saying.*

*She wasn't sure what the scenario was he was imagining. Her wanting to leave the island? Go get a job somewhere else? Even then, with Harper Studios on her resume and being able to say she was trained by Sal Santelli, she figured she'd be able to get work without the piece of paper.*

*But she was still going. Partly for the challenge of it, partly to live somewhere else for a little while—though that part made her stomach churn—and partly because she'd figured that maybe if she was away from here, it wouldn't be so obvious that Faith and Zach were gone too.*

*Zach had been gone before. At college in New York because Grey, like Sal, had been big on education. Leah still wasn't sure how Faith had managed to weasel her way out of going this year. At a guess, she'd promised that she'd go next year. But somehow, Leah didn't think that was her plan. But even from the East Coast, Zach had managed to come home regularly, turning up randomly on weekends.*

*Easy enough when you were as rich as the Harpers. He'd been home for every holiday and even spent most of the summers here when he wasn't at a music festival or tagging along with the Blacklight juggernaut if the band was touring. But this. This was different. If Faith and Zach were successful—and why wouldn't they be?—then they'd have a whole new life outside Lansing. One that didn't involve her.*

*Lifting the bottle, she took one last mouthful. No thinking about tomorrow. Tomorrow was not the Leah of tonight's problem. The future Leah could deal with that one.*

*Bubbles tingled down her throat as she swallowed. She wasn't entirely convinced she liked champagne. Her parents drank Prosecco sometimes and she'd tasted that—sort of sweet and fruity—but this was dry and almost reminded her of . . . toast. It had an edge she wasn't quite sure she was ready for. She set the bottle down. Zach didn't drink champagne as far as she knew. Didn't drink much of anything. Neither did Faith. And the small amount she'd had was just enough to give her a little more courage.*

*She was finally eighteen. There was nothing stopping her doing what she wanted.*

*Other than the man she wanted.*

*She moved around the lighthouse and there he was. Zach Harper, sitting cross-legged on the grass, guitar in his lap, staring out to sea. The perfect picture of the moody musician. It should have been a cliché. It would have been a cliché except he looked too damn good to be a cliché.*

*It was weird. Zach looked like a surfer on the surface, longish brown hair streaked from sun and salt water, skin always looking slightly tanned—and now in summer actually tanned—easy smile, seawater eyes. You'd think the sun was his element. But really, he was a creature of nighttime and moonlight. Something in him only came truly awake after sundown. In the silvery light, the angles of his face—that she'd seen morph from boy to something older over the last few years— were sharper, the lines of them adding up to something more than just the handsome guy he was in daylight.*

*She'd seen him on stage, and somehow the stage lights did the same thing. Transformed him. Making him something not quite real but at the same time primal. Something that made her blood heat and her heart want. Rock star genes. Potent things.*

*One more step and she was out of the shadow of the lighthouse.*

*"Hey, Zach."*

*The music died and he swung around, face startled. It eased when he saw who it was.*

*"Hey, birthday girl." He put the guitar down in the case lying open on the grass. "Isn't the party back that way?" He tipped his head in the direction of the house.*

*"It's winding down. I wanted some air."*

*"Too much champagne?"*

*She shook her head. She wanted him to be clear on that point. "No."*

*"Young people today, no idea how to party.".*

*"Tell me, oh ancient twenty-one-year-old, of the ways of your people."*

*He laughed at that. "That's ancient twenty-one-year-and-four-month-old to you, grasshopper."*

*"I bow to your superior knowledge," she said and sat down on the grass next to him, choosing a spot maybe a smidge closer than she would usually. Her shoulder, bared by the strapless dress she wore—she spent hours choosing exactly the right one in her favorite new-leaf*

*shade—was only a few inches from his. The warmth rising from him was a startling contrast to the night air.*

*It made her want to lean closer. But, no. Not yet.*

*This was enough to start. At least her heart thought it was from the way it was suddenly pounding in her ears.* God. *What was she doing? She stared out at the water, trying to remember how to breathe.*

*What she was doing was what she'd wanted to do since she'd been about fifteen, looked up one day, and realized, to her horror, that she had a hopeless, ridiculous, full-blown crush on Zach. Her best friend's brother.*

*Zach was looking out at the water too. "Score lots of good birthday loot?"*

*"I haven't opened any of it yet," she said. "But Mom and Dad got me a car."*

*"That's cool," Zach said.*

*"Yes," she agreed. She doubted he understood how cool. Her parents had refused to buy her a car when she'd first started driving, arguing that they lived a whole fifteen-minute walk from the high school and that nowhere on the island was far enough away that she couldn't ride her bike. Which was true but deeply uncool. Faith and Zach, of course, had cars. Plus Grey owned a bunch of them, so really, they had their pick. Which was good for them and good for her because Faith never minded giving her a ride. And face it, usually wherever Leah was going, Faith was going too.*

*But that wouldn't be true much longer.*

*Faith was leaving. So was Zach.*

*And she'd need a car in L.A.*

*She took a breath. No letting the conversation get*

*sidetracked. If she started a nice friendly chat with Zach, then she'd lose her nerve.*

*"Of course, there's one thing I really want for my birthday," she said.*

*"Oh?"*

*Maybe he'd heard something in her voice because his head turned. Which put his face very close to hers. Those famous gray-green Harper eyes turned an odd luminous moonlit shade at night.*

*She'd never seen them this close.*

*She could fall right into them. Never come up for air. Drown herself in Zach.*

*Even if it was for just one night.*

*Her heart pounded harder, her body caught between bravery and terror as they just stared at each other.*

*This was the moment. The one she'd pictured. Time to find out if she was brave enough to see if she could get to the things she'd pictured happening after this one.*

Now or never.

Damn.

*She shouldn't have left that champagne back there. She could use another hit right now. She swallowed. "Yes. Yes, there is. This." And she leaned toward him. Closed those last few vital inches. Such a small distance. And such a huge one at the same time.*

*And then she kissed him.*

*She heard his half-surprised noise, felt the shock of it to run through his body even though the only thing touching was their lips. For a moment his mouth stayed still beneath hers, not responding. But then he kissed her back.*

# chapter fourteen

"Earth to Leah?" Zach said, watching Leah as she stood, staring down at the picnic basket, her expression oddly . . . well, he wasn't exactly sure.

"What?" she blinked at him, clearly miles away.

He gestured at the blanket he'd spread. "Dinner is about to be served." He knelt and started pulling food out of the basket. With a party to go to afterward, he hadn't wanted too much. But he hadn't wanted Leah to get suspicious either, so there was plenty. Plus a birthday cake, just big enough for two, courtesy of Stella. She'd made a bigger one for the party, but this was just for him and Leah.

"Leah?" he said. "Food?"

She blew out a breath. "Food. Right." She focused on him, eyes catching his. Was he imagining things or were her cheeks pinker than they had been?

He'd chosen the lighthouse because it was the best view of the ocean. He hadn't thought about the memories that came with it. Leah. In that green dress.

She was wearing green again tonight. A sundress or whatever women called it. Cotton. Straps. Not much to it. It skimmed around her body leaving plenty of tanned skin on display. Legs, arms, collarbones. All calling to him. If he had his way he'd take it off. But that wouldn't get them to the party. Though it might make it easier to keep his hands off her once they were there.

He patted the blanket. "Come here."

"You trying to get friendly, Harper?" she said as she sank to her knees with a smile that told him she wouldn't be against the idea.

"How about we refuel, then we can think about that part?" he said, grinning back.

Leah nodded and reached for a plate. They ate mostly in silence until Zach rolled onto his back, staring up at the just darkening sky. "This is the life," he said.

"It's hard to beat Lansing in summer," Leah agreed. She put her plate aside and eased down beside him.

"You never wanted to leave?" he asked, curious. After all, she'd gone away to college. But she'd come back. And stayed.

"Like you said, hard to beat. I love my job, my family's here. I've traveled when I wanted to. Why would I want to leave?"

He waved a hand toward the horizon. "See what's out beyond that?"

"Lots of ocean, Hawaii, and then Australia," she said. "Seen those."

"Where's your spirit of adventure?"

"Outnumbered by my spirits of contented and happy." She rolled onto her stomach, propping herself up on her elbows so she was looking at him.

"You could work anywhere," he said. "You're talented, you've got a solid rep as an engineer. When this album comes out, hopefully you'll have an even bigger one as a producer. Do you really want to stay here?"

"Artists travel to work with producers all the time. Not hard to coax people to come work on an island, after all."

"I guess." He probably shouldn't push. After all, it wasn't as though he was asking her to come with him. She wanted temporary after all. He just wasn't sure why that was getting harder to swallow.

But he didn't want to ruin the mood, so he pushed himself up and went back to the picnic basket for the birthday cake. "Right. Cake—then I have a surprise." He passed the box to Leah.

"You got me cake?"

"You said you wanted cake. You ask, I deliver." He leaned down and kissed her.

She smiled happily at him as she opened the small cake box. "Chocolate?"

"With salted caramel frosting and chocolate cream."

"Awesome." She took the knife he passed her and lifted it toward the cake.

"Hey, make a wish first," he said, putting his hands over hers.

She rolled her eyes. "I wish that this surprise of yours involves you naked."

"You're not supposed to tell anyone what your wish is. And I'm serious," he said, "you have to make a wish on your birthday. Bad luck not to. Grey used to make us all close our eyes and make a wish every year."

"Bossy," she said, but she closed her eyes and her face

relaxed for a minute before her eyes sprang open again. "And now, cake."

Cake for two took time, Zach torn between wanting to stay here enjoying himself with Leah and needing to make sure they got to the party so all his—and Faith and Lou's—hard work wouldn't go to waste.

It was close to eight. They really needed to make a move. But looking at Leah in the sunset light, he was very tempted to stay right where they were.

But nope. Hopefully if the party went the way he wanted, the smile on Leah's face would be even wider when they got there. And after the party was done, he could take her back to the guesthouse and take that oh-so-tempting dress off her and do all the things he'd been thinking about.

"You look like you're plotting something evil," Leah said.

He shook his head. "Not evil. Hopefully good." He started gathering up the food and the plates and glasses. "But for my plan to work, we need to get going."

Her eyebrows lifted but her smile widened. "Is it time for some of those things we were discussing earlier?"

"You really do have a one-track mind, Santelli."

She stuck out her tongue. "And you still like that track."

"Absolutely. But no, I have something else planned before we get to those particular things."

Leah pretended to pout. "If you wait too long, my mind may change."

He snorted. "I doubt it. Face it, you want me bad."

"That goes both ways," she retorted, but didn't look annoyed.

"Truth. But anticipation makes things better, or so they tell me."

"Who's 'they'? Not Grey. Grey wasn't a big believer in delayed gratification."

That was true. His dad had been of the "see it, go for it, get it" school of life. He'd died too young, but no one could accuse him of having missed out on much in the time he had.

Other than being a better dad perhaps.

Zach shook off the thought. Tonight was about Leah.

He put the last glass back into the basket and climbed to his feet, holding out his hand to help her up. "Come on, Santelli, it'll be fun."

When they got back to the guesthouse and he just put the basket on the front steps and came back to her, pulling the keys to Grey's old truck—which Faith had loaned him for the duration of his stay—from his pocket, Leah laughed.

"That old thing? Doing it in style, Harper."

"Don't knock a classic." He patted the truck's hood. It was old and kind of ugly, and Faith should have traded it in by now, but he was glad she hadn't. He had too many memories of Grey telling him to get in the truck and taking him off on some wild escapade to want it gone. "Hop in," he said to Leah.

"Where are we going? Down to the harbor?" she asked as they headed down the drive.

"You'll see when we get there." Short of blindfolding her again—he wasn't sure she'd go for that twice in one night, not to mention that if any of the locals spot-

ted him driving a blindfolded Leah, it was going to attract the kinds of questions she wanted to avoid—there
wasn't really any way of hiding their destination once
he headed toward Billy's place. There were only four
houses on this tip of the island and Leah knew them all.

"Billy's having a Fourth of July party?" Leah said as
they turned into the drive.

He made a noncommittal noise, hoping she'd take it
for a yes.

"And we're stopping in?" she said, sounding confused.

Understandable when he'd told her they'd spend the
day alone.

"It won't take long." He parked the truck.

Leah looked puzzled when he came around and
opened the door for her but she didn't protest. "Sounds
like they're having a good time." The sounds of music
and laughter were spilling from the house.

If everything was according to plan, everyone would
be gathered inside, waiting for them to arrive. He and
Faith had agreed that no one actually wanted to walk
into a darkened room and have the life scared out of
them by their nearest and dearest yelling "Surprise!" at
them, but he still wanted everyone there for Leah to see
as soon as she got inside.

"There'd better be fireworks," Leah said as they
walked into the house.

"Billy loves blowing things up," Zach said. "So, I
think you're pretty safe there. Besides, if he hasn't organized anything, we can still make our own fireworks
later."

Leah rolled her eyes at him. "You know, your rock
star sex god thing needs work if that's your best line."

"Oh, but I don't need a line," he said softly, bending down to kiss her fast while they still could. "Because you can't get enough of me, remember?"

Before she could answer, he opened the door that led into Billy's huge living room and waved her through. "Happy birthday, Leah."

The smile that streaked across her face as she took in the crowd of people and the huge red and white and blue HAPPY BIRTHDAY banner strung across the room, told him he'd made the right decision.

About an hour later, Zach came back into the living room, looking for Leah, wanting to check whether she was actually as pleased by the surprise as she'd seemed. The first part of the party had passed in a haze of hellos and he'd soon found out that Caterina had taken charge of the caterers and Billy had the house entertainment system cranking and there was little for him to do but enjoy himself.

But there was no sign of a green dress and long dark hair. Lou was standing near the door he came in, so he stopped to talk to her for a few moments, still searching the room.

"Looking for someone?" Lou asked, eyes crinkling as she studied his face.

Zach stiffened. He'd thought Lou was out of the loop as far as he and Leah were concerned, but it was possible that Faith or Mina had let something slip. But he didn't know, so he was sticking to a strict "reveal nothing" policy. Faith was standing over near the doors to the deck, Caleb at her side, smiling and talking to Stella. Caleb looked like he was having a good time, but Faith looked a little tense. "I, um, need to talk to Faith about something. Recording stuff."

"At a party?" Lou shook her head at him, looking resigned. She was used to musicians.

"It won't take long. Look, there she is. Excuse me, while I grab her." He dropped a kiss on Lou's cheek and left her, trying to work out the quickest way to make it across the room to Faith. She hadn't moved, which was good, but she hadn't relaxed either.

She'd seemed happy when they had arrived at the party. So had something changed her mood or had she just been hiding it better then?

And if it was the former, then what exactly had happened? She and Caleb were holding hands, and there was no sign of strain on Caleb's face, so it didn't seem likely they'd had a fight. He watched as Faith scanned the room. At first he assumed she was looking for Leah too, but when she spotted Mina standing in the far corner with Will and Stefan, she grimaced a little. That didn't do anything to change Zach's impression that something was bugging her.

Maybe Leah had said something to her about the party?

Crap. If he'd screwed this up, better to know about it sooner rather than later.

He headed for Faith and after a minute or so of small talk, leaned over and said, "Can I talk to you?"

He watched her face as he spoke and saw a flicker of a wince.

There. He wasn't imagining it. His gut tightened while he waited for her response.

Faith nodded and they moved away from the others.

"Something wrong?" he said once they were mostly alone. Or alone as they could be in a room full of people. "Did Leah say something to you about the party? Is she pissed?"

"No," Faith said, eyes widening. "Why would she be?"

"I thought maybe she didn't like the surprise." She'd seemed pleased. But who knew? Maybe she was a very good actress.

"Well, if she doesn't, she hasn't said anything to me about it."

"Okay, then why do you look like you're not having fun?"

Faith's mouth flattened. "I'm having fun." She shook her head at him, sending the fringey sparkly earrings she wore shimmying.

"Faith, I may have been away from the island for a while but I still know you. And I know how you look when something's bugging you."

"It's nothing."

"It's not nothing."

She rubbed the back of her neck briefly. "I was going to wait and tell you and Mina tomorrow. This is a party."

"A party you don't exactly look like you're enjoying."

"If I tell you now, then all three of us might not enjoy it."

That sounded ominous. Which meant it was Harper business. He glanced around the room. Still no sign of Leah. Which meant she was probably out back where there was a bar and tables set up around a small dance floor—it wouldn't be a Santelli party without some dancing after all—or maybe on the deck. Either way, there were plenty of people for her to talk to and he wasn't allowed to hover at her side anyway with her parents here. "Well, I've asked now. So you might as well spill the beans."

She sighed. "Okay. Let me go get Mina. Why don't you go out front, meet us there? If all three of us leave at once, we'll attract attention."

He didn't argue but he waited and watched as Faith walked over to Mina, gave her a quick hug, and then pulled her away from the Fraser brothers. Mina's expression changed from smiling and pleased to a frown as Faith said something in her ear.

Then he turned and headed out, trying to ignore the twist in his gut that told him he wasn't going to like what Faith had to say. Something must have happened. But what? Or to whom? Lou was here at the party, he'd just seen her five minutes ago talking to Billy, so she was fine. But that didn't mean something hadn't happened to somebody else.

There was no one out front of the house, which was good. Meant he didn't have to chase anyone off so that he and his sisters could have privacy. But the minute or so it took for Faith and Mina to join him seemed a long time, leaving him with nothing to do but stare at the dark stretch of ocean, breathe in the night air, and wonder if Faith was about to drop a real bombshell.

# chapter fifteen

"So what's up?" Zach asked as his sisters reached him. They took up position together, standing opposite him, Mina closer to Faith than she was to him. When they'd been kids they'd been a sturdy triangle, each side supporting the others. Zach and Faith and Mina. The Harpers. On paper their lives had been golden. Privileged. Lucky. Money. Travel. A famous dad. In reality, it had been that but there was also a less-stable side. A side where parents disappeared for weeks or months and strangers came and went in the house. The three of them had relied on one another. Stood together. He'd been the one who'd pulled their trio apart when he'd left. But now he was back and yes, their triangle was battered and lopsided. But he hoped it was mending. They were here together. He just hoped whatever Faith had to say wasn't going to throw them any farther out of balance.

Faith smiled tightly. "You sure you want to do this now? We can wait until tomorrow."

"No," Mina said. She tugged at the silver *M* she wore around her neck. "We're here now."

Faith nodded. "Okay. " She took a breath.

"Just tell me if anyone's sick," Zach said before Faith could say anything else.

Her eyebrows flew upward. "God no. I would've told you straight out if it was something that bad." Her expression turned apologetic.

Relief swept through him. "Good. Anything else we can handle." He hoped.

Faith blew out a breath. "Well, I don't really know if there is anything to handle yet." She paused, as if unsure what to say next. Her mouth twisted, as she twined one hand through a lock of her hair.

Nervous.

"Is this about the archives again?" Mina asked.

*The archives?* He hadn't been thinking about them.

Faith nodded. "Had a call from the lawyers yesterday."

"While that sounds ominous," he said. He moved to stand next to Mina—who was chewing her lip and watching Faith intently—reaching out to put an arm around her. "What did they want? Was it about that payment Grey made?" He hadn't had to think about that for months. Or he'd done his best not to. Because there weren't many good reasons for Grey to have paid half a million dollars to an unknown recipient not long before he died.

Faith nodded. "It's taken them awhile to dig into the recipient. They kept looking for other big purchases but nothing came up, and it was a Swiss account, so it took some . . . effort to track down the recipient.".

"Anyone we know?" Zach asked. Mina's shoulders

were still like steel under his arm and he tightened his grip on her but kept his eyes on Faith who didn't look happy.

Faith shook her head. "The account the money went to was held in the name of a woman named Ree Vacek. She lives in some town in Illinois—"

"Illinois?" Mina said, eyes widening. "But then why was the paperwork in Jersey?" She stopped, then shook her head. "Never mind. It was Dad. It doesn't have to make sense." She made a little "go on" gesture.

"Well, this town is where the bank account that received the money was opened apparently. But I guess that doesn't mean she still lives there. Or ever lived there, maybe. The name doesn't ring any bells with me and it doesn't show up in any of the estate records anywhere. I told them to go ahead and see if they can track her down," Faith said. "Maybe it'll turn out to be a donation or something." She didn't sound like she believed that was likely.

Zach's stomach sank. Fuck. The payment had gone to a woman. It was a scenario they'd discussed when they'd first found out about the money. But part of him had hoped it wouldn't turn out to be that. Call him cynical, but there was one very obvious reason why Grey would be making a payment that big to a woman none of them had heard of. A child. Or the claim of one. But that last twelve months, he'd been starting to go downhill fast. Sure he'd made a few trips off-island, insistent on being an independent old bastard to the end, and yes, Grey had gotten Zoe and Lou and Emmy pregnant without any planning, but it seemed unlikely he'd been off knocking up random women when he'd been dying of liver cancer. But hell, it did seem like the most likely reason.

Unless this Ree Vacek, whoever she was, had something over him.

But Grey had never really given a shit about his reputation. And Zach couldn't see his dad giving into that sort of thing when he knew he only had a year or two left. And, if he was honest with himself, somewhere in the back of his mind, there had always been a part of him that had wondered if one day another Harper kid might turn up. A legacy of his father's charm and libido, that maybe even Grey himself might never have known about.

So maybe he was jumping to conclusions and, like Faith said, there were other perfectly legitimate reasons why Grey might have given someone half a million dollars.

"Do they think they can find her?" he asked as Mina slipped out from under his arm and walked a few steps away before turning and coming back, positioning herself, arms folded, beside him again.

Damn. Mina was the one who didn't have experience of this. She was the youngest. Sure, Grey had divorced Emmy in the end, but he'd never replaced her with anyone long term. And there hadn't been another kid to really hit the point home that Grey had screwed up again when Mina's mom had left. Not like Faith had been for Zach or Mina had been for Faith. Though he and Faith had been younger. Back then, he'd been excited at the thought of another sibling. And thankful that Lou had appeared to fill the mom-sized gap in his life Zoe had left behind her.

Faith nodded. "It's an unusual name, it shouldn't be that hard."

"Hell," he said. "Not to be the first to mention the elephant in the room, but do we want to talk about this?"

"That depends what you mean by 'this,'" Mina said, looking unhappy. Zach put his arm around her again.

"What we talked about before," Faith said.

"You really think Dad had another kid?" Mina asked, looking at him for confirmation.

Interesting. He would've expected Faith to be the first one to say it out loud, not Mina.

Zach squeezed Mina a little tighter. "I don't know, kiddo. It's not like Dad to ignore a child. I mean, he never bailed on any of us."

"That's assuming he knew about it," Faith said. "But I agree, he always took care of things in that department. And he'd gotten pretty careful, after Mina." She shot an apologetic look at her little sister. "I always got the impression he thought three not-so-planned kids was enough. Or maybe that he just didn't want a fourth marriage. He told me once that he'd gotten the snip to be safe, but I have no idea if he was serious or not. And knowing how sneaky he could be, I doubt there's anyway of finding out whether he did."

She was probably right. And really, the truth about whether or not Grey had been shooting blanks later in life was not something he needed to know.

"Did the lawyers give you a timeframe?"

Faith shook her head. "Not too long—weeks, maybe a bit longer—but they couldn't be exact."

Which meant they were stuck with not knowing for now and there was nothing that any of them could do about it. A burst of noise came from the house, as though someone had cranked up the music a notch or two.

Party. Leah. Right. Focus on the now. Don't borrow trouble. The future would take care of itself. "Okay. Then I think the best plan is to wait and see what the lawyers come up with. We can drive ourselves crazy speculating or we can just forget about it until we need to actually do something." He nodded back toward the house. "There's a party waiting for us back there, not to mention Leah's probably wondering where the hell we are. I vote for booze and cake and letting the lawyers do their thing."

Neither sister looked convinced. But then Faith nodded. "Yeah, you're right. We'll just drive ourselves crazy if we worry about it. Booze and cake sounds good to me." She smiled at Mina. "You can have cake and Will. He's a good distraction."

Her voice was overly cheerful. But he was pretty sure he'd sounded the same. But hell. Fake it until you make it, or whatever that shit was. If he had to pretend to be okay with this for the moment so that Faith and Mina could be okay with it, then he would. And, if he actually got something decent to drink and Leah back by his side, he might even be okay with it for real.

Leah was sipping a margarita and listening to Stella and Ivy wax lyrical about the latest superhero movie when she saw Zach, Faith, and Mina come back into the room together. The three of them looked somewhat strained. And they were coming from the front of the house, not the deck or out back where the party had spilled out in both directions.

Where had they been? She hadn't noticed them

leaving. Of course, she'd been somewhat distracted trying to say hello to everyone and get her head around the fact that Zach had organized a party for her.

She knew it was him. Even though Faith had been the one who'd taken charge when they'd arrived, there was no way Faith would have set this whole thing up without warning her.

So, it had to be Zach.

And she didn't really know how to feel about that. It was sweet of him—and yes, she was having a good time—but it wasn't the sort of thing that someone who was just a fling did, was it? So what did that mean?

That maybe there was something more? Or was that just wishful thinking on her part?

And how was she supposed to figure it out without flat out asking him? Which was not an option when this was supposed to be casual.

So things were confusing enough without trying to figure out what was going on with the Harpers. But if something had happened, she wanted to know. It wasn't like Faith or Zach to bail on a party and even Mina had been socializing more since she and Will had gotten together. Zach had his arm around Mina and was laughing at something she'd said and Faith was smiling too, but something about her best friend's posture made Leah think that the smiles weren't one hundred percent real.

"Hey, there's Faith," she said, interrupting the superhero talk. "I need to ask her something. You two excuse me a minute, okay?"

Ivy and Stella nodded and waved her off, still too interested in comparing notes on which superhero had the best biceps to be really paying much attention to

Leah. Leah appreciated Chris Evans and Chris Hems-
worth as much as the next gal but she wasn't a super
geek like Ivy or a die-hard Marvel fan like Stella, so she
drained her margarita, put the glass down on the nearest table, and started across the room toward the three
Harpers.

It was slow going to get there, everyone wanted to say
"hello" and "happy birthday," which was lovely, but having to stop every thirty seconds gave Faith, Mina, and
Zach time to split up before she could reach them.

She hesitated, making small talk with Theo King, the
Harper Inc. COO, who'd been the last person to step into
her path, and wondering whether she should go after
Faith or try to talk to Zach.

At that moment, Zach caught her eye and lifted one
eyebrow, as though asking if it would be okay if he came
over and joined them. She flashed him a smile and nodded slightly. She trusted that he'd play it cool. Sure, some
of the people here already knew and something about
the way she'd caught her mom looking at Zach earlier
made her think that Caterina at least suspected but she
wasn't looking for a big pronouncement.

As he made his way across the room, looking beyond gorgeous, she almost regretted that decision. It
would've been nice if she could've planted a big fat kiss
on him, and claimed him as her birthday present for
the second time in her life. But, she only had herself to
blame for the fact that that wasn't going to happen. Zach
said hello to Theo as he reached them and then bent
and kissed Leah's cheek, taking a moment to slip his
hand around her waist and squeeze gently before he
straightened again.

"Happy birthday," he said. "Having a good time?"

She smiled up at him, torn between wishing that kiss could've been more and being grateful that he was playing by the rules. "Yes, thanks," she said. "Remind me to thank whoever is responsible." She hoped he'd get the hint that she knew it was him.

Zach nodded. "I will."

Did that mean he understood?

"Faith tells me your recording sessions are going well, Zach," Theo said.

Zach shrugged. "It's good. But I don't want to talk about it too much. Don't want to jinx something, you know," he said, looking a little sheepish.

Theo laughed. "You musicians are all so superstitious. Give me a nice well-behaved spreadsheet any day rather than trying to do this creative shit that you do."

Zach grinned. "Trust me, I'm very happy to just keep doing my job and you do yours, Theo," he said. "Spreadsheets are kind of my idea of hell."

Leah rolled her eyes at him. "That's not entirely true. You got all your song stuff and music ideas and all that stuff pretty well documented."

"Maybe. But not in spreadsheets," Zach said. "You're the one who does all that detail stuff." He grinned. "She's a bit of a slave driver. I'm lucky she let me out of the studio tonight."

Well that was just an outright lie, but not one she could call him on in front of Theo. "Well, that's because I didn't know there was a party on," she said. Which was also kind of a fib. But one that Zach couldn't call her on either. So she'd call that even.

Zach shook his head, pretending to look disappointed. "Too busy to have a birthday party. I don't know what you're putting in the water around here, Theo. But it's turning everyone into workaholics."

"Busy time of year, with the festival." Theo said. "You know that."

"Just as well I came back to remind you all how to have some fun."

From the other side of the room came the sound of Billy cheering, though she couldn't make out what he was saying. Zach looked over and grinned. "Or maybe I'll just leave that up to Billy."

"Please don't," Theo said. "God knows what would happen if Billy was left in charge."

"Don't worry, he has plenty of adult supervision," Zach said just as the music cut off and the sound of a guitar rippled through the room. Zach turned in the direction of the sound.

"Is that him?" Leah asked. Eli played guitar, but his hand was still recovering. Billy, though a drummer at heart, was one of those musicians who could turn his hand to most instruments. As evidenced by the number of them hanging on the walls throughout the house—though she was pretty sure he didn't actually play tuba—and by the sleek black Steinway grand piano that sat in a corner of this very room and always made her hands itch to play it. Billy mostly kept his experiments offstage, but he was a damn good guitarist when he put his mind to it—maybe not near Grey's or Danny's or even Zach's level—but he could more than hold his own.

"Sounds like it," Zach said as the random guitar noises turned into the riff from an old Erroneous song.

"Hey birthday girl, get over here," Billy bellowed across the room.

Leah stayed where she was.

Zach laughed and pushed her gently in Billy's direction. "I don't think you're getting out of this. It's birthday serenade time."

Oh God. She'd never really liked being the center of attention. She liked people just fine. She liked parties just fine. She just never wanted all the people at the party to be staring at her. But Zach was right. Billy wasn't likely to quit until he got his way. She made her way over to him. He'd made himself at home on a chair beside the piano, guitar resting on one knee.

"Happy birthday, kiddo," he said and launched into a flamboyant cascade of chords that morphed into a round of "Happy Birthday" that everyone joined in.

Zach was standing beside her and even though there was a room full of people around her, his voice was really the only one she focused on. Was there a little extra stress on "Dear Leah" as he sang? Or was she just an idiot who'd already had two margaritas too fast? But he'd organized this party for her . . .

The song ended and everyone cheered and then Billy started playing another Erroneous song about party girls and summer nights that had everyone clapping along and could have provided her the perfect cover to ease back out of the spotlight. But she stayed where she was besides Zach, not wanting to move away while everybody was too focused on Billy to notice her lingering next to him.

Billy ran through two more songs then paused, looking over to Zach. "How about you, Zach?" he asked. "Got a song you want to play for us? Maybe one of those new ones you're working on?"

This got another cheer from the crowd. Which was

kind of dirty pool on Billy's part. If someone was working on new material, it was up to them to volunteer to
share it or not. Zach was very still beside her and she
wanted to tell him he didn't have to, but Billy was holding out the guitar and everyone was making encourag-
ing noises. Zach stepped forward and reached for the
guitar. She wasn't entirely convinced by the smile on his
face. Billy vacated the chair with a grin that made her
uneasy. Why was he poking at Zach?

Zach sat and then he said, "Well, maybe I can play
something new. But I'm going to need some help. And
it seems unfair to put the birthday girl to work, so, Faith,
wanna help me out?"

Leah's head whipped around, looking for Faith. She
found her standing next to Caleb, eyes wide, obviously
startled by Zach's request. For years Faith had refused
to perform in public. She'd broken that streak by agreeing to sing with Danny last year at CloudFest, but it
wasn't like she'd been going out of her way to repeat
that performance. But as someone in the back of the
room yelled "Yeah, Faith!" and someone else whistled,
she smiled and went to join Zach, taking a seat at the
piano.

Leah's heart started to pound as Faith bent her head
toward Zach and the two Harpers had a short, whispered
conversation before Faith straightened and put her hands
on the keys.

Zach cleared his throat. "So. Like most of you here,
Faith and I have known Leah a long time. She's always
been there when we needed her and I, for one, know I'm
a lucky son of a bitch to call her a friend. So, in honor
of her birthday, the day on which Sal and Caterina managed to give us all someone very special, I want to play

a song that she's been helping me with." He glanced over at Faith who was watching him with an intrigued expression. "So. This is " 'Falling Through.' "

The smile he directed at her as he started the opening chords—as familiar to her now as the lines of his face—made her heart clutch.

*Not here. Not now.*

That was all she could think, scared that she was going to give herself away. That she couldn't stand here and listen to Zach singing a love song at her—*to her*—and pretend that all she appreciated about it was the music and not the man himself.

So she stood and smiled and tried not to look transfixed by him. And the fact that he was singing for *her.* Because he was. Yes, he was putting on a show. She didn't think either he or Faith were capable of singing to a room full of people and not putting on a show, but he kept coming back to her, those sea-storm eyes finding her, that smile twisting in just the way he knew she was helpless against, his fingers putting in the extra little run on the opening line of the second verse that she'd tried to convince him to add, that voice working its magic.

Every girl's dream. That drop-dead sexy rock star singing just for her, telling her he was hers.

She wanted to believe it. Oh, so badly. Even though she knew it wasn't true. Knew he was going to leave. And, even worse, she realized that part of her did believe it. That despite all her good intentions and determination to be logical about this, somewhere, he'd snuck up on her again, crept under all those carefully constructed defenses. Made her do just about the dumbest thing she could think of.

Fall for him all over again.

Apparently she was really just that dumb.

Apparently Zach Harper was Leah's kryptonite. The one who was going to drag her down to her doom. Or at least leave her world blown to smithereens when he took off back to where he belonged.

Not here.

Not with her.

And so, she listened to the song, wondering how it was possible to be so happy and so shattered at the same time. She managed to smile. She managed to applaud at the end with everyone else and make the right noises while Faith got up from the piano and came over to hug her. Resisted the temptation to bury her head against her best friend's shoulder and confess just how dumb she'd been.

That wasn't going to help.

So she watched Zach hand Billy back his guitar over Faith's shoulder and then, after everyone's attention started to drift away from him, went in search of another drink.

# chapter sixteen

"You're quiet," Zach said many hours later as they drove back toward the Harper estate.

Leah turned back from the open car window. "Big night." She'd been staring out at nothing in particular, pretending to be focused on the night sky. It was easier than talking to Zach. She'd managed to avoid talking to him for most of the rest of the party after his song. The whole being-the-birthday-girl-and-having-to-talk-to-everyone-who'd-showed-up routine was actually the perfect cover. She only hoped most of them had missed the fact that she was distracted, keeping half an eye out for Zach so that she could move out of his path when he appeared.

She hadn't entirely succeeded. She'd wound up in the same small group as him a couple of times and had chatted and smiled and laughed like nothing was wrong. But she had avoided being alone with him until she'd realized that the only ones still left at the party other than Billy and Eli were herself, Zach, Faith, and Caleb.

And while she was one hundred percent sure she could have begged a ride home from Faith and Caleb, she was also one hundred percent sure she didn't want to explain to Faith why she was not going home with Zach. Which was how she'd wound up in the car with him, staring out at the darkness and wondering what the hell she was going to do next.

"Did you have a good time?" Zach asked.

There. That was the opening she needed. If she wanted it. Ask Zach why he'd thrown the party. But if she asked—if she pushed—then she would most likely let him know why she wanted to know. And maybe she'd been dumb enough to fall for Zach all over again, but she wasn't going to be dumb enough to tell him that.

She was, however, going to be dumb enough not to let him go until she had to. A braver woman would cut her losses and run. But she knew she couldn't. Even if there hadn't been the record to think of, she wasn't going to be the one to tell him to go. She'd keep the heartbreak to herself until he was safely off the island and couldn't see just how dumb she'd been.

"It was lovely," she said. Which was the truth. Apart from her realization about Zach, it had been a great party. But she didn't want to talk about it. Talking about it might stray back into the territory of who had come up with the idea and then she'd be right back where she didn't want to be. So she needed a different subject. And, like a gift, the memory of Zach and Faith and Mina returning to the party together came back to her as Zach turned the car into the Harper drive. "You know, before Billy decided to start the entertainment portion of the evening, I saw you and Faith and Mina together. Faith looked upset. Is everything okay?"

Zach glanced over at her, expression unreadable in the dim light, then looked away again as he turned into the entrance to the Harper estate.

"You might as well tell me," Leah said. "Faith will eventually."

That made his mouth quirk. "Dad always did say he might as well adopt you and Ivy given how close the three of you were." The gates swung open in front of them, and he set the car into motion again.

"Well, let's be glad he didn't," she said. "That would have made this"—she moved her hand back and forth between them—"all kinds of wrong. But I think you're changing the subject. What's going on?"

"Just Grey shit," Zach said.

"That covers a pretty wide range of possibilities," Leah pointed out. She tried to think of some of them. She knew that the business of tying up the loose ends of Grey's estate had been dragging on. "Is this about the archive business? Faith said something about another storage locker ages ago. And a bank account?"

"She told you that?" He sounded startled.

"Well, who is she supposed to talk to?" Leah said. "You haven't been around and Faith was trying to keep Mina out of the business hassles where she could. You know, with the whole dead husband thing? You can't be mad at Faith for finding other people to confide in."

Zach pulled up in front of the guesthouse. "I'm not mad . . . I guess I just hadn't thought about it."

"You not thinking about it is kind of the reason why she needed people like me to talk to," Leah said, the words coming out sharper than she intended. She reached for the door and got out of the truck before she could say anything else. She was tired. And upset. But she didn't want to fight with him.

Zach caught up with her as she was climbing the front steps. "Hey," he said. "Slow down."

She made herself stop. Turned to face him. "It's been a long day."

"I thought you wanted to hear about this?" He climbed two steps past her and sat down at the top, patting the wood next to him.

It was probably not a good idea to sit beside him. These steps and Zach were a dangerous combination, it seemed. But she sat anyway. "All right. Spill."

He was leaning forward over his knees, hands clasped. She thought she saw his knuckles whiten briefly, but it was hard to tell in the moonlight. "Zach?"

"To answer your question, yes, it's about the bank account. Turns out Grey paid a huge chunk of change to a woman named Ree Vacek six months or so before he died."

Grey. Not Dad. So, not a good thing, necessarily. All three of the Harpers tended to use Grey when they were talking about Grey the alcoholic problem-child rock star rather than Grey the sometimes-decent dad. "Ree Vacek?" she said. "That's not a name I know."

Zach shifted on the step. "It's not a name any of us know. The lawyers are looking into it. They've found the place where her bank account was opened. But not her. Not yet."

"How much money?" she asked softly.

"Half a million," Zach said flatly. "The lawyers can't find any records of any sort of purchase or title transfer around that time, so it looks like it was just the money."

*Half a million dollars.* That was a lot of money. She'd grown up in the music industry. She knew it wasn't all music and happiness. There was a seedier side that went with famous men who women were happy to throw themselves at and who didn't stop to think too hard about saying "yes" when they did. A side that involved lawsuits and paternity tests and . . . settlements. She had never heard that any of the Blacklight guys had had anything like that happen, but it didn't mean it hadn't. But Grey? Grey had never been shy about admitting he'd fathered a child. Hell, he tended to turn around and marry the women he knocked up. Lou and Emmy and Zoe were proof of that. But still . . .

"I take it by that silence that you're thinking exactly what the three of us are thinking," Zach said.

"There are lots of possible explanations. Maybe it was a charity. One of those internet good causes you see. You know he spent a lot of time in that last couple of years trying to make up for lost time and sort some of his stuff out. Maybe he felt like he could help someone?"

"Maybe," Zach said. "But why hide it, if that was what he was doing? He did this in secret."

"You really think Grey got some woman pregnant before he died?"

"I don't know," Zach said. "But my gut says maybe yes."

If it were true, that meant there was another Harper sibling out there. Holy crap. No wonder Faith had looked upset. Faith was fierce about family. She would want to know. "What do the lawyers think?"

"I gather they think that we shouldn't jump to conclusions while they find out more," Zach said. "I tend to agree with them. We can drive ourselves crazy speculating or just wait until we have some facts."

Did he really think that? Or was that just what he'd told Mina and Faith to make them feel better? She searched his face, but he wasn't giving anything away. "I think you're right," she said. Hell, she could hardly tell him not to bury his head in the sand when she was intent on burying hers.

He hitched a shoulder slightly in acknowledgment then scrubbed a hand over his face. "So now you know as much as we do." He shook his head. "You know, sometimes I wonder what it would be like to have a normal family."

"I think almost everyone wonders that at some point. All families have their quirks."

"Yeah, but you have to admit, mine has quirks with a capital quirk."

"I don't know," she said. "I'm kind of fond of you all. Granted, Grey was original but hell"—she stopped and waved her arm toward the garden and the ocean beyond—"he gave you all of this. And he gave you Faith and Mina. And Lou. That's not so bad."

"Not going to let me feel sorry for myself, huh?"

"Nope. It's my birthday. No being a downer."

That made him laugh. "All right then." He twisted, body angling toward her. "It is past midnight, though, so technically it's not your birthday any more."

She shook her head. "Oh no. It's my birthday until I go to bed and fall asleep, that's the rule."

"You make the rules now?"

"It's my birthday." She bumped him with her shoulder. "I am the birthday queen."

He reached across, gently tugged one of the strands

of hair that was coming down from the updo she'd
wound it into. The scent of his skin made her catch her
breath. God. Why did she want him so much when it
was all going to end in disaster?

"And what does Your Majesty require on her birthday?" he asked.

There was only one answer to that question. "This,"
she said, hearing the echoes of memory as she leaned in.

"Ah, that old line," he said, closing the distance
between them, stopping just short, so his mouth was just
one tantalizing inch above hers. "Say it again."

"This," she breathed and pressed her mouth to his.

"This," she said again as his arms came around her
and the kiss sank through her and washed away every
last shred of common sense in its wake.

"You got it," Zach said and then somehow, he was
lifting her, walking toward the door. There was a slightly
awkward maneuver as he shifted his weight to free his
palm and scan the door open, but she just tightened her
legs around his waist and held on. Held on as he kissed
her again and walked through the darkened guesthouse
without pausing until they reached the bedroom and he
let her down, so they were standing there, kissing wildly
like they had that very first time they'd stood here so
many years ago.

Eventually she had to come up for air and they broke
apart, breathing heavily, eyes locked.

"I like your birthday," Zach said softly. "It often
works out well for me."

She laughed. "I'm quite fond of it too." She stepped
back in, reached for the first button on his shirt. "But
ssssh, I'm unwrapping my present."

The rumble of his laugh vibrated against her fingers

as they moved against cotton and skin. But he didn't speak. Just stood there and let her do what she wanted, those eyes watching her, their color drowned in the moonlight but the heat in them unmistakable every time she glanced up.

By the time she reached the last button, her fingers were trembling.

"Leah," Zach said, putting his hands over hers. He was warm and strong and hot against her and she swayed toward him, wanting his kiss. She thought it would be wild again, drive them forward, but instead Zach turned things slow. Patient.

Fierce but sweet. Sweeter than that first time. Their first night had been hungry and fumbling and sweet and glorious and hot. Bound up in longing and hope and youthful optimism. There was still longing. Still heat that sent her melting every time his fingers moved across her skin. But she wasn't eighteen anymore.

And she knew he wasn't forever.

She knew she couldn't hope it would work out differently. All she could do was bank this memory. Add it to the store that might help after he was gone. Hope that she wasn't just adding to the thoughts that might break her at three a.m. when she was alone again and he was thousands of miles away.

But if she was going to be foolish—and when it came to Zach, it seemed that was always what she was going to be—she would err on the side of hope. And take as much time from him as he was willing to give. Time and whatever else he offered her.

She let herself give in to the pace he was setting, sinking into each sensation. Each moment stretched as mouths met and skin brushed and clothes vanished, each sensation savored until it dissolved into the next. By the time they laid on the bed she felt as though she was dissolving as he lay above her and then pushed, oh-so-slowly, inside, the expression on his face reverent and heated, and her world became Zach and the feel of him. The taste of him as he moved with her, slow and sure, steady as a drumbeat, setting up the perfect rhythm between them with the same certainty he had when he played his guitar. Sure of himself. Sure of her. Sure of *them*.

So sure she let herself believe him. Wrapped herself around him and let herself memorize him, feel him. All hers. The pleasure of it flowed through her, pushing her higher and closer and hotter until she couldn't resist any more and let it blow through her like the perfect chord, taking both of them away.

"Are you ready for this?" Eli asked Zach as they pulled up at the studio on Friday.

Zach looked across at his friend and grinned. "Abso-fucking-lutely." He drummed his fingers on the wheel a moment then killed the engine. In a few hours the musicians he'd hired to back him at CloudFest would be arriving and they'd start rehearsing. Less than two weeks to go, but they could pull it off. Six songs wasn't a long set. But even though he knew he could do it, nerves had been riding him the last few days. He'd been working through the arrangements, running things by Eli and Leah, trying to maximize the time he had left.

"Must be hard to be so full of self-doubt," Eli said, rolling his eyes.

"Yeah, like you're such a shy and retiring type," Zach

retorted as he pushed his door open. "Anyway, self-doubt's for losers."

"Ah, now that's a Grey Harper quote I recognize," Eli said. "Like father, like son?"

Zach ignored him. He didn't want to be like Grey. He wanted to be himself. Zach. Sure, he wouldn't say no to finding the kind of success with his music that Black-light had found, but he'd pass on the addiction and self-destructive tendencies. "Let's do this," he said and headed toward the studio.

Leah was working with Nessa and her band today but it was their last day of recording and she'd said she'd be around to give him a hand after she wrapped it up with them. She'd been a little quiet this week but the last two weeks before CloudFest were always kind of insane and she had a full studio to deal with as well as trying to fit in some extra work helping out at the Harper Inc. offices with all the last-minute organizing that went on in the background to get CloudFest to the starting line smoothly.

And after the CloudFest, they'd get some time to-gether.

The thought stopped him a moment. Would they? He'd need to get moving after CloudFest. Get a single out, climb onto the promo train, and hustle. He wouldn't be around. But he'd still have to finish the album with Leah too. So he could come back to her. Would come back to her. They'd started this thing with her crazy idea that it would only be until he left, but that thought didn't sit so well with him any more. He wasn't ready to let her go. Wasn't ready to not have her quick smile and her teasing and her musical mind around him. Definitely wasn't ready to not have her in his bed.

Hell no to that.

So he'd just change her mind. That would be easy enough. She talked a good game but he knew she wasn't ready either. She hadn't said it, but things were too good between them. So he'd turn on the Harper charm and convince her.

"Earth to Zach?" Eli said and Zach stopped walking. Realized they were inside the studio foyer and he hadn't even noticed. He saw Leah through the window in the wall that blocked off this area from the recording studios. She was sitting at the board outside the main studio, her hair half-falling down around her face as usual as she listened intently to something Nessa was saying. Faith was sitting beside her. Huh. He hadn't expected his sister to be here. If anyone had absolutely no time at all in the weeks leading up to CloudFest, it was Faith. But then again, Nessa was her protégé. So maybe she was turning over a new leaf and trying not to work quite so hard on the festival so she had time for the other new things in her life. Like Nessa. Like Caleb.

"Earth to Zach," Eli repeated and Zach shook his head.

"Sorry, was thinking about that piano section again in 'Air and Breath,'" he said. "I'm going to grab a coffee before we set up."

"Good idea," Eli said, stifling a yawn.

They'd been up until nearly two, talking through the songs, so neither of them had had enough sleep.

"Better make yours a double shot," Zach said. He headed for the kitchen and the sweet caffeine-producing goodness of the coffee machine. He was pulling down cups from the cabinet over the counter when he saw Billy come through the studio door.

He nudged Eli. "What's he doing here?" If it was early for Zach and Eli to be at the studio before ten it was definitely unusual to see Billy up and coherent at this hour. He started working the coffee machine.

Eli shrugged. "No idea. But you know Billy. He likes nosing around other people's sessions."

That was true. Though he hadn't showed up for any of Zach's sessions so far. But maybe he was here to hear Nessa. Give Faith a hand. Zach turned his attention back to the coffee, producing two coffees strong enough to dissolve steel. Eli took one sip then put his down and shoveled a few spoons of sugar into it. "Dude, are you trying to give us ulcers?"

Zach laughed. "We're too young for ulcers. Got to be on our game though."

"You need to relax," Eli muttered. "You've picked guys who know what they're doing. It will be fine."

Zach sipped his own coffee, trying to ignore the fact that Eli was right and it was way too strong. He was allowed to be nervous. CloudFest was a big deal. It was the kick-start he needed. And he hadn't played with a whole new band in a while. What if they didn't click? There was no time to fix it if it turned into a disaster. He'd spent an hour earlier in the week trying to convince Faith that she should play with him but she'd turned him down.

"Not for this," she'd said. "This needs to be all you. Not take two on the two of us playing together. You need the person you want to tour with you. And that's something I'm definitely not going to do."

She'd looked happy that he'd asked though, softening her rejection with a hug that had felt as easy as it had when they were kids and that was something. He liked seeing his sisters happy, seeing them thriving again. Something else he'd miss when he left.

"Bring the coffee," he said. "We should get started."

But when he walked through the doors into the hall-way that stretched along the length of the studios and recording rooms, Billy was talking to Faith.

Billy nodded at Zach. "Zach. Morning."

"Billy," Zach said. "Sis."

Faith smiled at him but he thought the expression looked a little tight. "Billy was just telling me he needs to talk to us, Zach."

"Us?" Zach said. He looked at Eli. "The three of us?"

"Just you and me," Faith said, shaking her head.

Zach's gut tightened. "What's up?" he said just as Eli said, "Dad? Something wrong?"

"Nothing's wrong," Billy said. "I just want to talk to these two." He jerked his head toward the studio man-ager's office. "Why don't we go in there?"

He wanted to talk privately? Zach didn't like the sound of that. Billy wasn't the "let's talk in private" type. What the hell was going on?

The studio manager's office, which had been Sal's do-main for years and was now Leah's, was tiny. Barely big enough for the three of them. Faith slid around behind the small desk, leaving Zach standing near Billy. Billy closed the door behind them.

"What's this all about?" Zach asked. He wasn't in the mood for small talk.

Billy stared at him a moment then folded his arms. "Well, it's like this. I'm taking the secret slot at Cloud-Fest."

"What the hell?" Zach said, just as Faith said, "What?"

Billy didn't move an inch. Didn't look away. "You heard me."

Faith sat down in the chair behind the desk with a thud. "Billy—" she started to say, but Billy cut her off with a gesture.

"No point arguing, sweetheart, it's my right."

Zach stared at Billy, gut tensing. "What the hell are you talking about?"

"He means the festival trust," Faith said.

"None the wiser," Zach said tightly.

"Harper Inc. runs CloudFest," Faith said. "But the profits go through a trust that was set up for Blacklight. For all four of them. And part of the trust rules is that a member of Blacklight can play at the festival if they want to."

"I thought that was the headline slot?" Zach said. He'd never seen the legal documents but he'd thought the agreement was for the headline slot. And as far as he knew none of the guys had ever used the clause. It was a non-issue when Grey was alive and they were still all playing together. They took whatever slot in their own festival they wanted. Since then until last year when Danny had stepped in to cover Zach's screwup, none of them had played at CloudFest since Grey had died. "*I'm* doing the secret set."

"The agreement specifies a desired slot, not the headline slot," Billy said, sounding certain. "And I got my lawyer to check yesterday. I can have any damn slot I want. So the secret gig is mine if I want it and I do."

# chapter seventeen

"That slot's mine," Zach said, fighting to sound calm. "I need it to launch my album."

Billy's expression didn't change. "Sorry, kid. I'm taking it."

It would have been easier if Billy had punched him, maybe. Might have been easier to take than this casual pulling the rug out from under him. "Like hell you are."

"Zach," Faith said softly.

He didn't want to look at her but he did.

Her eyes were huge. And apologetic. "Billy's right. It's his if he wants it." She bit her lip. "I'm sorry."

"What the actual fuck?" Zach said. "Did the two of you cook this up? Some nice little revenge for me bailing last year? Giving me a taste of my own medicine?"

"No!" Faith said. "Don't be stupid. I'd never do that to you."

He wanted to believe her. He wasn't entirely sure he did. In her place, he might well want a little payback.

"Back off, Zach," Billy said. "This isn't personal. And Faith had nothing to do with it."

"Not personal?" Zach said, incredulous. "You've watched me all this time, seen what I'm trying to do. You knew how I wanted to launch this album and now you're going to tell me it's not fucking personal when you fucking bury it all?" He stepped closer to Billy, anger driving him forward. "Tell you what, Billy. It feels pretty damn fucking personal. And there's no earthly reason for you to do this. You have more money than you know what to do with. You're one of the most famous drummers on the planet. You don't need this. I do." His voice cracked and he curled his hands into fists.

"I don't have to give you an explanation," Billy growled, standing his ground.

"No, but I think you owe me one," Zach said, gritting his teeth. He was focused on Billy but he could see Faith out of the corner of his eye. She looked pale. And miserable. He should try and calm down for her sake but he was too damn angry.

"Owe you? What the fuck do I owe you?" Billy said. "Shit. You really are like your old man. Think the Harpers are the center of the universe. Sorry, kid, but the rest of us have things we want too. And you don't always get to have your way."

Zach stared at him. "What the hell does that mean?"

"Just that you lost your Dad. I lost my best friend. And my career."

"You have a new band," Zach said. "Your career is just fine."

Billy shook his head. "Erroneous isn't Blacklight. And no, I don't mean the money. It's not the money.

You're right, I don't need that. And neither do you. It's the music. Erroneous. We're doing okay. We can do better. Get to more people. And if I can kick that along by getting us a nice splash of publicity at CloudFest, then that's what I'm going to do."

"And you don't care that you're being an utter prick and ruining my shot in the process?"

Billy lifted his chin. "You know what, Zach? Maybe I am a prick. But so are you. You know what this business takes. And you've done what you thought you had to to get to where you are so far. Just look at Faith here and the career she doesn't have because you left her behind. So don't bust my balls for doing exactly what you'd do. It's not going to change my mind."

"Fuck you, Billy," Zach said and then pulled the door open before he put his fist through Billy's face or the wall.

When Leah knocked on the door of the guesthouse there was no answer. But she could hear Zach's voice somewhere inside. She hesitated, not entirely sure if she should just go in even though the door was ajar. It had only been about half an hour since Zach had stormed out of the studio, with Billy stalking out only a couple of minutes later.

Leah had gone in to see what on earth was going on and found Faith looking kind of shaky behind the desk in Leah's office. Once Faith had explained to her what Billy had just done, Leah had felt pretty shaky herself. Billy had taken Zach's slot at CloudFest. She had no idea what that meant other than it screwed Zach's plans to launch his songs. *Their* songs.

What the hell was Billy thinking? Faith's retelling of

the reason he'd given made no sense. All she knew was she needed to know if Zach was okay. But now that she was here, she wasn't so sure of her welcome.

She wanted to talk this out with him. What it meant for the songs they'd worked so hard on. What it meant for Zach. He was the one she wanted to turn to, to figure this out. To come up with the plan. Because that was what you did when you had a problem. You went to the person you loved and figured it out. The trouble was Zach didn't love her.

But he needed someone right now. So she was going to be it.

She pushed open the door. "Zach?"

No answer. The rumble of his voice seemed to be coming from the kitchen so she headed in that direction. Zach was standing by the counter, facing the window, phone to his ear. She couldn't see his face but his posture was tense.

"Just get him to call me, Katie," he growled and then ended the call, shoving his phone into his pocket. For a moment he just stood there, staring out the window. Then his shoulders slumped and he muttered, "Fuck."

"Zach," she said again.

He whirled, staring at her like she was the last person on earth he expected to see. "What are you doing here?"

The tone of his words stung a little. Did he think she wouldn't come? Or just didn't care if she came or not? "I came to see if you're okay," she said.

"Just perfect," he said grimly. "I assume Faith told you what happened?"

"Yes," Leah said. "Though it wasn't exactly hard to

figure out that something was wrong. You kind of slammed out of there."

"Nice of her to share my business."

Okay, he was upset. But she wasn't going to let him take it out on her. "Well, firstly, I happen to work for Harper Inc. and I have been doing a lot of the scheduling work, so I needed to know, and secondly, seeing as Faith knows that you and I are seeing each other, it's not exactly unreasonable for her to tell me. She's worried about you."

"If that's true, she should be the one here checking on me, shouldn't she?"

Leah frowned at him. "She didn't tell me exactly what happened, other than Billy pulling the king of all dick moves, but I got the impression she thinks you're mad at her."

"So she sent you?"

"Yes." She folded her arms to match his. "Though I can leave if you prefer. I just thought—"

There was a muscle clenching on and off at the side of his jaw. She held her breath, wondering if he was actually going to say "yes, go." But then he relaxed and sat down on one of the stools by the counter. "No. Stay. Sorry. I'm in a foul mood but I shouldn't take this out on you."

"Anything I can do to help? Were you calling Jay?" It seemed the most likely option.

"Yes," Zach said. "But apparently he's in meetings for another hour. So I just have to sit on my hands until then. No, scratch that, first I have to go meet the guys I'd hired for the band at the ferry and tell them they might as well turn around and go home."

What the hell? "What are you talking about?"

"They're here to play with me at CloudFest. No CloudFest, no need for a band."

*No need for him to stay on Lansing any longer.* The thought flashed into her head and she almost lost her breath. No. Not yet. She wasn't ready for him to leave just yet. So she had to convince him to stay. "That's ridiculous. We'll find you another gig. And in the meantime you can rehearse with the guys. We can even spend more time recording." She was talking too fast. She made herself stop. Breathe.

"Isn't the studio booked pretty solid around Cloud-Fest?"

"Yes, but a lot of the acts bring their own producers and engineers. Besides"—she waved her hand in the direction of Grey's studio—"you have another studio you can use."

"Recording requires a producer. And you can't tell me you have much spare time from now until the festival starts."

"I'll have some." She moved over to stand beside him. She wanted to put her arms around him, but the tension radiating from him didn't exactly invite her any closer. "And I'm happy to spend it with you. Besides, you'll need to rehearse before we can record the arrangements."

Zach looked unconvinced but a little more tension drained out of him. Good. More relaxed meant that he wasn't going to do anything crazy. Like leave. At least she hoped not. She moved in, put her arms around him. "Billy's a prick," she said. "But we'll figure this out. The music is too good. You're too good. It will be fine."

His arms came around her and she hugged him harder. She had no idea if what she'd said was true or not. Truth was, the music business was a fickle bitch and no having a pedigree and talent like Zach was guarantee of success. They both needed this album to work. She didn't want to think about what it might do to her chances of building a producing career if the album failed. Zach could bounce back from that but the fact that he'd taken a chance on a rookie producer and then not delivered the goods would blow back on her. So even more reason to make sure it was perfect. That he stayed until they had it right.

And call her crazy but now that they didn't have the looming deadline of CloudFest hanging over them, she was hoping that might just take quite some time.

"Are you coming back to the studio?" she asked, letting go of him.

Zach straightened. Shook his head. "I'm going to stay here. Talk to Jay. Then I'll come back. Tell Eli to go meet the guys. I'll meet them back at the studio later today."

She nodded. Faith had told Eli at the same time as her. She'd never seen Eli truly angry before but he'd gone lethally quiet, his brown eyes turning cold when Faith had delivered the news of what Billy had done. She'd always thought of Eli as Billy's sidekick. Her first thought was that he'd most likely side with his dad, but he'd been horrified. He'd left to see if he could talk Billy out of it at the same time she'd left to find Zach. But she wasn't going to tell Zach that. No point getting his hopes up. Sal had always said Billy was stubborn as a herd of donkeys, so she didn't think Eli was likely to succeed in changing his dad's mind.

"Okay. I'll see you back there." She leaned in again.

Kissed him, fast and hard. "Everything will work out. Trust me."

Faith was waiting outside for Leah when she got back to the studio. She looked worried.

How long had she been standing there? Since Leah had left?

"How is he?" Faith asked.

"Angry. But still here," Leah replied. The flash of relief on Faith's face told her she wasn't the only one who'd been wondering if Zach would just pack up and go.

Faith scowled. "I could strangle Billy." Her hands flexed at her side as though she was imagining doing just that.

"I think there's a line forming for that privilege," Leah said. "You think Eli will be able to get him to back down?"

Faith shook her head. "Grey was about the only person I ever knew who could really talk Billy out of something when he'd made up his mind. And even he only succeeded about half the time. I don't like Eli's chances. Not even if he drags his mom into it. She's never really put her foot down with Billy about this kind of thing. Family stuff, yes. Business, not so much."

Eli's mom, Nina, was kind of a force of nature. But Faith was right. She gave Billy his freedom. "And he can really do this? Just take any slot he wants?"

Faith nodded. "Yep. I rang the lawyers. They checked the wording. He's right. I can't stop him. In a way it's easier that he wants the secret gig. It would be all kinds of awkward to have to bump the closing act this late. At least a change in the secret act doesn't screw up all the promo."

No, it just screwed over Zach. "I still don't understand why he'd do this now," Leah said. "He could have told you months ago if he wanted the secret gig. Or the headline slot for that matter. Why wait until now?"

"Your guess is as good as mine. I put some feelers out. Tickets for the Erroneous tour aren't moving as fast as they'd like, but it's not like they're bombing."

"You think there's something else going on?"

"I have no idea. I tried to call Nina but she's in court today. So I think we just have to go ahead and assume Billy's not going to alter his course. Theo's waiting to hear about logistics for getting all of Erroneous's shit here in time."

"And Zach's just screwed." Leah rubbed her chest, trying to chase away the sick sensation lingering there. It didn't work.

"I'll offer him another slot—I can't bump any of the main acts, but we could squeeze him in on another stage. But I don't think he'll take it. He wants a main-stage, big-excitement gig to launch his solo stuff. Low key won't cut it. If I had to guess, he'll look for another big show somewhere."

"Which means he'll be leaving." Leah tried to sound normal about it. She didn't entirely succeed. Her throat was suddenly too dry and her voice squeaked.

Faith's expression turned sympathetic. "You need to finish recording first. You've got time."

Time for what exactly? Convincing Zach to stay? To give it all up for her? That seemed as unlikely as Billy changing his mind. She tried to smile. "I always knew this was short term."

That didn't chase the sympathy off Faith's face. "You could try telling him how you feel," she said.

"Who says I feel something?" Denial. It was a long shot but worth a try.

"I've known you since we were babies, Leah. I've seen you with him these last few weeks. You're happy. Very happy. And not just 'I've got a crush' kind of happy."

"You really think me telling Zach that I was dumb enough to let myself—" She stopped, not wanting to say the word out loud. That made it real. Would only make it harder when the time came. "I mean, you really think some sort of big declaration would make a difference? This is Zach we're talking about. Something tells me that's more likely to make him run away even faster."

Faith winced. Which meant she didn't really have a counter-argument. "Okay. I won't butt in. I'm here if you need me, though."

Leah smiled at that. "I know."

"So what exactly are you saying, Jay?" Zach stared down at the phone on the kitchen table in frustration. He wished he could see his manager's face, but Jay was in a car somewhere in L.A. on the way to the airport to go to New York for another client. So far, this morning's conference call wasn't proving any less frustrating than yesterday. "Are they pulling the deal?"

"No." Jay's voice was thin through the phone's speaker. "But I have to be honest with you, Zach. Without the whole CloudFest, Blacklight, going-back-to-your-roots thing, I got the feeling their enthusiasm was way down."

Fucking perfect. Without a big label really wanting

to push him and give him the kind of promo he wanted—
that would be hard to achieve on his own—he was all
kinds of screwed. The deal Jay had been chasing was
one with the focus on the marketing side. He had enough
money to record but he didn't have the reach that a huge
label's marketing machine could get him.

"And what would it take to get their enthusiasm back
up?" he asked.

"At this point, I'm not sure. You need something
flashy. Something to catch their attention. If you've got
any favors to pull in, I'd go asking. See what you can
come up with. Otherwise—Harper or not—you're just
going to be another act to them. And we're not going to
get the same deal."

That was clear enough. Prove he could bring something to the table or else. He asked Jay a few more
questions then ended the call. It was nearly midday. He
needed to get to the studio. Leah was already there, finishing up with Nessa. The rest of the guys would be there
at one. He'd broken the news yesterday that there would
be no CloudFest gig and managed to convince them
all to stay regardless to work with him on the rest of
the album. It hadn't been easy. Pete, the drummer, had
been ready to bail, to go looking for another gig. But
this was one area where Zach's money could do some
good and the guy had agreed to stay when Zach had
offered more cash. They'd have to see how it worked out
in the long run.

He bent to pick up the messenger bag with his laptop
and other crap in it, shoved the phone into one of the
pockets, and looked around. Had he forgotten anything?
He couldn't think. Sleep had been hard to come by last

night, he'd been so mad. Leah had come over, and the worried look in her eyes had only made him feel worse. He'd taken her to bed and they'd indulged in some mutual distraction for a while, but he'd lain awake for a long time after she'd fallen asleep curled up against him. But other than his guitar, he didn't think he'd missed anything. So. Time to suck it up and go over to the studio and rehearse like he was just fine with the crap Billy had pulled.

Be an adult.

When for once, he could entirely see the appeal Grey had found in alcohol. Anything to calm the storm in his head so he could think.

His hand clenched around the strap of the messenger bag. No booze. He was better than that.

Still, he couldn't quite make himself walk to the front door and get in the damn truck.

While he was standing there, telling himself to just do it, someone banged on the front door.

Who the hell was coming to see him? It had to be someone he knew or the gate guard would've called up. Leah wouldn't knock. Neither would Faith or Mina. Eli hadn't answered his calls yesterday, so God only knew where he was. Probably with his dick of a dad.

He stalked down toward the door, ready to tell whoever it was to go the hell away. But when he pulled it open, he found Billy on the other side, and the curses on his lips changed to a whole other level of angry.

"What the fu—"

"Save it." Billy said harshly before Zach could complete the sentence. "You're pissed at me. Fine. I don't blame you."

"Then what the hell are you doing on my doorstep?" Zach said. "Not a smart move. You have about ten seconds to leave."

"You gonna call security on me?" Billy didn't look worried.

"I doubt I'd need security to deal with you, old man."

Billy shrugged. "Better men than you have tried, kid. So we can stand here having a pissing contest or you can let me in and I'll tell you why I'm here."

He reached for the handle of the screen door, which was locked. It rattled as Billy tugged at it.

Zach made no move to unlock it. "You have something to say to me? Say it from there."

One side of Billy's mouth curled up. "You really are just like your dad, aren't you? Arrogant little shit. All right. But you're going to let me in."

"Why?"

Billy held up a piece of paper that looked like it had been torn from a notebook. It was folded in half, nothing to be seen but the pale blue lines on the white paper. "Because of this."

"You trying to give me your phone number, Billy?" Zach said. "Don't bother. I've got your number now."

"Yeah but do you have Davis Lewis's?" Billy said.

Zach's eyes dropped back down to the piece of paper, he couldn't help it. Davis Lewis? What the hell was Billy doing with Davis's number?

"Got your attention, did I?" Billy said. "So. Let me in and we'll talk."

Zach had never wanted to tell someone to go screw himself quite badly. But over the desire to kick Billy to the curb, Jay's voice floated through his head. *You need something flashy.* Something to get attention. Like the most famous producer in the world.

He reached down and unlocked the door. "Come on in," he said and turned and walked back to the kitchen without stopping to see if Billy was following him. He still didn't look when he reached the fridge, pulled it open, extracted a beer, and twisted the top off.

When he turned back, the chilled bottle too cold in his tightly clenched hand, Billy stood on the other side of the counter. "So talk," Zach said, and took a swig of the beer.

"Start drinking at this time of day and you're going to end up more like your old man than you might want," Billy said.

Zach raised his eyebrows. "Yeah, well, coming from you that's pretty much the pot calling the fucking kettle black, so let's skip the part where you try to give me life advice like you care."

"Look, Zach, I realize you don't like what I did." Billy's mouth flattened. "Hell, I'm not sure I like it myself."

"Then give me back the fucking slot."

"No can do. I told you. I need that slot. But I feel bad. And I know you want to make a splash, so I'm giving you this." Billy held out the piece of paper.

"Why do I want Davis Lewis's number?"

Dark eyes rolled at him. "Everybody wants that number."

"What makes you think I don't already have it?" Zach asked. He took another sip of beer. The sour taste didn't do much to mask the sour feeling in his stomach.

"Maybe you do. But if you used it, he turned you

down. Otherwise you wouldn't be here recording with Eli and Leah, would you now?" Billy's voice was matter of fact.

Zach kept his face still with an effort. He wasn't going to give Billy the satisfaction of seeing that he'd scored a hit. "Eli and Leah are doing an amazing job," he said coldly.

Billy shrugged. "I'm sure they're good. But they can't get you the same sort of buzz Davis will. He hasn't worked with anyone new in quite some time. Doing your album with him will get you all the attention you need. Much more than just doing CloudFest would. There isn't a record company on the planet who doesn't want the next act anointed by Davis." He put the paper down on the counter, pushed it toward Zach. "Take that. Make the call. He'll take it."

"Him taking the call isn't the same as him agreeing to work with me."

"I talked to him. I played him one of your tracks. You won't have a problem."

"How the hell did you get one of my tracks?" Zach growled.

"Eli was working on your stuff on the house system," Billy said. "It wasn't hard to find."

Apparently Zach was going to have to have a word with Eli about appropriate security measures. But that could wait. First he had to get his head around what Billy was offering him. "So you think I should just ditch Eli and Leah and go work with Davis?"

"Eli won't care, he'll be happy for you," Billy said.

Zach wasn't so sure about that. Eli's producing was more important to him than he let on. "I'm pretty sure Leah will care."

"Because you're sleeping with her?"

Zach coughed, almost dropping the beer.

"I'm not blind," Billy said. "You two haven't exactly been subtle about it. But you weren't planning to stay here, were you? And she's a smart girl. She knows that."

"I think it's the me screwing her over professionally that she'll be upset about," Zach said.

"So, pay her what you agreed. She's no worse off than she was before."

That sounded so neat and tidy. But it wouldn't be. It wasn't money Leah wanted. She wanted the credit. The success that would make people want to work with her.

"Look, Zach," Billy said. "This is business. If you want what I think you want, if you want the fame and glory—the kind that Blacklight had—then there's only one choice for you to make here. Call Davis. Then pack your bags and go wherever he wants you to go and make the best album you can." His mouth twisted. "Trust me, you'll regret it if you don't. Spending your life thinking what might have been sucks. That's what Danny and Shane and I have been doing since we lost Grey. And maybe I can never find what Blacklight had again but I'm damn well going to try. And you should try to. You're good. You can be one of the best. But you have to be willing to pay the price."

The price being taking what he wanted and living with the consequences. He stared down at the piece of paper. Such a small thing. But then maybe all of life came to small things. Big choices in small moments.

"You've worked for this for years," Billy said. "Don't fuck it up now because of sentiment. Make the call." And then he turned and walked away.

# chapter eighteen

By the time it hit two o'clock and Zach hadn't made it to the studio, Leah was beginning to feel sick all over again. She'd settled his band into the rehearsal room and set them up with the tapes of the songs they'd recorded so far as well as some of her ideas about how the other parts should go, and that was keeping them occupied, but she could tell they were wondering what the hell was going on. So was she.

Eli hadn't shown up either. That was less surprising. Zach hadn't answered any of Eli's calls last night, and there'd been a few. Until the two of them talked, Leah suspected Eli would lay low. She couldn't entirely blame him. He was between a very big rock and a very hard place stuck in the middle of Zach and Billy. But lack of Eli didn't explain the lack of Zach.

She looked at her phone. No messages. Should she call him? And what, have him avoid her calls too? He'd let her in last night but he'd been a million miles away, even when she'd been wrapped around him. She'd gone to bed with a sense of dread coiling in her gut that she hadn't been able to shake. But Zach clearly hadn't been ready to talk. Pushing wasn't going to help. So she'd left him alone and come to the studio.

But maybe that had been the wrong approach. Whatever was going on, they needed to talk. She hit the intercom button. All the studios were full at the moment, as were the rehearsal rooms but she could see from the system that no one was actively recording. And all the acts were bands or singers that had been here before and knew their way around the studio.

"Hey everyone," she said. "I have to go out. On my cell if anyone has any dramas. Or call the Harper Inc. offices. All the numbers are on the wall in the kitchen."

The sick curl of dread was back, stronger than before, when she pulled up outside the guesthouse. It wasn't closed up, so that was good, and Grey's old truck was still out front. Though it wasn't like Zach would've taken that with him if he'd gone.

*He's not going anywhere*, she told herself firmly. But the first thing she saw when she opened the door was a stack of guitar cases, and the chill that shivered down her spine stopped her in her tracks.

*Just taking them to the studio. That was all.*

She took a breath. Made herself move. She didn't call out to Zach, just walked slowly through the house until she found him in the bedroom. Standing at the end of the bed, staring down at a nearly full suitcase.

Her knees wobbled and she had to grab for the doorframe. He hadn't seen her yet, which gave her a few seconds to remember how to breathe. How to speak.

"Going somewhere?" she said eventually. The words stung her throat.

Zach froze, a pile of jeans in his hands. He put them in the suitcase, very slowly closed the lid, and then zipped it shut. Then, just as slowly, turned around to face her. "Leah."

It was more breath than word.

She needed to be calm. Not let him see she was freaked out already. She swallowed. Hard. "That's me. But not an answer to my question."

"I—"

"You're leaving."

He nodded. "Davis Lewis changed his mind. He wants to work with me." His voice was flat. Guarded. Cold.

There was a chair near the door. She made it there before her knees gave out for real. He wasn't just leaving. He was going to throw the work they'd done under the bus as well. "The album's half done already."

"You'll still get paid," he said, looking back down at the suitcase. Not at her.

The pain of it was like a slap. Unexpectedly ferocious. Followed by an equally unexpected rush of anger. He'd been planning to just bail. Not just on them. But on their work.

"That isn't the fucking point, Zach. I wanted the credit not the money." It was easier to focus on the business part of this. It hurt slightly less than thinking about the other part. The part where he'd do this to her. The woman he was sleeping with. She'd thought he cared about her. Could she have been so wrong? She couldn't think about that. She couldn't make it through the conversation if she thought about that.

"There'll be other albums."

"Not like this. And maybe not at all if this gets out. You do this, you change your mind and go record with Davis and throw what we did away and that gets out, then everyone will think that I can't cut it." Her throat was burning with the effort to sound reasonable.

"No one will know."

That wasn't true. "This industry leaks like a sieve. You know it will get out." Though she wasn't sure which was worse. Not having anybody know he'd chosen her in the first place or having everybody think he'd ditched her.

She thought he winced. Just ever so slightly. But then the cool mask was back in place. No emotion on his face. Eyes the color of the sea in a winter storm. She shivered. "Please, Zach. Don't do this to me. To *us.*"

This time he did wince. But somehow the emotion didn't give her any hope.

"I have to do what's right for my music. It's a business decision," he said. His voice hadn't changed and she had to fight not to wince herself.

"But it's not just business. It's you and me. There's more to us than business and sex, Zach." God. What could she say to get through to him? To bring back the man who'd shared her bed, who'd thrown her a party to make her feel special, and banish the one who was standing before her, willing to throw her away in a second.

"You said this was temporary," he said. "In fact, you insisted on it."

"Newsflash. I lied," she said desperately. "You know I lied. You know how I feel about you, Zach. Don't say you don't. It's been so good between us. And it's not just

sex. There's more to us. There could be so much more."
Her voice cracked on the last word and she bit down,
fighting for control. "Please, Zach. I love—"

"Don't say it," he said and the words were so cold she
could practically see them glinting in the air like icicles.
"You don't mean it. You shouldn't mean it. You know
me. I'm like Grey. I want the big dream."

"You can have it," she said. "You don't have to do
it the same way he did. You can have music and be
happy. You can be more than he was. God, Zach, don't
you see? You've been running from him your whole
life, trying to get out from under his shadow. Well, you
can. You can be better than him. All you have to do is
stay."

He looked like he was made of stone. Hardly breathing. Hardly moving. Totally out of reach. "I need this,
Leah. I need what Davis can do for me."

"More than me?" It was just a whisper. A whisper
was all she was capable of.

"More than anything," he said. He turned back then.
Lifted the case off the bed. Set it down on the floor.
Pulled the handle up.

The click of it locking into place might as well have
been a gunshot. Blowing everything she'd thought they'd
had apart. Foolish. So foolish to think he might change.
Why was her heart so very very stupid?

"Please don't go," she said one more time. One last
try. Everyone was allowed one last try. Even when they
knew there was no hope of victory.

He shook his head. "I can't stay," he said. He walked
out of the room without touching her, knuckles white
where they gripped the suitcase.

She stayed where she was on the chair, frozen, feeling her world break apart, listening to the sound of him packing the truck. When the front door shut one last time and the roar of the engine rumbled to life, she went to the window. Stupid.

But she had to see it for herself. Had to see that he was really leaving.

He was. The big truck was pulling away and Zach didn't even glance back at the house as he headed down the drive.

She dug her hands into the window frame, willing herself to stay upright. She'd spent a lot of time waiting for Zach Harper to come back home. And now he was leaving her behind again. As she watched his car pull away, she knew he was taking her heart with him and didn't even try to stop the tears.

Four days later, Faith arrived on Leah's doorstep at nine p.m. Leah opened the door before Faith could knock. She had, after all, been expecting her. She'd been turning up there, like clockwork, every night since Zach had left. Ivy had come too the first three nights, but she was stuck down at the festival site doing security briefings tonight.

Faith held up a grocery sack. "Ice cream."

At least tonight it was only ice cream. The first two nights it had been ice cream and tequila. Which had been a temporary fix, but really only resulted in adding a hangover to her misery.

"I think I'm just about over the ice cream and crying part," Leah said. The second part of that wasn't strictly true. She had a feeling she'd be crying over Zach Fucking Harper for a long time. But she was definitely done wallowing.

She led the way back into her small living room. Waited for the inevitable question.

"What happened here?" Faith said, staring around at the piles of books and papers and knickknacks piled on the sofa and the floor.

"I'm sorting some stuff out," Leah said, trying to sound casual.

"O-kay," Faith said carefully. "Why, exactly?"

"Because I'm leaving after CloudFest."

Faith dropped the grocery bag on the floor, eyes going wide. "Excuse me?"

Leah took a deep breath. "I'm leaving. I'm going back to L.A, see what I can rustle up for producing gigs."

"You have a perfectly good studio for that right here," Faith said. She sounded bewildered.

Leah pointed at the lone armchair that wasn't full of crap. "Sit down."

Faith shook her head. "Not until you start making sense."

"I can't stay here, Faith," Leah said. She didn't want to have this conversation. She'd known she'd have to, but that didn't make it any easier.

"But Lansing is your home. You can produce here. Hell, between your dad and me and Ziggy we can find you producing work in a heartbeat."

"It's not that," Leah said. "Though I'd prefer to do it on my own, if I can." She wanted to try. She needed to try. To prove that she was good enough. If news about Zach ditching her as producer got out then it wouldn't help her reputation any if she turned around and got her next producing job through pulling on the strings of the very well connected Blacklight web.

"Then what?" Faith asked. "I know my brother is a

world-class asshole, but that doesn't mean you have to run."

"It's not running," Leah said. "It's choosing not to stay anymore."

Faith frowned. "I don't understand."

Leah cleared a space on the chair nearest her. Maybe Faith didn't want to sit, but Leah had been at the studio all day and then spent the last two hours in a decluttering frenzy. All that on way too little sleep, and she was wiped. "I've had a lot of time to think these last few days. And while there's plenty about what just happened that I don't understand, I did realize one thing."

"Which was?"

"That the reason—the real reason I came back to Lansing after college—wasn't just that Mom and Dad are here or that the studio was here. Or even that you and Ivy were here." God. Was she really going to say this out loud? It was mortifying enough to realize it in the darkness of her bedroom at two a.m. two nights ago. It had nearly sent her to the tequila again. She swallowed. Fought the heat that rose in her cheeks even now. "I came back because, I think—no, I know—that part of me was always waiting for Zach to come back here. That if I waited long enough, he'd come home and we'd work it out somehow. That we'd make it work."

Faith was looking at her like she'd gone insane.

"I know it sounds dumb. Believe me, I know it *is* dumb. Beyond dumb."

"But—you married Joey."

"I did. I didn't know that I was waiting for Zach. Not until he actually did come back. And then he left again. I loved Joey. But not enough. Not like I—" She made herself stop talking. Faith was Zach's sister. It wasn't fair to put her in the middle of this mess. The mess that Leah only had herself to blame for. "But anyway. I have to go stop waiting. Because he's not coming back for me. And I have to find out what my life is supposed to be like when I know that. Right now, I can't do that here on Lansing."

Faith looked like she might cry. But then she shook her head, sat a little straighter in her chair. "I hate my brother right now."

"Don't be mad at him. He didn't do this. I did." She didn't want to be the reason for Faith and Zach to fight again. That would only make her feel worse.

"Are you ever going to come back?" Faith asked.

Leah let out a breath, suddenly swamped with relief. Faith wasn't going to talk her out of it. Maybe she understood. Which meant maybe Leah wasn't crazy to want to do it. "For good? I don't know. But I'm not going to get on the ferry and never come back. I have a lot here. Not to mention you're getting married here. It's just . . . right now I need to know what else there is."

Faith nodded slowly. "Okay. I don't like it. In fact, I pretty much hate it." She bent and reached for the grocery bag. "And I think I'm going to need to eat about half this ice cream. But I understand." She looked at Leah, managed a smile. "But you're staying until Cloud-Fest?"

"Yes," Leah said. "I wouldn't bail on you. That would be shitty of me." There'd been too much bailing on people. She wasn't going to do that to anyone she loved. "So I'm here for the festival and maybe a little after that, while I pack up my stuff and get myself organized." She was half-thinking she'd rent the place out. It was hers, it was the one thing she'd wanted in the divorce and

Joey, thank God, hadn't fought her on that. But she hadn't figured out all the details.

"Good," Faith said. "Then first things first. Ice cream. And then we focus on having as good a time as possible until you leave."

# chapter nineteen

London had never felt quite so far away before. Zach had spent plenty of time in the city. He liked it. He always had. Well, every time he'd been here before now. And, staring at his computer screen where he could just make out some of the gardens back home behind Mina and Faith who were sitting in Faith's kitchen with the French doors open, he'd never wished quite so badly for a teleport. The sky he could see above his sisters' heads was brilliant blue, not gray like London had been almost the entire time since he'd arrived. Not that he'd seen much sunlight with all the time he'd been spending in the studio.

He'd thought the drizzling rain and clouds had suited his mood, but seeing the sun only brought home everything he was missing so badly.

But he was here now. He'd made his choice. He had to live with it. The work he was doing with Davis was great. The part of him that was the music knew that.

That it was good. Even if the rest of him couldn't feel it yet.

It would come. It was what he kept telling himself. He'd feel it. Feel satisfied. Feel happy. When he wasn't so tired. He just had to get past this stupid stage where everything just felt . . . empty. And learn to sleep again. He'd been here for ten days. Too long to keep blaming jet lag. He'd never really suffered too much from that. And jet lag didn't come with endless memories of Leah running through his head or the creeping knowledge that maybe the cost of his choice was too high. Or the constant battle to not pick up his phone and check if she had called him. But he didn't want Faith and Mina seeing any of that so he summoned a smile for his sisters and saluted them with his coffee mug.

"Shouldn't you be drinking tea?" Faith said, smiling.

"I haven't been gone that long," he said. "They haven't converted me yet." Her smile flickered briefly but he didn't let her see that he'd noticed. "I'll stick to coffee."

Plenty of triple shot espresso was about the only thing getting him through each endless day. Davis didn't believe in wasting time. They'd broken for dinner just now but they'd be starting up again in an hour. But he hadn't been hungry, so he'd decided to reply to the message Faith had sent the night before.

"What's up?" he asked.

"Maybe we're just checking up on you," Mina said. She leaned closer, as though she was studying his image. He hoped Faith's screen needed cleaning. He hadn't shaved since he got here and between that and the long days and lack of sleep, he wasn't going to be winning any beauty contests any time soon.

"I'm fine," he said. "But checking up on me doesn't take both of you." He shifted in his seat. His sisters had been checking in with him—separately—just about every day since he'd arrived in England. So far neither of them had raised the subject of Leah. He hoped today wasn't the day when they'd finally decided to tag team him on the subject of his spectacular fail in that department. He didn't need to be told.

"How's it going over there?" Faith asked after a few seconds.

Small talk. Not exactly what he'd expected from her message. Was she stalling? What was going on? "It's good," he said. "Davis is brilliant. How's it going there?" CloudFest started in three days. But Faith looked surprisingly calm. Of course, this year, she hadn't had to deal with things like him pulling out at the last minute. And she had Caleb now. Someone she could rely on. Someone who loved her and would be there for her.

"We're good," Faith said. Then she shook her head slightly. "So. We heard from the lawyers again. About Ree Vacek."

He'd forgotten all about Grey's mystery payment. He had enough on his plate without trying to figure out the weirdness that was his dad's legacy. "They found her?"

Mina nodded, eyes serious. "Yes. Turns out she still lives in Illinois."

"And?" They wouldn't have called him if that was all the news they had. Not unless they really were just checking up on him.

Faith's expression turned frustrated. "And she declined to tell us anything about the money."

Well, shit. He hadn't spent much time thinking about

what might happen if they found Grey's mystery woman. But the vague thoughts he'd had definitely hadn't included her not wanting to play ball. "She declined?"

"According to the lawyers she said it wasn't anybody's business," Faith said.

Maybe he should have been relieved. But he wasn't. Because "none of your business" didn't sound to him like the answer of someone who had nothing to hide. "Did they find out anything about her?"

Faith shook her head. "Not a lot. She works for a realtor. Her husband's a lawyer. They've been married over thirty years. Two kids."

In other words, not the sort of woman who sounded like she'd had a wild fling with a rock star. "Can we find out more?"

Mina shrugged, leaned a little closer to the screen. "They found the kids' birth certificates. The husband is listed as the father on both. The oldest one—a girl—was born seven and half months after they were married but they wouldn't be the first couple to have that happen. All very normal and boring."

"Except for the half a million dollars Grey paid her," he said. "There's got to be something more there."

"I agree," Faith said. "But we can't make her tell us. We're not the mob. She hasn't done anything wrong. There's no proof she extorted the money or did anything else to Dad to get it. She's certainly not threatened to reveal anything or ever asked for anything more since. I don't like it any more than you do, but I'm not sure there's anything we can do about it without straying into an area that's all kinds of gray."

Zach winced. *All kinds of gray.* When it came to

understanding Grey—and untangling whatever this was that he'd left behind—that was far too appropriate. Faith's point was reasonable, but looking at her—and at Mina who was more obviously not happy—he didn't think she was as calm about the news as she was making out. "What are we talking about? If we wanted to find out, I mean."

"More digging. Private investigators. That kind of thing. I'm not sure I want to go there," Faith said.

Beside her, Mina nodded, though her mouth was flat. "If there's a secret, it's her secret. Dad didn't tell us before he died. So maybe he thought it was her secret too."

And trying to find out what that secret was had the potential to hurt Ree Vacek, whoever she was, and her family. Grey had hurt people his entire life. Zach wasn't proud of himself that he'd just added to that legacy by hurting Leah. So maybe it was time for the Harpers to turn over a new leaf. "Okay. If that's what you both think, then I agree. If there's something there, we'll find out eventually. Or we won't. Let's leave it alone." As he said the words, he knew it was the right thing to do. The first thing that had made him feel something approaching happy since he'd left Lansing.

The near identical smiles of approval Faith and Mina shot at him only cemented the feeling.

"I definitely think it's the right way to go. Let the past be the past," Mina said. She blew him a kiss. "And I have to run. My shift at Search and Rescue starts in twenty minutes." She waved at the screen, then stood and disappeared from view.

*Let the past be the past.* He could do that when it

came to Grey's mistakes. He wasn't finding it quite so easy to do with his own most recent screwups. He ignored that and focused on his screen. "What about you?" he asked Faith. "Don't you have CloudFest stuff to do?"

Faith tilted her head. "I've got a bit of time."

Something about her tone made him uneasy. "I have to be back in the studio soon."

"Where it's all going just 'fine'?"

He could practically hear the quotes around "fine" in her voice. He wasn't fooling her. He'd have to try harder. "Yes."

"Then why do you look like crap?" She pointed at him. "Your face is not the face of a man blissfully happy making an album with his dream producer."

Zach set his jaw. "I'm just tired. Jet lag." Even to him, his voice sounded unconvincing.

Faith snorted. "You want to try that again? You look miserable."

"I'm fine."

"You're not fine. Neither of you is fine." Faith said then clamped her lips together as though she wasn't supposed to say that last part.

*Leah.* He'd told himself he wouldn't ask. But he had to know. "Is she okay?"

Faith scowled. "No. She looks the same as you. You should come home. Fix it."

"I need this album."

"So make it with Leah," Faith said. "Is Davis really so much better? Do you like what he's doing more? Because you don't look like you do."

He could always rely on Faith to see right through

him. But it didn't really matter how he felt, did it? Not after what Billy had done. "I need his rep."

She shook her head fiercely, hair flying around her face. "That's crap. You need to be happy. The music won't make you happy if you screw up the rest of your life. You have money. You have resources of your own. You can make this album work. You don't need Davis Lewis or anybody else. Except Leah. You were so happy when you were here with her, Zach. That means something."

It did. And he wanted to feel that way again. But he'd made a choice. "I can come back when I'm done."

Faith opened her mouth. Then closed it. Then sighed. "If you wait that long she won't be here."

"Excuse me?" *What the hell did that mean?*

"Leah's leaving after CloudFest."

Leaving? Leah was leaving Lansing? That felt like a fist to the gut. Stole his breath. Leah gone? God. Had part of him been banking on going back to her? "Going where?"

"I'm not telling you that," Faith said.

"But why would she go?"

"Because there's nothing keeping her here."

Not with him gone, is that what she meant? His gut clenched again, as though a second blow had landed. Leah gone. Out of his reach. Because of him she was blowing up her life. Shit. Maybe Billy was right. Maybe he was just like Grey. He didn't want to be. Grey had always put music first, not people. Zach had never had the guts to ask him if he'd thought it was worth it. But somehow he knew it wouldn't be for him. But he didn't know if he could be different.

But, he realized, he wanted to try. There had to be a

way. To do both. To be great at music and at life. To do it with Leah. And suddenly, he had an idea how.

He straightened. "You know, I read the festival agreement, after Billy pulled his stunt." It hadn't done any good at the time. It had only said what Faith had already confirmed. Though now . . .

Faith leaned forward. "And?"

"Do you have it there?" He was pretty sure he'd deleted the e-mail that Faith had sent him with the documents. Which wasn't nearly as satisfying as tearing it into pieces. It felt like weeks ago.

"Yes. Give me a minute." Faith got up and disappeared from view. But not for long. She sat back down and waved a document at him.

"Can you remind me what exactly it says about Blacklight members' rights? And about the secret slot?" His memory of those couple of days was hazy. Raw fury apparently stopped him remembering.

Faith shrugged, flipped a few pages, and then looked down, reading intently for thirty seconds or so. "It says the Blacklight guys have a right to any slot they want. It doesn't actually talk about the secret slot directly. Grey started that as a one-off thing and it became a tradition. I don't think it ever got added into the trust agreement. Why?"

"And Harper Inc. controls the scheduling—the guys don't have any veto power on that?"

"No. We're currently appointed by the trust to do the administration. I guess the three of them could vote to change that but they can't pull any extra strings as things stand."

He didn't think that was likely to happen. He'd had an e-mail from Danny telling him that he thought Billy

was being a world-class shit. And Shane would probably side with Danny over Billy if push ever came to
shove.

Faith was looking curious now. "Why do you want
to know?"

"Because I was wondering if there was any way you
could squeeze in another secret gig. I mean, Billy gets
the traditional spot for the secret gig, before the closing
act, fine. But there's nothing to stop you giving me a surprise slot as well, is there?" Two secret acts at Cloud-
Fest would generate some buzz for him. He could get
the CloudFest social media machine behind him. Get
them to drop a few hints that there might be some extra
surprises this year. After that, if he was good enough
on the day, the buzz might take care of itself. And if it
didn't, well, screw Jay, screw the record companies. He
wanted Leah. He'd figure the rest out.

Faith's eyes widened. "No-o-o," she said. Then she
began to smile. "No, there isn't." She paused for a moment, frowning as though she was trying to figure something out in her head. "I think I could make it work. If
you came back, that is." Then her head tilted. "Is your
stuff with Davis ready, though?

He didn't care about Davis. Not anymore. Maybe he
never had. He'd made a bad choice. But he was going to
fix it. "No, but the stuff I did with Leah is. I can keep
the arrangements simple, that's how they're built. Come
home. Fix things."

Faith's squee of approval almost deafened him. But
it also gave him a shred of hope that his plan wasn't
crazy. It sounded easy on the face of it. Come home,
perform. Launch his music the way he wanted it to
be. Win back his girl. It sounded easy, but it would be

complicated. Leah might not forgive him. But as he thought about it, he suddenly knew that complicated with Leah was better than simple alone.

"You feel like this every year," Leah muttered to herself as she lay in the middle of her living room and watched the ceiling fan spinning lazily above her. She was so tired she'd gone beyond aching body parts into a phase where her body didn't feel entirely real any more. She'd thrown herself into CloudFest preparation with a vengeance—needing the distraction—and whenever she'd found a spare minute from that, she'd been working on her L.A. plans and cleaning out her house. Every part of her ached. And in about twenty minutes she needed to pull herself up off the floor, and put on a pretty dress, and go and make nice at Faith's CloudFest Eve party like she wasn't exhausted and brokenhearted.

She needed a shower, about two gallons of coffee, and then a margarita or three. At least at the party, she could hang with Ivy and Mina and Will and her other friends. Who all knew how she was feeling and wouldn't mind if she wasn't totally the life of the party.

But until she had to move, she was going to lie here, watch the ceiling fan, and try not to think. It was a skill she'd been working hard to perfect since Zach had left. Sometimes it even worked. Sometimes, for a moment, she forgot exactly how many days and hours and minutes it was since he'd left her behind. Sometimes, for a moment, her hands didn't itch to pick up the phone and call him or beg Faith to tell her where exactly he was so she could run to the nearest airport and buy a ticket and go there.

And each of those moments that she managed not to

think about that gave her a little bit of hope that she could make it to the next moment. That there would be more moments. Longer moments. That she wouldn't always feel this crappy.

"See the ceiling fan. *Be* the ceiling fan." She wasn't exactly sure if watching the spinning blade was soothing or making her vaguely queasy. She closed her eyes. Maybe she could nap instead.

A power nap. That was a thing that people did. *Normal* people. Not the kind of people who'd let themselves fall for Zach Harper all over again. Maybe if she napped, she could be normal too.

But just as she was wrestling with the idea that, if she was going to nap, she needed to tell her phone to set an alarm, someone knocked on her front door.

Her eyes flew open. "Dammit." She kept her voice down. Maybe whoever it was wouldn't hear her. Maybe they'd go *away*. The knock came again.

Whoever it was, it had better be good. She got up with an effort and walked to the door, trying to summon a polite expression. When she opened the door and saw Zach standing there, her attempt at a smile vanished in a heartbeat, replaced by sheer blinding panic.

She shut the door instinctively, trying to think through the sudden deafening roar of blood in her ears. *Zach was here. Why the hell was Zach here?*

"Leah?" Zach called through the door.

She opened it again. "What do you want?" She tried to sound angry rather than shocked. She wasn't sure how well she was pulling it off when all she could do was stare at him, taking in every last detail. His clothes were rumpled and he needed a shave. The dark circles under his eyes matched her own. And she wanted to throw her arms around him and never let him go.

She stayed where she was. She couldn't wreck herself a third time.

"You're mad," he said.

"No shit."

"I should have brought doughnuts."

He was trying to charm her. She wasn't going to let him. "There are not enough doughnuts in the world, Zachary."

"I know, I'm sorry." He spread his hands. "You may have noticed I tend to fall back on charm and baked goods when I'm nervous."

"I find myself immune to your charms. And we already covered the baked goods." She stopped. Played back his sentence in her head. "Wait. Why are you nervous?"

"Because I'm worried that, like doughnuts, there might not be enough groveling in the world to make you forgive me."

She felt her mouth drop open. Made herself close it. Tried to remember how to talk while her brain repeated *"forgive me, forgive me, forgive me"* on a loop. "Maybe you should be worried."

He stepped a little closer. Dammit. He might look rumpled and travel-stained but he smelled far too good.

"Only maybe?" he said softly.

She closed her eyes. She couldn't be dumb again. She had to be strong. Had to send him away. "What do you want, Zach?"

"I wanted to tell you I'm back."

"So I see. But based on our last conversation I'm

forced to conclude that you being back isn't any of my business."

"You know what they say about jumping to conclusions." He offered her a tentative smile.

"You're trying to be charming again."

"Sorry."

He didn't look sorry.

"Zach, I'm busy. Welcome home and all that but I have somewhere I need to be." His sister's party. Where he was probably headed, she realized with sudden horror. Oh God. She could not go if he was going to be there. She wouldn't be able to pretend everything was sunshine and roses with Zach standing in the same room reminding her it really, really wasn't.

"Wait," Zach said. "I haven't said what I came to say."

"If you mention doughnuts again, I'm going to have to hurt you."

He shook his head. "No doughnuts. No pastry of any kind. Just a confession."

A confession? She didn't know what to say so she just made a little "go on" gesture.

"I'm a world-class idiot."

"I'm aware." She was also aware of her fingers clenching by her side, of the tremble in her skin, of the foolish foolish hope starting to grow in her chest.

"I treated you like crap. I ran away."

"Still not news, Zach."

"Well, maybe this part will be. I know I can say 'sorry.' I am saying 'sorry.' Sorry," he added. "But I need you to know why I came back."

"Why?" Oh, that stupid, stupid heart of hers. It wanted to step closer to him. Grab him. Hold onto him so he couldn't leave again. She made herself stay right where she was. Was she never going to learn?

"Because I was miserable without you. Because I need you. Because I don't give a crap about Davis Lewis and his reputation. I want you. I want to make music with you and love with you and . . ." He trailed off. "I just want you."

She was trying to think. This seemed so surreal. Maybe she was napping after all? She dug her finger-nails into her palm. Felt the sting of it. So, apparently she was awake. And Zach was standing there. Telling her he—

"Say something," Zach said.

"You left me," she said. "Twice."

"I came back," he said. "Granted the first time took me far too long, but I wasn't so stupid this time."

"You've been gone nearly two weeks." Two weeks that had felt like several centuries.

"That's better than years," he said with another half-smile. "If it helps, I hated every second of it."

"So did I," she blurted, then clapped a hand over her mouth.

Zach laughed. Then reached out and pulled her fin-gers gently away. "Say that again."

"I'm not sure I want to."

"Say it again and I promise you, you won't regret it."

She stared up at him. She wanted to say it. Wanted to hear him saying it again too. But if she just said it, nothing would change. "I'm leaving Lansing," she said. "I want to produce."

"I know. And hey, to get you started I know this guy who has this half-finished album. They say it's pretty good. Probably due to the producer he was working with."

"I mean it, Zach. I want to get away from Lansing for a while."

"That's good," he said. "Because I kind of have this job where I need to travel."

"I don't want to follow you around. I'm done waiting for Zach Harper."

"Maybe I want to follow you around."

He hadn't let go of her hand, she realized. And her fingers were tangling with his, the familiar feel of his hand so good it made her want to cry. "You need to be in the spotlight."

"Not all the time. Sometimes I just need you. I love you, Leah Santelli. Wherever you are, that's where I want to be." He straightened. "So we can leave. And we can come back." He hitched a shoulder. "I made Shane an offer to buy his house. He accepted."

"You bought a house here? You bought *Shane's* house?" He wanted a house on Lansing? He wanted her? Disbelief was battling with sheer delighted joy.

"This is home," he said. "I want somewhere to come back to." His fingers tightened and he pulled her toward him. "I want *us* to have somewhere to come back to. So what do you say? Make a life with me, Leah. Make music and memories and mistakes with me. Figure it out with me. Don't make me go away again."

Maybe she *was* dreaming. If she was, she didn't want to wake up. And maybe, when it came to Zach, there was no way she would ever wake up. So maybe there was no other choice to make. Only him.

She tightened her grip on his hand. "I have three conditions."

The smile that spread across his face was all she needed to see. "Yes?" he said.

"No more running. We figure things out together."

"I can live with that," he said, mouth quirking. "Next."

"Be my date to Faith's party tonight."

"Try to stop me."

She grinned at him then, so happy she wasn't sure why she hadn't exploded.

"And the third?" Zach asked.

"Kiss me."

"Always," he said and then he did.

# epilogue

*Two weeks later . . .*

Zach was starting to think he knew the drive between the Harper house and Shane's—no, *his* house—by heart. He'd been driving or walking it several times a day since he'd bought the place. Whenever he could steal a few hours from the studio or the rapidly escalating round of festivities that were leading up to Faith and Caleb's wedding, he headed there. Walked around. Still getting used to the idea. Both the house and the fact that Leah would be living there with him when they were on Lansing. Which would be for the next few months at least while they finished his album.

There was plenty of buzz about it after the gig at CloudFest. More buzz about them than about Erroneous. And maybe it made him a petty motherfucker, but part of him was happy about that. But after the album was done, well, they'd play things by ear. He wanted to tour. She wanted to do some more producing. That was a portable profession. They could make it work.

He looked over to Leah, who was slouching back in her seat, her feet up on the dashboard and a goofy, day-dreaming expression on her face. "Happy?" he asked.

She smiled. "How many times a day are you going to ask me that?"

"Quite a few. All of the times." Zach said, still not quite believing she was his. He'd almost fucked this up. He wasn't going to let himself be so stupid again.

Her cheeks turned pink but her smile turned a little smug. "Good. I might ask a few times myself."

"Sounds like a plan," Zach said. They'd reached the guesthouse and he turned the car off. "Still want to go down to the beach?"

"Absolutely," Leah said. "Summer won't last forever. And I'm feeling kind of sticky."

Zach grinned at her.

They could have swum at the pool at Shane's place, but they'd gotten sidetracked when they'd been checking out one of the guest bedrooms. Shane believed in huge beds apparently. Zach approved. Leah had insisted they bring the sheets back to the guesthouse. He'd buy Shane a new set and include it in the stuff they were shipping back to him. Which wasn't as much as Zach had expected. Shane had said they could have most of the stuff in the house. So now he had to decide if there was anything he wanted to keep in the house or whether he wanted a clean slate. Maybe he could keep that bed. For sentimental reasons.

"Five minutes to grab your suit," Zach said. "Last one into the water has to—" He broke off as Leah pulled her T-shirt up, revealing that she was already wearing a bikini top. "When did you put that on?"

"I had it in my bag. And my panties were toast. You owe me new lingerie, Harper."

"That is one thing I'm more than happy to provide. Right. So new plan. I'll go change and you can grab beer. And whatever else you want."

"Deal," Leah said. And, true to her word, she was waiting with a six-pack and a cooler when he came back out of the house. He took the beer from her and extended his free hand, tangling his fingers with hers when she took it.

"Are you going to miss this?" he asked as they walked through the garden toward the beach path.

"Probably," she said. "But Lansing isn't going anywhere. And I have time to get used to the idea."

"We'll come back as much as you want to," Zach said. He didn't want to stay away too long either. He'd miss Faith and Mina and Lou too much. And Eli was sticking around a bit longer too. Billy had left after CloudFest. Zach had expected Eli to go with him, to get ready to go out on tour again. But Eli had claimed his ankle wasn't ready. Which Zach read as he and Billy hadn't patched things up yet. Well, that was Billy's problem, even though it sucked for Eli.

Leah pulled her sunglasses down to give him a mock-stern look. "I want some of that rock star glamorous jet-setting lifestyle first."

He laughed and swatted her butt. "Then we'd better make this swim short and get back to work." They'd reached the crest in the path where the beach suddenly opened up beneath them, the pale sand gleaming in the sun until the point where it turned into blue blue water stretching endlessly out to the horizon. He paused for a moment, drinking in the view. The view from Shane's end of the island was more dramatic than this, maybe, but this was always going to be his favorite part of Lansing. This and the woman beside him.

He turned to say something to Leah and that was when he noticed the woman sitting on the beach, looking out at the water. Long dark hair flowed over a red-and-white striped T-shirt. Her legs were bare. He couldn't really see her face but there was nothing in her posture that he recognized. His smile turned to a frown. The beach along the Harper property was technically private but they never bothered enforcing that with the locals. This time of year though, when there were still lingering tourists from CloudFest, their security guys were strict about keeping anyone they didn't know off the beach. Too easy to get up to the house from there. So how the hell had this woman gotten past them?

He nudged Leah. "Do you know who that is?"

Leah looked where he was pointing. Then shook her head. "I don't think so."

Zach patted his pocket. "I should call the gate guys."

"Don't be silly," Leah said. "She's alone. She's looking at the water, not staring up at the house with crazed-fan face. Why don't we just go down and say hello?"

He hesitated. He knew it would be smarter to call security, but Leah was right. There was nothing in the woman's body language that read "dangerous" to him. Quite the opposite in fact. She seemed totally calm. Grounded, though that was an odd thought to have just by looking at her. Odd but right. She seemed solid. Like she was part of the landscape.

Leah was already headed down the steps to the beach.

He caught up to her as she hit the sand. "Let me do the talking."

"Yeah, right," she snorted. "Look, if she does anything weird you can clock her on the head with one of your beers and call for backup."

Her voice must have caught the woman's attention because she turned, then stood, brushing sand off her legs as she watched them approach. She had sunglasses on, which made her expression hard to read, but she wasn't surging forward with the type of "oh my God, you're Zach Harper" shrieks of excitement that the more . . . enthusiastic . . . fans used.

"Hey," he said when they were only a few feet away. "Nice day."

"Yes, it is," she said. Her voice was low for a woman's. Kind of husky. There was something familiar about it. Did he know her after all?

"I'm—"

"Zach Harper," she said, finishing the sentence for him.

His stomach tightened. Dammit. Maybe she was a fan, after all.

But then she pulled off her sunglasses and he found himself staring into a pair of large gray-green eyes that were the exact color of his own.

"My name's Jane Vacek," the mystery woman said. "And I think I'm your sister."

**THE END**